SAND
AND
SHADOW

SAND
AND
SHADOW

LAURISA WHITE REYES

Santa Clarita, CA

Skyrocket Press
28020 Newbird Drive
Santa Clarita, CA 91350
www.SkyrocketPress.com

Cover design by Barbara Groves
www.BrokenCandleBookDesigns.com
Interior design by Laurisa Reyes

ISBN: 978-1-947394-02-5

ALSO BY LAURISA WHITE REYES

THE CELESTINE CHRONICLES SERIES
Book I: The Rock of Ivanore
Book II: The Last Enchanter
Book III: Seer of the Guilde

THE CRYSTAL KEEPER SERIES
Book I: Exile
Book II: Betrayal
Book III: Vengeance
Book IV: Hidden
Book V: Defiant
Book VI: Fallen

YA & CHILDREN'S FICTION
Contact
Memorable
Petals
The Storytellers
Mickey Malloy, Wonder Boy!

NON-FICTION
8 Secrets to Successful Self-Publishing
The Kids' Guide to Writing Fiction
Teaching Kids to Write Well: Six Secrets Every Grown-Up
Should Know

FUTURE RELEASES
Last Summer in Algonac

To my children:
Carissa, Marc, Stuart, Brennah & Jarett
Thank you for making my life worth living.

"We see our sins reflected everywhere: in the pallor of our intimates' faces, in the scratching of tree branches against windows, in the strange movements of everyday objects."

— Anna Godbersen, *The Luxe*

1

He did not belong.

That was the first conscious thought in Adán's head. Before he sensed that he was breathing or that his heart was pumping, he knew he shouldn't be there. He'd known it for a long time but had kept it to himself. Hadn't said a word right up to the moment the acrylic screen had come down and the icy serum entered his vein, but his apprehension was abruptly interrupted as he succumbed to the anesthetic that prepared him for cryo-hibernation.

Adán opened his eyes to a disorienting darkness. *Light,* he thought. *There is supposed to be light.* He squeezed his eyes shut, and then opened them again, straining to detect even the slightest glimmer. He felt his own hot breath collecting in the narrow space between his face and the cover above him. Had the respiratory system failed? Was that why his cryo had been terminated? He had been asleep only moments. At least it felt like moments. He awoke to his half-finished thought, still feeling the tightness in his gut, what Colonel Foster had deemed nerves.

"It'll pass," she had assured him. "It's as easy as going to sleep."

He breathed harder, faster. The moist air from his lungs condensed on his skin. Or was he perspiring? He lifted his right hand to wipe the sheen of sweat away, and his knuckles hit the underside of the screen. A dull thud reverberated through Adán's unit, and something shifted just at waist level. Adán couldn't raise his head more than a few inches, but it was enough to see the sudden speck of green light above his body. With his hand, he struck the acrylic over and over. With each collision, the spot of light grew larger.

It took a minute for Adán's mind to clear, to recall his training, his protocol. He tried to speak, but his throat was dry. He swallowed and tried again.

"Systems on. 4-ENG-003." His voice uttering his personal systems key in this confined space sounded too loud. "Computer, open cryo screen."

Nothing happened. He tried again, but still his unit remained closed.

Adán struck the acrylic cover a few more times until enough light had filtered into his unit that he could make out the emergency control panel at his left just beside his fingertips. On it was a rectangular button marked COMM and a lever marked RELEASE. They were crude apparatuses compared to the vocal commands he was used to, but he would use them if necessary. They'd gone over this in training, but even the simplest of thoughts resisted recall, a temporary effect of coming out of cryo. Gradually, as memories coalesced in his mind, he pressed his thumb against the COMM button.

"Hello? Can anyone hear me?" Adán forced himself to control his breathing to slow as he waited for a reply.

Nothing. "This is Mission Specialist Adán Fuentes. My unit seems to be malfunctioning."

Again, he waited. Adán re-adjusted his thumb. "Hello? Hello?"

The screen, so close to his face, seemed to press in on him. He should wait for confirmation to clear his unit and that the Med Squad was ready for him, but he had to get out. He had to get out *now*.

Adán hooked two of his fingers around the emergency release lever and pulled. The dull *click* of the latch resonated through his enclosure. With a sucking sound, the screen slid open, pushing what seemed to be a layer of dust to the floor.

For a moment, Adán saw only green, and it reminded him of the time he and Saul had gone scuba diving off Catalina Island—how under water everything had that odd seaweed-like tint to it. Then the overhead lights blinked on, and the dim oceany color evaporated. The sudden brightness stung Adán's eyes, and he shielded them with his elbow. When he thought he could tolerate the light, he lowered his arm and cautiously sat up.

He was in the Quarters just as he should be, the vast cavern-like hibernation compartment housing two rows of twelve identical cryo units each—twenty-four in all—and the main control panel at the far end. This room was the last image he'd had before his cover came down, but it had looked nothing like this.

The overhead lights that ran the length of the room blinked and dimmed at irregular intervals. The intermittent light made it difficult for Adán's vision to fully adjust. Then, instead of cryo units, all he saw were two dozen oblong heaps of rust-colored dirt—his own open unit the only exception—like the mounds of earth on freshly filled graves.

What the hell?

The next thing he noticed was a thick, long bulge along the starboard wall, extending from the far end of the room to just past midway. The bulge was so large it had displaced several of the units.

Adán felt weak and lightheaded, which he had been told to expect. After the initial dose of anesthesia, the needle in his arm had first replaced the water in his body with a low temperature-tolerant liquid, and then later reversed the process, providing a nutrient-infused solution to revive his body once the three-year journey to Europa was complete. Even so, upon waking, his stomach felt horribly empty, as if the very core of him was missing. Adán ignored it. As he sat up, his muscles cramped, and his fingertips tingled. He made a weak fist and then cautiously unfolded each finger, allowing time for normal sensation to return. Once it had, he turned his attention to the I.V. needle in his arm.

Where were the medics? The MED squad was supposed to awaken first and help the others. They were supposed to follow protocol, otherwise how could they successfully fulfill the mission? But from what he could tell, none of the others had awakened yet. He looked at the bulge and the dust and swallowed back the panic rising in his throat.

Something had gone terribly wrong.

Adán walked his fingers up his arm to the circular silicon patch that tracked his vitals and peeled it off. He did the same for the one on his temple, the one that had recorded and archived his brain activity during hibernation. Then he slid his fingers around the needle above his wrist.

He considered just yanking it out, like tearing off a band-aid, but couldn't quite get up the nerve. Instead, he tugged, gently at first. An acute pain rippled up his arm. He released the needle, gasping.

No wonder the medics were supposed to remove the I.V.s and *then* wake up the crew.

He tried again, this time sucking in a deep breath while sliding the metal tube out of his skin.

Adán pressed the heel of his hand against the small wound to stop the bleeding and shifted his legs over the side of the unit. As he set his bare feet on the floor, a cloud of dust puffed up, staining the hem of his white pants burnt orange. As he took his first step, the muscles in both calves seized, and pain stabbed at the backs of his legs and knees. Cramps. He had been warned about the cramps.

"Pull your toes up," Colonel Foster had told him. "Stretch out those muscles."

Adán let go of his arm and reached down to pull on his feet, straightening each leg as he did so. It took a minute or two, but eventually the cramping subsided.

He stood up, taking a few unsteady steps between the two rows of cryo units. If he was awake, then maybe others were, too. At least the ones whose lights were on, though after the MED squad, they were all scheduled to wake at the same time, but none of the other units were open yet.

He studied the pale green glow beneath the dust on his own unit. The light signaled that his body systems had stabilized and that he was ready to be released from cryo. He turned to the unit beside his own and wiped the dust away from the light panel with his arm. There was no green, no light at all. Not even the yellow LED that should have indicated the unit was in use.

The mound of dust on the unit's cover had formed a sort of crust, like the plates of caked earth in a dry riverbed. Adán touched it with the tip of his finger, and the crust crumbled leaving just a thin layer of dirt behind. Taking a pinch of it, he rubbed the powder against the pad of this thumb. He remembered how the Apollo astronauts had described lunar soil: fine as flour, rough as sandpaper. This stuff was like that. The coating of it on the cover seemed so delicate that if he blew on it, it might all just float away, but something inside of him resisted. Instead, he stepped away from the unit and moved to the next one.

The green light was like a beacon. Adán was so relieved he had to steady himself. He wasn't the only one awake. He was not alone. Scraping the dust from the cover with the side of his hand, he peered inside.

A pair of bewildered brown eyes gazed back at him.

NASA-NGIS COALITION
Planetary Colonization Division
Washington D.C.

Inter-Department Memo

Attention: Robert Herrera, Lead Project Manager

Robert,

Screening for project candidates begins on Monday. Applications should be verified via a photo I.D. and Social Security number. No exceptions. Be advised that we expect to be notified of all qualified applicants.

Despite the public's belief that crew members will be selected at random from those applicants who pass the initial health screening, the project heads agree that it will be most beneficial to the program and to the human race if the crews consist of those with superior physical and intellectual abilities. Therefore, please only forward files to us of those who score in the top tier in BOTH academic and athletic screenings.

In addition, please ensure that the registration clerks check the appropriate ethnic and gender codes on the application forms. Ideal crews will have a balance of diverse members, where possible.

Addendum: From this time forward, please refer to colonization crews as 'teams' in your press releases, as that term will elicit a more reassuring and positive effect on the media and the public.

Signed,

Megan A. Whitlock

Vice-President, Northrop Grumman Innovation Systems

2

"Tink!" Adán laughed at himself when he realized the occupant of the cryo unit couldn't hear him. He didn't have authorization for vocal command on anyone else's unit, only the MED squad and the Commander did, but each unit had an exterior emergency release, like the ones inside. Adán reached for the lever on this chamber and pulled. The screen slid away.

"Tink," said Adán, "are you all right?"

Tink was on the engineering squad with Adán. The patch on his uniform read H. SEOUNG, but thanks to his genius with electronics during training, he'd been christened with his nickname, the Tinkerer.

Tink moaned. "My arms are numb. I can't feel my fingers."

"Give it a minute. You'll be fine."

Tink rubbed his arms and rolled his ankles. His Asian straight hair stuck out at haphazard angles like black porcupine quills. He ran his fingers through it trying to smooth it down. "I feel gross," he said. "And hungry."

"Me, too. Just hang on."

"Hey, where are the medics? And what's with all this dirt?"

Adán moved across the aisle to unit #14 and rubbed the lights clean. *Please be awake*, he whispered, thinking of the person he knew lay inside. He felt a shudder of relief on seeing green and pulled the release.

The dark-haired woman lying inside snapped her eyes shut against the sudden light. Her face was round and pale with a sprinkling of freckles. "Damn it. What the—"

"Dema, are you awake?" It was a stupid question, Adán realized the moment he said it. Of course, she was awake.

"What do you think?" she said with a yawn. "Yeah, I'm awake, but—" She blinked her eyes open. It was the first time Adán had seen her eyes so close up, and he realized he'd been wrong about their color. He'd assumed they were brown, but they were more the shade of dark honey.

"What's happened?" Dema asked, gazing around the compartment.

"I don't know," said Adán, forcing his mind to stay on track, "but we're going to need your help."

While Dema expertly detached her I.V. and retrieved gauze and medical tape from the first aid kit under her unit, Adán moved from chamber to chamber, brushing the dirt from each pair of LEDs.

"There are only six green lights on," he called out from the far end of the room. "Six out of twenty-four."

"Only six of us awake?" asked Tink, climbing awkwardly out of his unit. He grabbed hold of it, steadying himself, and closed his eyes. "Ugh. Did that too fast. Dizzy."

"Take it slow, Tink," said Adán. "The rest of the units' lights aren't on."

"What do you mean their lights aren't on?" Dema pushed a tangled strand of brown hair out of her eyes. The ID on her

10

jumper read D. SARKISSIAN 7-MED-002. Below that was a simple red cross on a black background. She was far more level-headed than Adán, a characteristic he had always admired about her.

Adán hesitated responding to Dema's question, not ready to accept the answer that had been niggling at the back of his brain.

"And where's the rest of my squad?" Dema continued. "We were supposed to revive first."

"I woke up first," said Adán. "I have no idea why. We're the only ones so far. FYI, the units aren't responding to vocal commands. Go manual."

After a little help from Tink, Dema was on her feet. She seemed more stable than either Adán or Tink, but then again, she had ranked first in the physical trials. She moved to the remaining three units with green lights, wiped away the dust with her sleeve, and released their covers. The occupants each responded with uncomfortable moans.

Dema leaned over one of the open chambers. "You all right, Fess?" she asked, pressing her fingers against the young man's throat. A sheen of perspiration glistened on his dark skin.

At eighteen, Fess was the youngest member of the crew and had only joined them a month before departure. All the others had been selected by lottery two years before that and had been training together ever since. From what Adán had heard, the kid's test scores were so high that the government had flagged him. Usually that didn't mean much. Like most flaggers, he was assigned as an alternate, but when a first-string crew member came down sick, Fess joined Carpathia's team at the eleventh hour. He was tall and lean with coffee-colored skin and a head full of tight curls that looked like tiny springs. His real name was Ray, but everyone referred to him as the Professor. Fess for short.

Fess nodded, his eyes still shut tight. "Yeah, I'm fine. Just got to get my bearings, is all. I'm a little woozy."

"All right," said Dema. "Just stay here while I check the others. I'll be back in a minute."

The last two open units were occupied by a female and a male. Lainie Turner was on the agricultural squad and specialized in hydroponics. She had worn her auburn hair in a braid when they were put down, but the braid had come loose somehow. As she eased herself into a sitting position, her hair fell across her shoulders in soft waves. She remained silent as she took in the other crew members and the strangeness of their surroundings.

"Is she okay?" Tink asked as Dema checked her vitals.

"She's fine," Dema replied, quickly moving to the next unit.

Lainie responded with a weak, confirming smile. "I'm all good," she said uncertainly. "Where did all this dust come from?"

"I think there's a breach in the hull," said Adán, pointing to the bulge in the wall. "Something perforated the shuttle, allowing dust to blow in during a storm or something."

"A crash landing?" asked Tink.

"Maybe," replied Adán. "Though we'd have to examine the rest of the ship to be sure."

"A breach doesn't make sense," said Lainie. "Our air would have leaked out."

Tink dragged a finger across his unit. "It's far-fetched, I know, but the shuttle is constantly producing oxygen. Maybe it's been compensating for the imbalance?"

Adán wasn't sure if Tink was right, but for now it was as plausible an explanation as any.

"Is there anything I can do to help?" Lainie asked Dema, who had turned her attention to the man in the last open unit.

"Would you mind checking their arms?" Dema said, nodding toward Tink and Adán. "Make sure they've been properly disinfected."

Surveyor Specialist Jonah Smith remained prone in his cryo unit, his eyes pressed closed. Adán considered him one of the more intense members of the crew, giving them judgmental looks when they used profanity or laughed about "inappropriate" things, like sex. As a result, Jonah had seemed like an outsider to the rest of them, never quite connecting the way most of them had.

"Can you feel your fingers? Toes?" Dema asked.

"Yes."

"Any headache or pain anywhere else in your body?"

"No. Just dizzy."

After clearing Jonah, Dema let out a relieved breath. "Except for the muscle spasms and stomach cramps, which were expected, everyone seems all right."

"All done," said Lainie, securing a fresh piece of gauze to Adán's I.V. wound. "What next?"

Dema scanned the room with an intense urgency in her eyes. "We've got to check them all," she said, indicating the closed units.

"But the lights are off," said Adán. "They're not—they're not ready."

Dema stepped over to the next unit, examining the LEDs. Then she shot a questioning glance over her shoulder at Tink.

"No yellow light," he told her. "Means the power's off."

"No power at all? Any of them?"

Adán knew what Dema was thinking. He'd been trying to push the idea away, but he could tell Tink was thinking it too.

"They're gone, Dema," Tink said, a catch in his voice. "Something went wrong. Look at the way the lights keep flickering."

"But that doesn't mean—"

"The shuttle's damaged," Tink added. "The power grid's impaired. Life support needs power. Damn it!" He banged a fist against his cryo unit.

For a moment, Dema's gaze remained fixed in front of her. Then her eyes darted from one unit to the next. "I have to check all of them," she said again, determination in her voice. "There might still be a chance."

Lainie stepped up beside her and gave her arm a tender squeeze. "We'll check them together."

Dema smiled appreciatively. Then she approached the next nearest unit and swept her entire arm down the full length of its cover. The dust sloughed off into a soft pile, leaving just a thin sheet of powder behind. This Dema blew away with a single breath. Then she and Lainie both stepped back with surprised gasps.

Adán leaned forward a little so he could see into the unit, but he wished he hadn't. Its occupant resembled something made of papier-mâché, its skin as dry and brittle as aged parchment. The severe contour of cheekbones and eye sockets jutted out from its face like tiny mountain ranges. The only thing Adán had ever seen like it was an Egyptian mummy at the Museum of Natural History. If not for the ID patch, it would have been impossible to tell who it was.

Adán recoiled from the sight and backed up a few steps. Dema pressed her hand against her mouth. Her eyes wide with shock, she stared at the thing beneath the shield.

"What the hell's going on?"

Adán hadn't noticed Fess standing behind them. He looked both scared and angry at the same time as he paced nervously between the rows of cryo units.

"What *is* that? I mean, shit man, that guy's—you know—shit!"

Jonah still sat inside his unit, his arms wrapped around his knees. "Shut it, Fess," he said. "He's just dead. All right?"

"Yeah, he's dead!" Fess stopped his pacing and flung his arms out in a frantic gesture. "What about the rest of 'em. Are they all dead?"

Dema rested her hand on the dead man's cover. "Tink?" she asked in a surprisingly steady voice. "Why don't you take a look at the control panel. We must be missing something."

Adán caught Tink casting a questioning glance at Lainie, who responded with a silent, reassuring nod. Then Tink crossed the Quarters to the solitary desk and screen standing at the far end. After wiping the screen free of dust, he slid his index finger across the glass plate, studying the data.

"Just our six," he said, shaking his head. "Ours are the only functioning units."

Adán studied the damaged wall. "Whatever hit us hit us hard," he said.

"Or we hit *it*," said Jonah, who was finally easing his way out of his unit. "Maybe we crashed like Tink suggested. Maybe the landing system malfunctioned."

"We might have struck an asteroid," suggested Lainie, twisting her loose hair into a knot at the nape of her neck. Despite her composure, it looked like she was fighting back tears. Adán couldn't blame her. After training together for so long, most of the crew had formed tight friendships, and now most of them were dead. Of his own close circle, only Tink remained. The realization filled his stomach with rocks.

Swallowing back the rising fear in his throat, Adán turned his attention back to Tink. "Life support. Power. Who knows what else has been damaged? We need to evaluate our situation before we decide what to do next."

"Evaluate what situation?" Fess's voice was taut and shaky. He turned to the unit beside him and pushed away a swath of dust. He did the same with several units in a row, each time revealing another mummified crew member. "Look at them!" he said. "They're all dead! That's our situation!"

"Calm down, kid," said Adán, concerned Fess's panic might spread to the rest of them, but Fess would not quiet down.

"We're it, man. Six out of twenty-four! There aren't enough of us to *do* anything!"

No one replied to Fess's revelation. They all knew what he said was true. There were six squads tasked with specific responsibilities, each dependent upon the others for a successful mission. Each squad had four members—three core members and one alternate. NGIS had made sure there were enough people to function even if someone got injured, or worse—died. But no one could have foreseen something like this.

"Hold on." Tink stared at the control panel.

"What is it?" asked Adán.

Tink didn't answer at first, his eyes fixed on the panel. Then he scanned the room, his gaze finally resting on unit #24. It was the last unit in Adán's row, at the end of the bulge, one of the displaced units. Adán wondered what Tink saw there. What was he looking at?

Then he saw it, too. A momentary flash of green, barely visible beneath the swath of dust. It blinked on again, holding steady for a few seconds before switching off.

"I think that one's still functioning," said Tink. "The indicator light keeps going on and off, but the yellow LED is holding."

Dema hurried over to the unit. A moment later, Adán was beside her, wiping the lights clean. Yes, there was the faint yellow light just like Tink said. How had he missed it before? Maybe it hadn't been on, but it was on now. As they stood there watching, the green light turned on again.

Dema didn't waste another second. She pulled the release, and the screen slid open. Dust sloughed to the floor, and soft clouds of it billowed up around their feet. Inside lay a man with thinning blonde hair. He was unconscious, but he was most definitely alive.

3

Scott Dryker was the education team's squad leader and Carpathia's mission commander. Seeing his face instead of one more mummy sent a wave of relief through Adán. So, there were seven of them. Seven survivors.

Lainie had come to stand beside him and was peering over his shoulder at Scott. Tink watched the monitor, but everyone else had gathered around Scott's unit. They all wanted to know the same thing.

"Is he—?" Fess folded and unfolded his arms, restless and worried. His voice cut off, like he didn't dare utter what should follow.

"He's alive," said Dema, glancing at Tink for confirmation.

Tink's eyes were riveted on the monitor. "His vitals are holding, but his brain activity—there's something odd—"

Suddenly, the green light above Scott's unit switched off. Tink's head shot up. "It's off!" he shouted. "Everything just shut off!"

He was right, Adán realized. The green—the yellow. Both lights were off now. Lainie gripped his arm. "Oh my God!" she said. "Is he breathing?"

Tink was shouting again. "His vitals are slowing. Power's been cut off. We're losing him!"

All eyes turned to Dema. She was the sole medic, the only one who knew what to do, but she wasn't moving. She stood frozen, staring at Commander Dryker's still form like she was in some sort of a trance.

"Dema," said Adán. She didn't respond. A look of confusion passed over her face.

"Dema, tell us what to do," said Lainie desperately.

Adán touched Dema's arm, which seemed to shake her out of her stupor. Her face changed, her expression resolved.

"Okay. Everyone back away!" ordered Dema. She squeezed Scott's wrist, feeling for a pulse. "Scott, do you hear me? Tink, look at the vitals again. Do you see anything?"

"Power to that unit is off. His heart rate is dropping."

Dema released Dryker's limp wrist. Adán felt a wave of nausea. They'd lost their commander. What the hell would they do now?

But then Dema was moving, shouting, pointing. Adán blinked, trying to refocus his thoughts. She was shouting at *him*.

"Adán! See that line there? Brush off the dust. It's red. You can't miss it. Follow it to the crash box and hand me the paddles inside."

Adán did what he was told. They had practiced such scenarios in training. He followed the power cord, thick as his thumb, to where it connected to the red box on the shuttle wall. He flipped up the latch and threw open the cover. Inside were two squarish paddles connected to the box and each other by a spiral cord. He handed them to Dema.

"Push that button inside. That's right," Dema instructed. "The charge has to build for a minute. Let's hope to God these things still work."

The crash box emitted a high-pitched beeping. Dema instructed Adán to unzip Scott's uniform, which he did. Then Dema placed the paddles on the commander's chest, the skin bare and pale. Then they waited.

"Dema, you've got to do something," called Tink. "He's flat lined!"

Dema didn't respond. Her eyes were fixed on Dryker's face. The beeping changed to a steady hum.

"Clear!" Dema shouted.

There was a loud *umf* as the paddles shocked him. Scott's chest jolted like something had slammed into him hard. At the same time, the lights in the room dimmed so low Adán could hardly see at all. The defibrillator had drawn too much power from the already damaged grid.

Everyone waited. Adán hardly dared to breathe.

C'mon. C'mon.

The lights eased back up. Dema reset the paddles. "Tink, any change?"

Tink was shaking, and sweat trickled down his temples. "Nothing. Oh, God," he whispered. "Please."

"Again!" Dema shouted.

Adán pressed the button again. Lainie finally broke down and started sobbing. Jonah crossed himself. Fess muttered "Christ" under his breath.

Again, Scott's body jerked with the electric shock. And again, the lights dimmed low.

They all held their collective breaths waiting for confirmation from Tink that the shocks had worked. Except for the beeping from the crash box, the room filled with a tense silence.

Then suddenly, there was a loud *BANG* followed by a violent jolt.

Adrenalin blasted through Adán's body, and he felt the fire down to his fingertips.

"What was that?" Jonah asked in a hesitant whisper.

A moment passed, then came another sharp *bang*. The walls of the Quarters shuddered as if something had grabbed hold and was shaking it. Then as suddenly as it started, it stopped, and the room was again in silence.

"Wow," said Tink, letting out an agitated breath. "I don't think the shuttle can handle the defibrillator's power surge."

"Is that what that was?" asked Lainie, drying her eyes with the heel of her hand.

"Yeah," said Fess nervously. "Had to be, right?"

Tink continued. "Next time, there might not be enough power to get the lights back on."

Dema was breathing hard, as they all were, but she set the paddles aside and positioned her palms on the commander's chest, depressing his ribcage several times in succession. They had all practiced giving CPR in mission training, but this was the first time any of them had ever witnessed it for real.

Dema gave Scott four more compressions. On the last one, the green light on Scott's unit clicked on again. All eyes focused on that small, green glow. The yellow light beside it came on, too, but flickered unsteadily.

C'mon. C'mon. Adán was ready to make a deal with God— or the devil—for the life of their commander, if that's what it would take. But then Dryker took a sudden gasping breath.

"Quick!" said Dema. "I've got to disconnect him! If this thing shorts out one more time, he'll flat line again."

Adán knew what she meant. They could not risk draining what little power the shuttle might have left. If Dryker's heart stopped beating again, that would be the end for him. Adán didn't wait to be told what to do next. He fumbled through Scott's first aid box and got two sterile pads of gauze. Tearing them open, he held them ready as Dema removed the needle. A bubble of red formed just as Adán pressed the gauze to the wound. A moment later, Adán had the gauze taped in place. Dema pulled the silicon patch off Dryker's upper arm, but just as Dema reached for the patch at his temple, the unit's lights flicked off again. Dema grasped the edge of the patch and yanked it off. A small strip of skin came with it, but Scott was still breathing. He was safe.

"We need to move him," said Dema.

"Move him?" asked Adán. "Where? Why?

"He's unconscious. Who knows for how long? He still needs the I.V. and the monitors, but his unit has malfunctioned."

"We could move him to one of our units," Lainie suggested. "Give him mine."

"That's a good idea, but let's choose one that's closer," said Dema. "Adán, Fess, c'mon you guys. Give me a hand."

Tink and the other three men followed Dema's directions, lifting the commander out of his cryo unit. The nearest functioning one was Adán's, so they carried him there and laid him inside.

"Watch his head," Dema ordered.

While Dema set about connecting Adán's monitoring patches to Dryker's body, Tink made sure the readings showed up on the control panel. Then Dema sterilized the I.V. needle with alcohol swabs from Adán's first aid kit and inserted it into Scott's arm. Meanwhile, Adán stood aside, watching the entire process in disbelief. It seemed strange to see their mission commander lying in the unit that had kept Adán alive throughout their journey. It didn't feel right somehow, but Adán shook it off.

Scott Dryker had survived, barely. But seventeen others were dead, most likely from an electrical system malfunction caused by whatever had dented the shuttle.

Adán stepped over to the now empty unit #24. The distended section of the wall extended into the compartment by as much as twelve or thirteen inches, enough to have pushed four units away from the wall, including Dryker's, which Adán realized had been slightly crushed on contact. But he spotted something else as well.

The end of the bulge was a mangled mass of twisted metal and wires, and at the center of it, a two-foot-long gap caked solid with orange dust. Adán poked at it with his finger, and, to his surprise, it sifted away like powdered sugar, leaving a jagged breach clean through the entire hull.

He bent low until his eyes were level with the opening and peered through it. What he saw was a narrow slice of more orange. His view was limited, but from what he could tell, the outside didn't look much different from inside. Just dust as far as the eye could see.

The air coming through the opening was frigid.

Air? It couldn't be, he thought. There was no breathable atmosphere on Europa. Adán thought of Tink's explanation about the pressure being balanced, preventing their air from escaping. But air was coming *in*, not going out, which would explain why so much dust had blown into the shuttle. To play it safe, he would seal off the hole until a more permanent patch could be installed.

Reaching into Dryker's unit, he pulled out the foam pad on which he'd lain and rolled it into a long cylinder. Then he pressed it into the gap. Just before he got the last bit crammed in, a small puff of air escaped through the narrow space, and with it—a smell.

Adán bent closer and sniffed.

Impossible.

Before he could second guess himself, the smell was gone, replaced with the bland scent of arid dust. But for that moment, that single moment, that smell had seemed as real as anything—the unmistakable aroma of cinnamon.

Tink

Umma sets four china plates on the table and carefully arranges the sujeo beside them. Tonight, we are having a guest. Commander Travis Berkeley will be joining us. Appa arranged it. Refused to allow me to join the shuttle team without first meeting with the person in charge. I'm embarrassed, but out of respect do not contradict my father. I never contradict him.

It helps that we live in Falls Church, just twenty minutes outside DC, and Appa has worked at Northrop Grumman as a flight engineer since before I was born. He thinks this gives him some clout. I suppose it might, though I don't think that is why Commander Berkeley agreed to come. I'm only twenty-two, but I earned my masters in Aeronautics and Astronautics at MIT last year. I'd already been accepted to work in my father's department when NASA went public with the colonization recruitment program. There was never a question whether or not I would apply.

I carry the bowl of steaming rice to the dining table and place it in the center next to the platters already there. Earlier, I helped Umma with the mandu, my favorite.

Commander Berkeley arrives promptly at five o'clock. He greets my parents with respect, and I can tell Appa's suspicion is already fading. By the end of dinner, he has given his blessing for me to join the team.

Throughout the evening, Commander Berkeley speaks primarily to Appa. Occasionally he addresses my mother, but the only thing he says to me directly is on his way out the door. "I'll see *you* in training on Monday."

I'm ecstatic, of course, and after he leaves, my parents shower me with praise and honor. Their only son, an astronaut. They are proud.

Later, in my room, doubt sets in. I have felt it before, when I accepted my undergraduate diploma two years ago, when Appa urged me to apply for the program, when I hesitated before filling out the application. It's not that I don't know what I'm doing. I do. I'm confident enough and have proven my capabilities many times over, haven't I? But school wasn't easy for me. High school was a breeze, graduated early and already had my college GEs done by graduation. So, everyone expected me to excel at MIT.

When I got those first term results, I couldn't bear to tell my parents. I couldn't shame them like that. So, I buckled down and threw myself into my studies so that I'd never have to. The truth is, I never wanted to be an engineer. I don't want to work for NASA. I don't want to leave Earth. My friend, Cody, dropped out of school to open his own business. His dream has always been to have his own café. When I told Appa, he scoffed and told me I was wasting my time hanging around someone like that. I didn't tell Cody what he'd said, of course.

The truth is, I admire Cody and others who do what they want to do regardless of prestige or money. What would I do if I had the freedom, and the balls, to do it?

Honestly, I really don't know. I hadn't really thought about it much until Appa invited the Commander over for dinner. No one had ever asked me what I wanted to do. I'd never even asked myself.

Cody says I should start my own business too. Something to do with computers, but I don't know. I think back to that first term at MIT, the mistakes I made, how hard I had to work to stay on top. It doesn't come easy for me. I'm not a genius, I just work my ass off.

Now, sitting in my room with a suitcase open on my bed, my clothes folded neatly in separate piles, I feel the weight of what is to come. This is not just some classroom experiment, a slate where mistakes can be wiped clean. There will be others all depending on me. An error could mean someone's life, maybe my own.

I'm not the right guy for this job. I know it even if no one else does. Maybe I should tell Berkeley to select someone else. There's got to be plenty of qualified engineers out there, but what would I tell Appa? Could I bear his disappointment, the disgrace?

I slip a hand beneath the pile of button-down shirts and arrange it in the corner of the suitcase. Each successive stack fits neatly beside the others, like pieces of a puzzle. Organized. Precise. No room for imperfection.

Once my toiletries have been added and an extra pair of shoes, I shut the case and zip it closed. I'll try to sleep tonight before calling an Uber in the morning, but I'm not tired. So, I lay on my bed and stare at the ceiling until the sun rises through my window.

4

"Commander Dryker? Can you hear me?" Lainie leaned over the open cryo unit and gently shook him by the shoulder.

"He's really out," said Dema. "I'm leaving these monitors in place until he revives so I can keep an eye on him."

Lainie nodded and then withdrew, her arms wrapped tightly around herself. Tink moved to her side, telling her everything would be okay, but from the dusty coffins containing his dead crewmates, some of whom were his friends, Adán knew things were not okay. Would never be okay.

"So, what do we do now?" asked Jonah, kicking the ball of his foot against his cryo unit's base. More dust rained onto the floor. "If the whole ship looks like this, we're in serious trouble."

"Maybe it doesn't," said Adán, indicating the padding he'd stuffed into the breach. "Something penetrated all the way through. The dust has been getting in through here, but this compartment is closed off from the rest of the shuttle."

"Europa's temperature is minus 160 degrees Celsius," scoffed Jonah. "If the hull was breached, we should have all been solid ice by now."

At five feet six, Jonah was the shortest man on the team, four inches shorter than Adán, and as light-skinned as Adán was Latino-dark, but he more than compensated for his lack of height by his bulk. During training, he'd spent twice as many hours in the gym as everyone else. With his angular features and close-cropped red hair, Adán always thought he looked like a human battering ram, so out of sync with his usual tranquil temperament. Then there was Tink who looked like a toothpick next to Jonah.

"We were protected," explained Tink. "Our units are individually regulated. And the shuttle's heating system probably switched on prior to our release, ensuring a habitable temperature and air pressure."

Fess snapped his fingers several times loudly. "Listen to yourselves! Everyone's dead, and you all are talking about dust and habitable temperatures!"

"Panicking isn't going to help," said Jonah.

Lainie placed a gentle hand on Fess's arm, and he quieted down.

"The other units clearly malfunctioned," said Lainie, turning her attention to Adán, as if expecting him to know something she didn't. "Is it possible that they froze?"

"Maybe. I don't know." Adán wished he had answers, but he didn't. He had questions. Too many questions. "Dema, what do you think?"

Dema shook her head. "I'm a medic, not a doctor. But if I didn't know any better, I'd say they died a long time ago. Decades, maybe."

"Decades? What?" Fess tugged nervously at the front of his uniform. He seemed to be growing more agitated by the minute. "That's crazy!"

It did sound crazy. Their journey was supposed to take three years, not decades. Three years to reach Jupiter's sixth moon. Cryo was supposed to help them pass the time, keep them safe, conserve fuel and provisions.

"What are you saying, Dema?" Adán asked.

"I don't know what I'm saying," answered Dema. "I just know that going under, we all went through the same vitrifying process. Water was removed from our cells to prevent crystals from forming during the cooling process. At negative 200 degrees, we were preserved, stored until the system slowly rehydrated us, raised our temperatures, woke us up. The whole ship was preserved in a state of low humidity. Look at them," she said, indicating the lightless cryo units. "Their bodies didn't decompose. They couldn't. I think that their units went through the motions of raising the temperatures but failed to rehydrate them, creating the ideal setting for mummification."

Adán considered Dema's explanation. How long would mummifying seventeen humans have taken? How long ago had the Carpathia been hit? And how long had the rest of them been lying there waiting to wake up?

"So, the system went all screwy," said Fess. "But mummies aren't made in just three years."

"No," said Dema, "they're not."

The air around them swelled with tension. This was sounding crazier by the second, but no one except Fess could say it. Finally, Jonah spoke up, but the composure in his voice unnerved Adán.

"So, we haven't been traveling for a few years," he said. "We've been traveling for tens of years." He shrugged casually. "Sounds like we missed our mark."

Adán had had enough of the cryo room, the room of death. He wanted to get out, get moving, get away. "We can't just stand around guessing. We still have a mission to accomplish, procedures to follow."

"What procedures?" asked Fess. "Most of our team is dead. Our shuttle is banged up. Hell, now we're not even sure if we landed on the right planet?"

"There's nothing concrete to suggest we landed somewhere other than Europa," said Adán. "So, let's stop guessing and instead do something constructive."

"Well, we're all hungry," said Jonah. "If we're going to follow procedures, then the first order of business is getting something to eat. Isn't that right, Dema?"

Dema hesitated, and then nodded. "That's right. Well, after our preliminary physical exams."

Jonah smirked and waved his arm, indicating the entire room. "I think most of us would pass the exam, don't you? As for the rest of them…"

"Jonah, that's disturbed, don't you think?" said Lainie, affronted. "We all spent two years in training together. The least you can do is show them a little respect."

"When did they show me any respect?" Jonah's grin vanished and his expression turned somber. "Sorry. I only meant that under the circumstances we should forgo the preliminaries and get down to what matters."

"Jonah's right," said Tink. "What matters is that we're all hungry as hell."

Fess jerked a nod. "Plus, this place is creeping me out."

Finally, something Adán agreed with. The IV that had rehydrated them had also provided fundamental nutrients, but if they didn't eat soon, they'd be too weak to be much good to one another. Adán stepped up to the compartment door. He wondered what he would find on the other side. More dust? The boogie man? He glanced back at everyone's anxious faces. Then he called out his code.

"4-ENG-003. Computer, open the Quarters access."

There was a *beep*, followed by a sucking *hiss* as the door slid open to the right. "Just the air pressure regulating," Adán said.

The area beyond the doorway was dark. For a moment, he hesitated. It looked like a deep dark hole. But the others were waiting, watching. He took one step forward. To his relief, the floor lights turned on, and in another moment, the central part of the shuttle was awash with light. And it was comfortably warm. The temperature regulation system seemed to be working fine.

"I'll stay with Scott," said Dema. "He shouldn't be left alone."

Adán stepped aside to let the others file past him through the doorway. "I'll bring something back, okay?"

Dema nodded uneasily. "Okay. Thanks."

The Common Room, or CR, was a long, narrow compartment approximately the same dimensions as the Quarters, with three long tables and six computer terminals along one wall. The other wall was floor-to-ceiling metal storage units with pull-handles on the doors. Adán opened one, sliding out a four-foot-long shallow drawer. White curls of frigid air spiraled above the acrylic containers within. Each had black lettering on its side. The first read MASH POT/GRA. Adán hauled out the container, which was surprisingly light weight for its size, and set it down on one of the tables. Unsealing the lid, he fished out a metallic pouch about four by six inches and tore it open.

"Our food is freeze-dried and has been stored in sub-zero temps. We'll need water to rehydrate it." Adán stuck his finger into his mouth, moistening it with spit, and then dipped it into the pouch. The cold white and beige flakes clung to his skin like chalk dust. Then he put his finger back into his mouth and sucked it all off.

"To hell with the water," said Fess, grabbing a pouch for himself. "I'll take it dry."

"Not a good idea," said Adán. "Tastes okay, but it's like eating wood shavings. It'll suck the moisture right out of you. The water dispenser is right behind you. As long as the oxygen and hydrogen tanks haven't been damaged, the aqua mixer should be functioning. Try it out, Tink."

Sculpted into the wall was something between a sink and a drinking fountain. It was white, the same color as everything else inside the shuttle, with a metal spigot. Tink tilted his head beneath it, waving his hand in front of the tiny sensor. It took a few seconds, but then a cool stream of water poured out into his open mouth.

"Yum," he said.

"Now listen," said Adán, "don't forget what we were told in training. There's enough dry food to last the team a full year, if we stick to the scheduled rations."

"Yeah, but now that there's only six of us—" said Fess.

"Seven," Tink corrected. "The commander makes seven."

"Okay, seven of us," answered Fess. "Then it should last three years, maybe more."

Adán opened another silver pouch, holding it briefly under the water stream. "True, but the protocol is for us to scout out land for agriculture. We need to dig the well, set up the irrigation system and green houses, plant the seeds so that down the road there will be a renewable food supply for the colony."

Fess straddled a bench and poured the contents of his pouch into his mouth. He brushed the crumbs off his lips. "What colony, Adán? Look at us," he said. "There aren't enough of us for a colony. Maybe we should get this shuttle off the ground and head back home."

"You know we're just the first. Pioneers," said Tink, stirring water into a pouch with a finger. "We pave the way for everyone else."

"And what about the rest of the fleet?" Lainie accepted the prepared pouch of food from Tink. "Where are the other eleven shuttles?"

Adán had always appreciated Lainie's direct way of looking at things. She'd come from a farm in Idaho where her father raised cows. Despite her background in agricultural engineering, at first, some of the others had poked fun of her, but she had quickly earned their respect with her keen problem-solving. She had a way of seeing the whole picture, which was probably why no one on the team had ever beaten her at chess.

Now her question about the shuttles triggered something in Adán's brain. He'd been so focused on himself and his own crew, but where were the other shuttles? Had they arrived yet? If they had, they might have tried comm-ing them. "I'll head to the comm station right after we've eaten something. Okay?" he said. "If the rest of the fleet has revived, they would have sent word."

That seemed to set everyone at ease, at least for the time being. Adán opened a second container, this one marked CIN APPLES, and passed the pouches around, setting aside one of each for Dema. For the most part, everyone prepared and ate their food in silence. Tink was the first one finished, which didn't surprise Adán at all. He had always been the first during training, too. While the rest of the team were dumping their trays, Tink was already at his desk devouring the next hour's lesson. That probably explained why he had gotten such high scores. Some team members had expected Tink to be named commander, and everyone was shocked when the position went to Scott Dryker. Scott was only a paper pusher, part of the EDU squad. But Adán had to admit Scott was better with people than Tink. He was a natural communicator, a born leader. But Tink didn't hold a grudge about it, so neither did anyone else.

"I'm going to check out the cockpit," said Tink, tossing his empty pouches into the pull-out recycling bin in the wall. Establishing a reciprocal system of reprocessing was another task on their agenda. "I can access the main connections to the shuttle's electrical from there. Adán, you want to come with me and retrieve the protocol, check the comm?"

"Sure," said Adán, hurrying to finish his apples. "I'm right behind you."

"What about the rest of us?" asked Lainie.

Adán took a moment to look at each of his teammates. Lainie, responsible for their long-term food supply. Fess, the lone survivor of the tech squad (or what the others lovingly referred to as the grunt squad), seemed calmer now that he had something in his stomach, but he was still agitated, tapping his fingers and thumb against the cabinet like it was a bongo drum. Beside him was Jonah, using his fingers to reach the very bottom of his mashed potatoes. He and Dryker represented half of the surviving educational squad and were responsible not only for maintaining the shuttle's virtual library, but also of keeping detailed records for the colony.

No one from the GEO or the BIO squads had survived, and the rest were trained to accomplish their missions with at least one additional squad member by their side.

"Lainie, would you mind taking this food back to Dema?" asked Adán. "Tink and I will learn what we can about the shuttle's condition. Fess and Jonah, maybe you should get outside and check things out."

In truth, Adán wasn't sure what was the right thing to do, but they had to do something to keep occupied, at least until they contacted the rest of the fleet and received their orders. For now, he just had to keep it together because the alternative would be—what would the alternative be? He had no idea.

Fess moved quickly, just as he'd been trained to do. He was made for it, for constructing things, for getting things done. "Get your gear on. I'll grab us some mix tanks," he told Jonah.

Jonah moved more slowly, giving Adán an annoyed look as he stood. "You're not the commander, Fuentes," he said under his breath, just loud enough for Adán to hear. He chose to ignore the comment. Of course, he wasn't the commander. Everyone knew that, no one more clearly than him, but what were they supposed to do? Sit around waiting for Dryker to wake up?

"Give Adán a break, Jonah," said Lainie. "He's just trying to help."

Fess held his palm up to the sensor on the gear compartment, a room parallel to the CR though not as long. In it were the showers and restrooms, lockers for each team member, space to change into their gear.

The door slid open, and Fess headed inside.

Lainie gathered up Dema's pouches and held each under the stream of water long enough to moisten them. Then she disappeared back into the Quarters.

Jonah sluggishly opened the recycle bin and dropped his pouches inside. Adán wondered if he'd have to be tougher on him to get him to move. Despite Lainie's comment, Jonah was right. He had no authority, but still—

Fess returned, breathing hard. "Can't go outside," he said frantically.

Not again, thought Adán. *This kid is like a mouse trap.* Every little thing set him off.

"Take it easy, Fess," Jonah said with more patience than Adán felt. "What are you talking about?"

Fess took several deep breaths in succession before answering. "The mixers," he said in measured syllables, "the tanks that give us air—"

"We know what mixers are." Adán cut him off impatiently. "What about them?"

Fess's eyes widened with growing panic.

"They're gone."

THE NEW YORK TIMES

NASA-NGIS PREPARES FOR LAUNCH OF FIRST PLANETARY COLONY

Written by Yemeni Bastien
8:39pm

The President announced Thursday that NASA & Northrop Grumman's Planetary Colonization Division has moved up its inaugural launch date by more than five years.

Plans are underway to send twelve international super shuttles to establish exploratory facilities and a provisional colony on Europa, Jupiter's fourth largest moon. The shuttles will carry all materials necessary to construct and maintain a fully operational laboratory and engineering station. The colonists will be placed into temporary cryo-hibernation for the three-year journey.

The proposed launch date for the U.S. shuttles Carpathia, Beacon, and Ensign is September 2nd. In addition, China and Russia are each providing three shuttles and teams to the mission, while Iran, Great Britain, and the United Nations of Korea will each contribute one. Launch dates for the other countries' shuttles are yet to be determined.

Senator Polk of Wisconsin issued a statement questioning NASA's decision, accusing the President of using the project to improve his chances for next year's re-election and claiming the hasty move may lead to possible disaster. However, others in Washington are wondering if the decision was influenced by the recent reports of increased solar radiation levels detected in Earth's atmosphere, but when questioned following the announcement, the President abruptly dismissed the idea as absurd.

5

Adán followed Tink out of the common room into the cockpit, where the main controls of the shuttle were housed. A pale overhead light blinked on at their entrance.

"Connection's weak," noted Tink. They also noted the condition of the shuttle's forward windshield, a rectangular glass window fitted in the front of the cockpit to be used for visual confirmation during surface landings and take offs. Through it Adán had expected to see the planet, but instead he saw nothing at all. Like the cryo shields, it was completely caked in dust.

Tink settled himself into one of the two cockpit chairs and studied the control panel. The commander and the pilot had sat here during lift off, overseeing the initial stage of Carpathia's mission. Once the shuttle was safely on course and maximum speed had been achieved, they had joined the rest of the crew in cryo. The pilot hadn't survived, and the Commander lay unconscious in Adán's cryo unit.

Above Tink, a clear acrylic screen jutted out from the ceiling. He typed a series of codes onto the panel keyboard, and the screen flickered to life.

"I don't understand it. No mixers. How could they forget to stock the shuttle with mixers?"

Tink's question was the same one Adán had been asking himself for the past half hour while he and the others had scoured every nook and cranny of the shuttle, hoping the devices meant to provide oxygen to the crew while outside had simply been misplaced. Yet unless NASA had stored them in the exterior cargo bays, which was a possibility, there wasn't a single mixer on board. And if they were in the cargo bays, how could they get to them?

"Not just the mixers," Tink pointed out. "You saw the suits? Those aren't anything like the EMU's we trained in."

"Yeah, I noticed. They're thinner, lighter weight. And the helmets—the visors aren't mirrored."

"Computer, access diagnostics," Tink said, followed by his personal code. Then to Adán he added, "This'll give us some idea of which systems are functioning and at what capacity."

He scrolled through several screens full of numbers and mathematic equations. "For the most part, it seems that the shuttle is in good shape," he said after a while. "Whatever caused that breach, though, did some serious damage to the electrical system, which may be why so many of the cryo units failed. Fortunately, the damage is isolated to that sector of the ship. Temperature regulation, data storage and collection, fuel systems, water development. Everything else seems fine."

Storage compartments ran along one wall near the ceiling. Adán opened three before he located the stash of E-Tabs, 9-inch rectangular touch screen devices. He pulled out six of them and tucked them under his arm. "Wish we could get a glimpse of what's outside. Can you access the planet's atmospheric readings?"

Tink nodded. "Yeah, but I'm not sure if I can interpret them correctly. That's the GEO squad's job."

"Well, pull it up anyway. Let's see what we've got."

Tink swiped his finger across the screen again. "Okay, here it is. Surface temp is negative twelve degrees Celsius. Humidity seven percent."

"Pretty damn cold out there."

"Yeah. And we're supposed to go out there and drill a well—without mixers, I might add."

"There's a layer of ice covering much of Europa's surface, anywhere between two to eighteen miles thick. Endless source of water with a drill and steamer. That's why they sent us here. Right?" Adán recalled the directives that had been drummed into them. "That's our mission. Well, one of 'em anyway. I'm going to pull up the comm link, okay?"

Tink fell silent for a moment, as if suddenly lost in thought.

"What is it?" asked Adán.

The skin between Tink's eyebrows pinched. "Negative twelve degrees. That's ten degrees Fahrenheit."

"Yeah?"

"That can't be right. Remember what Jonah said? At best, Europa is negative 160, negative 260 Fahrenheit."

"The monitor's gotta be wrong." Adán snapped a fingernail against the screen. "Maybe the collision did more damage than we realized."

"Yeah," said Tink, thoughtfully. "That has to be it. I'll run the diagnostics. Gotta know what needs to be fixed, right?"

"Right."

The comm stats turned up nothing. Adán had hoped there had been some attempt at contact from the fleet—a message or signal, something. With eleven other shuttles out there, it was hard to believe the Carpathia was the only one that had reached Europa so far. Earlier, Dema suggested they'd traveled far longer than three years, and Jonah had joked that they'd missed their mark. Now with the temperature glitch, a troubling thought wormed its way into Adán's brain: What if they weren't where they were supposed to be?

"You got anything?" asked Tink.

"Nope," said Adán. "You?"

"I'll have to work on this sector here if we don't want any more short outs." Tink pointed to the corner of the screen. "If Fess could repair the external damage at Panel Nine—if he had air, of course—I could get the circuits up and running again. It shouldn't be too difficult."

"Maybe he can do the repairs from inside. Can you manage your part alone? I mean, the simulations were all done in pairs."

"I can manage."

Adán switched off the comm link. He thought of the mixers and the hull breach. He thought too of what he'd seen through it. What he smelled through it.

"Hey Tink?"

"Yeah?"

"There's something else I need you to check. Could you pull up the atmospheric readings again?"

"Sure. Why?"

"Europa's atmosphere is composed solely of oxygen, isn't it? And it's thin, too thin to breathe without mix tanks. I still don't get how our air didn't leak out."

Tink scratched at his temple with his index finger. "Well, you said it was all jammed up with dust, right? The shuttle constantly produces our air. Maybe it has been leaking but the breach is too small to make much of a difference."

"You got those numbers up yet?"

Tink pointed at a series of digits on the bottom left of the screen. Adán leaned closer, narrowing his eyes at the list of elements: oxygen, nitrogen, carbon dioxide.

Tink looked at Adán, his eyebrows raised curiously. "I may be reading this wrong," he said. "I'm no meteorologist, but I'd say there's more than just oxygen out there."

Adán nodded. "That answers my question about the breach, but since when does any planet in our solar system, other than Earth, have a breathable atmosphere?"

"Are you sure this is accurate?" Dema slid a finger over her E-Tab screen, refreshing the calculations. "I mean, there has to be some glitch in the system, right?"

She was referring to the data Tink and Adán had just shared with the rest of Carpathia's crew. Adán was reviewing them now, as was everyone else.

"It doesn't make sense," said Lainie. "We can't breathe Europa's atmosphere, not without a mixer."

"Well, that explains that," snorted Jonah.

"What?" asked Adán.

Jonah set his E-Tab down on the table. "The missing mix tanks weren't an oversight. We've landed on a planet where we can breathe, and NASA sent us here on purpose."

"Those goddamn sons of bitches!" said Fess. "They knew we wouldn't need them! They knew it from the start."

"We don't know that for sure," Lainie replied cautiously.

"So, we don't need mixers," said Dema. "That still doesn't answer the big question. If we're not on Europa, then where are we?"

Adán looked from one set of questioning eyes to another. They all seemed to be waiting for him to say something, as if he had an explanation, or could tell them what to do. But why him? He wasn't the commander.

"What about the damage to the Quarters' hull?" asked Lainie. "Is it possible that whatever hit us threw us off course, and we landed on some other planet by mistake?"

Jonah gave an indifferent shrug. "So, some meteor hits us, we veer off course, and just happen to land on some random planet. One that just happens to have a breathable atmosphere. We'd have better odds of hitting a golf ball into a tin can from ten miles off. Get real."

Adán didn't like the way Jonah had spoken to Lainie just now, but this wasn't the time to confront anyone about their bad manners. They were all under a lot of stress.

"Whatever hit us," he suggested, "it must have happened during descent, once we'd already entered the planet's atmosphere, or even after we landed. If that breach had occurred in open space, it would have created a vacuum, instantly crushing this thing from the inside out."

"So, what did hit us?" The question Dema posed was one Adán couldn't answer.

"I don't know." It was all he could offer at the moment. "But listen, we've got plenty of food and water on board. Tink's going to work on getting the electrical back online. With air out there, Fess can work on patching up the breach."

"Has anyone tried to contact the others?" It was Fess again. "Have we heard from any of the other shuttles yet?"

Tink shook his head. "The comm link was set to off, but it's functioning now. I sent out a hail transmission, but so far, no response. Either they haven't landed yet or—"

"Or what?" asked Jonah.

"Or they're not going to land."

Adán didn't like the silence that followed. The unspoken questions and fears unnerved him. Had the other shuttles been hit by something, too? If they had, maybe they hadn't been as lucky as the Carpathia, which had sustained only a negligible breach.

He turned to face the wall of metal cabinets. He and Tink would have to search for answers to their exact location later. For now, the best way to keep everyone's minds occupied was to get to work.

"We've all gotten our fill of what some people might call food," Adán said. "Now we need to see to the next thing on our agenda. Shelter."

"Can't we just sleep in the shuttle?" asked Lainie. "At least it's warm."

"If you want to go back to your cryo unit and all that dust," replied Jonah, "you go right ahead."

"No way," Fess said. "I'm not spending a single night with all those coffins in there."

Adán opened the top cabinet on his right. "We could stay in the common room," he suggested, "but it'd be pretty

46

cramped with all these tables. There's plenty of room in the shelters, and we won't even have to connect them to the shuttle's oxygen tanks." He pulled out a canvas tool bag and dropped it on the floor beside him with a loud clank. Next, he removed a large bundle of metallic lightweight tarp. "The braces for the tent frame are in outer storage bay one, along with the heating units, cots, and other hardware. We'll only need one shelter now instead of all three, so that shouldn't take too long to put up."

The crew sat sullenly, hesitant to move. Adán couldn't blame them. They'd lost their friends, they didn't know where they were, nothing was going as planned. All the more reason to stick to protocol, keep busy and focused.

Tink, always the optimist, was the first to head for the locker room. "The good news is we won't have mix tanks, which will lighten our load a bit."

Still the others lagged.

"C'mon," added Tink, reaching for Lainie's hand. "Let's get suited up and head outside. Time to face our own brave new world."

6

Until they opened the hatch on the port side of the shuttle and stepped outside, Adán and the crew of the Carpathia weren't really sure what to expect. Due to the condition of the cockpit windows, it was the first look any of them had had of the planet's surface. According to Tink's diagnostic readings, there were mountain ranges forty-two kilometers to the west, longer and taller than those on earth. There also appeared to be a massive cleft in the planet's crust twice the width of the Grand Canyon located a little less than a mile away. More importantly, the presence of oxygen, nitrogen, and carbon in the planet's atmosphere suggested the possibility of life. The question was would it be microscopic forms of life or something bigger?

Adán clicked his bio-optic scanner into place on his visor and scanned the horizon. As he stepped onto the planet surface, he felt gravity's pull to be a little stronger than on Earth, though that had already been confirmed by the data that appeared at the edge of his visual field. His lightweight space suit felt heftier, his steps a bit more sluggish. He searched for anything that might suggest the presence of life: plant life, patterned formations, running water. But despite the mountains being visible in the distance, all around them, for miles in every direction, orange dunes lay as motionless as the painted landscapes he'd seen hanging in museums back home. Adán's father had taken him to one shortly before his call from NASA. He had felt drawn to a particular painting there. It was actually a painting of the sea, with a wide golden strip of sand and foamy white waves. In the air, gulls dipped down toward the water, presumably to catch fish. Adán had stared at that painting for several minutes. Though he knew it was nothing but acrylic and canvas, he was afraid that if he blinked, he might miss that wave breaking on the shore, or the gull snagging its dinner and swooping back up into the sky.

Adán felt that way now as he took in the 360-degree view all around him. He half expected the hills of dust to suddenly rear up and gallop toward him, but they didn't.

Carpathia's exterior was long and sleek, resembling the design of the shuttles used in the 1980s and 90s, only much larger. Standing below its nose and looking down the length of it, Adán felt dwarfed by the immense spacecraft. Though it left Earth the old-fashioned way, vertically, it was designed to land horizontally like an airplane and could take off that way from the planet surface. From what he could tell, the Carpathia had landed successfully but sustained more damage than could be determined from the inside. Adán located the source of the long bulge inside the cryo compartment, what could only be described as a fifteen-foot-long gash along the ship's side that ended where the rear hull had been breached. Larger than it looked from the inside, the gash itself was deep enough that Adán could easily spot where some wires and metal hardware had been severed. It would take days, if not weeks, to repair it, if they could repair it at all.

Adán stooped a little to walk beneath the belly of the ship in order to inspect the landing gear. While everything appeared to be in order, there was one thing that bothered him. He found tracks in the soil trailing behind each of the three massive wheels, as he had expected, but they were located at a distance to the right of the shuttle. Between these tracks and the wheels were three unmistakable swaths in the earth, as if something had shoved the Carpathia sideways four or five yards.

Adán stepped away from the shuttle, keeping its damaged flank in view. He walked backward until he could see it all at once—the shuttle, the gash in its side, the scars left in the dirt. Several thoughts hit him at once. First, the damage had indeed happened on the ground, not in flight. Second, whatever hit them was big enough and strong enough to move a shuttle the size of a jumbo jet. A meteor? Yet there were no rocks near the shuttle, big or small. And third, unless they could get the shuttle working again, they were stranded.

"Hey Adán, you out here?" Fess's voice in Adán's comm was a lifeline, a connection to what felt familiar and safe, but he did not reply. He knew the crew, at least what was left of it. What point would there be in worrying them about something he couldn't explain? He brushed his foot across the swath near the first wheel, back and forth along its length until it had vanished. He quickly did the same with the other two. The strange evidences—of what?—were gone.

"Found you!" Fess came around the end of the shuttle just as Adán was having second thoughts about what he'd done. When Fess caught sight of the wound in Carpathia's side, he whistled. "You see that?" he asked, casting nervous glances to his sides, like he expected to spot something sneaking up on them. "What the hell did that?"

Despite the gloves and suits they both wore, Adán was starting to feel the cold. "Your guess is as good as mine," he said. "The important question is can you fix it?"

Fess hastily examined the shredded metal, the severed wires, and crushed fixtures inside. "Maybe. The electrical is priority, of course." He raised a hand, indicating the damage. "Some of the connections have been severed, which explains the funky lighting in the cryo compartment, but the overall structure has been compromised as well. I'll have to improvise replacement parts with what we've got in the storage bays. Wouldn't do to get this thing in the air just to have it fall apart."

"When can you get started?"

"ASAP."

Adán considered this but changed his mind. Fess seemed more than a little skittish. "Get some sleep first. You noticed the sun hasn't changed position since we've been out here."

"Yeah, I noticed." Fess squinted skyward. "This planet's tidal-locked, like our moon back home. Same hemisphere always in daylight. Easy to lose track of time like that."

"We've been awake nearly ten hours. Everyone's feeling it. Is the shelter up?"

Fess nodded past the front of the shuttle. "It's up. Lainie, Tink, and Jonah are loading it now with the cots and generator. Dema's gone back inside to check on Dryker."

Adán followed Fess to where a large tent-like structure stood shining in the sun. The paper-thin metallic material was not only stronger and lighter weight than tarp, but it also acted as a solar cell gathering energy from the planet's sun and storing it in a portable generator, which Adán could already hear rumbling nearby.

It had taken more than an hour to set up the shelter and another hour to transport all necessities from the shuttle to the shelter: cots, blankets, a few days' worth of food, four 5-gallon containers of water, the E-Tabs, and other vital gear. Jonah had used a ladder from the Cargo Bay and cleaned off the shuttle cockpit's window. Fess had detached a table and its benches from the common room and set it up at one end of the shelter. On this, Tink set up a portable comm.

"Starting tomorrow," he said, "I'm going to program a signal to hail the other shuttles at regular intervals. If any of them come within range, they'll hear it and hopefully respond."

"Good thinking," said Adán. "We should sleep in shifts. You guys get some shut eye while I keep a look out."

Confused expressions appeared on everyone's faces. "Keep a look out for what?" asked Jonah, spreading out his arms to indicate the wasteland around them. "Dust devils?"

Adán thought of what he'd seen, how the shuttle had been pushed across the ground. He wondered if he'd done the right thing not mentioning it to the crew. They'd been so busy setting up the shelter no one else had noticed. He could tell them about it, but what good would it do? Things were bad enough as it was, with losing so many of the crew and having had no contact with the rest of the fleet. No, telling them now would only cause unnecessary panic. Besides, Adán thought, how did he know what had really happened? All he could do was speculate, and right now they needed facts. Solid, tangible facts. And the fact was they were all exhausted.

Adán tipped his head back and squinted toward the tiny sun. "I'd just feel better if someone's on watch," he said. "We've been awake less than a day." He bent over and picked up a clot of orange dirt which crumbled to a fine powder in his hand. "And the fact is, we have no idea what's out there."

Adán found Dema in the Quarters up to her elbows in dust. Using a mat from one of the abandoned units, she had managed to scrape much of the dust into a two-foot-high berm along one wall. Yet despite her efforts, a thin sheen of it decorated everything. She glanced up when Adán entered, giving him a "Don't say it, I already know" kind of smile. Her face was smudged red from the stuff, as if she'd gotten a horrific sunburn, and her once blue uniform looked more like desert camouflage.

"It's so fine," she said with a disapproving sigh. "Like corn starch. I think the only way to get rid of all this would be to hose it down or suck it up with an industrial vac."

"I'll check inventory later," said Adán, "see if we have something in the cargo bays that might help."

"Thanks."

Dema cast a wary glance over at Scott Dryker lying comatose in Adán's cryo unit. "He'll be fine for a few minutes," said Adán. "Why don't you grab a shower? You remember where the linens and clean uniforms are, right?"

Dema nodded, maneuvering a dirty strand of hair away from her face. "Is everything all right out there?" she asked.

"Shelter's up, if that's what you mean." Adán rested a hand on his—Scott's—cryo unit. "It's cold, which we expected. And there's no sign of life, which we also expected."

"Nothing green?"

"Not a single patch of moss. With water under the surface, we had hoped maybe." He smiled, attempting to reassure Dema that despite their circumstances, he still had his humor.

Adán couldn't find the right words to describe how Scott looked lying in his unit. Like the distant red mountains on this planet, he never moved except for the nearly indiscernible rise and fall of his chest. At least there was that—and the lines and spikes on the monitor proving that he was still alive. Adán thought of their fellow crewmates, the ones surrounding them now, the ones that hadn't survived. They couldn't leave them in here. Not only was it creepy, but it would be disrespectful. If the ground wasn't too frozen, they would have to bury them. Tomorrow's first order of business, he decided.

"You going to be all right in here tonight?" asked Adán. "Maybe I should stay, too."

"No, that's not necessary. I mean, yeah, the place needs some tidying up..."

"I meant with *them*."

Dema's smile faltered, but only for a second. "What can they do, rise from the dead and cannibalize me?"

"You watch too many horror flicks."

"I used to." Dema shrugged, and Adán saw a hint of wistful sadness in it. He didn't want to think about what they used to do. All he cared about was what they needed to do now.

"Go on," he said. "Get cleaned up. I'll babysit Commander Dryker while you're gone."

"You sure?"

"Yeah, I got it."

As soon as the door slid shut behind Dema, Adán felt an eerie feeling creep over him. The lights overhead still flickered from the damaged current. How could Dema stand being in here alone? But she wasn't alone. Not really. She was with Scott.

Adán ran his palm along the outside of the cryo unit. It was still his, wasn't it? He did spend the past however many years lying in it. Now Scott had taken his place. He shouldn't care, thought Adán. It wasn't like he'd need it again anytime soon, but even so, he couldn't help but feel just a twinge of— *mine.*

He and Scott had not been what anyone would call friends during training. Bonds were formed, of course. How could they not be when the crew had spent two years together? But Scott was always a bit of a loner. The girls seemed to like him all right, though. Those first few months at Northrop, they'd actually whisper and giggle when he walked into a room. Eventually that wore off. Thank God.

Originally there had been twelve men and twelve women. Though their mission was to prepare a home for future colonists, the unspoken directive was that some of them would pair up, choose to settle on Europa permanently, and propagate the human species. Yet despite clandestine meetups between some of the crew members, there was little time for romance. They hadn't been given enough spare time to do anything more than study protocol and learn the specifics of their particular team's responsibilities. All that mattered was the mission.

Adán looked around at the lifeless units and thought of himself and the other survivors: Scott, Dema, Lainie, Tink, Jonah, and Fess. With so few of them, he wondered how, and if, the mission could be completed now.

Once Dema had showered, Adán made sure she ate a good dinner and was safely settled in her cryo unit for the night before deciding to retrieve something from his personal storage bin.

"You play that?" asked Dema, noticing the instrument in his hand.

Adán held up a twelve-inch-long recorder and smiled. "Didn't we all learn to play these as kids?"

Dema shook her head. "Not me. I was never very good with music. I'd heard you were a musician though."

Adán sighed. "Not much time for it during training. I actually play a few instruments, though violin is—was—my passion."

"Why didn't you bring your violin then?"

Adán held the recorder to his lips and played a few notes. "This fit better in the box." It wasn't the whole truth, but it was close enough.

"You sure you'll be okay in here?" he asked, pausing at the door. "Because I can—"

Dema gave a soft laugh. "Go on."

Adán said goodnight and headed for the cockpit to start his watch. Through the now cleaned windows, he had a clear view of the shelter and of the surrounding terrain.

He thought of Dema, of the way her eyes had searched his in those first moments after he'd woken her, as if she expected him to answer all her unspoken questions. He hadn't been able to stop thinking about those eyes, or the face that framed them, with her high cheekbones and freckles. He'd known Dema for two years now, but she'd always had an eye for Scott Dryker, so he hadn't given her much thought. Yet after waking, he'd felt so desperate to make sure she was alive. And that moment when she'd looked at him, when he knew she was safe—he hadn't realized until then how much he cared about her.

Adán switched on the communications link and within moments heard Tink's voice. "Hey, don't fall asleep on the job."

Adán chuckled. "I won't. But you'd better relieve me on time, or I can't make any promises."

"No problem. I've turned off the portable comm in here so we can sleep. So, make sure to keep an eye on the beacon there in the cockpit. Let me know right away if any messages from the fleet come through."

"I will, though it's odd that we haven't heard from anyone yet. I wonder what happened?"

"Maybe the damage to our power grid interrupted the signal," suggested Tink. "I wouldn't worry about it since I'll have that fixed in no time. I'm sure the fleet's out there somewhere, trying to reach us right now."

"Maybe," replied Adán. "Hopefully."

He wished Tink a good night's sleep and switched off the comm, though he couldn't help but wonder if there was another explanation for the lack of communication from the fleet. The Carpathia had been damaged. What if something similar had happened to the other shuttles?

Adán immediately dismissed the thought. It was a near impossibility for all twelve shuttles to experience the same problem.

Still, what if—?

Adán leaned back in the pilot's seat and propped his feet up on the steering column. Then he picked up his E-Tab and clicked on an icon of a treble clef. Music. In the shuttle's archives, he found a collection of Beethoven's violin sonatas and synced it to the cockpit's speakers. Then he lifted the recorder to his lips and settled in for his three-hour shift of watching—nothing.

7

Adán was the first to wake in the morning. He looked at his watch. According to Earth, Pacific Standard Time at least, it was 6:14 AM. Around midnight, he'd finished his three-hour shift and was relieved by Tink who was followed by Jonah.

There was plenty to accomplish today, and Adán checked off each task in his mind. They would scout their immediate surroundings, begin repairs on the shuttle, clean out the Quarters. But first they needed to deal with the bodies of their crewmates. He shuddered at the thought. If he had any other option, he would prefer to leave them where they were, encased in their individual cryo units. But they needed the shuttle to rendezvous with the fleet, if and when the fleet signaled them, and it just wouldn't do to have seventeen mummified corpses coming along for the ride. And besides, their families would want them properly buried.

Adán and Fess were nearly done digging the five-foot-deep pit by the time Lainie, Tink, and Jonah emerged from the shelter. The porous ash-like soil was easy enough to excavate using the two shovels they'd found in the cargo bay.

"You just going to lay them in there all together?" asked Jonah.

"I suppose so," said Adán. He finished the pit and stuck the shovel upright in the soil. "All right," he said. "Let's do it."

They found Dema awake in the cryo compartment, checking Scott's vitals.

"How's he doing?" asked Adán.

"The same," she replied, "but stable. Did you guys sleep okay out there?"

"We slept fine. Have you had breakfast?"

"I got something that resembled scrambled eggs and sausage a little earlier. So, what's the plan for today?"

Adán nodded towards the other units. "It's time," he said.

Dema wrapped her arms around herself. "Oh."

They decided to start at the far end of the room. Adán brushed off the layer of dust from the shield and peered into the unit. "D. Anderson," he said. "It's Devin." He looked up at his fellow crewmates waiting for some response. Devin Anderson was an all-around nice guy, maybe a little on the nerdy side. Could never get his hair to lay flat due to a cowlick in the back, and he had a particular fondness for grape jelly.

No one spoke as Adán pulled the release. The moment the cover slid back, the air was corrupted by the putrid smell of dried flesh. Adán covered his nose with his arm and gagged. The others all did the same. Lainie turned away. Tink bent over with his hands pressed against his knees.

"We have to do this now," said Adán, choking on his words. "If we wait any longer, it will just get worse."

"We'll wrap him in a blanket," suggested Dema. "It'll be easier to transport him that way."

"God, I can't!" said Fess. "I can't touch it! I won't!"

"Get a grip," said Jonah. "It's not like he'll bleed all over you. At worst, you might get some dehydrated snot on your uniform." He reached into the unit and slipped a hand beneath the dead man's neck. Though the scowl on his face revealed some disgust, Adán was surprised with how gentle Jonah was. His movements were not abrupt or indifferent, but he seemed to take great care to avoid damaging the brittle body in any way. Once he had his other arm beneath the stiff thighs, Jonah cautiously lifted the body from the unit. A hush fell over the room as he laid it on the blanket Dema had spread out on the floor. Together, they wrapped it around Devin Anderson, then stepped back. Jonah's eyes met Adán's for just a moment before he looked away again, but in that moment, Adán caught just a hint of what he could swear was remorse.

It took three hours to remove all seventeen crewmembers and lay them in their mass grave. Each one was given as much care and respect as the one before. The surviving crew did their work in relative silence. These had once been their friends and teammates. They had willingly said farewell to their families, to their normal lives back on Earth, for the chance to colonize a new world, but things had ended tragically for them.

The fact that those remaining had been left to carry on their mission alone weighed on Adán with a physical force that knotted his insides. It was all he could do to not drop to his knees and vomit at the side of the grave, not because of all the death that surrounded him, but for all the unknowns that lay ahead. How long would it be, he wondered, before he and the others joined their deceased crewmates here?

Once all seventeen bodies had been respectfully arranged in their final resting place, the crew had gone through their storage units to collect personal items that should be buried with them: photographs, letters, journals, trinkets with sentimental value. Then Dema covered the bodies with the blanket in which they had been carried, but there were too many to cover with just one. So Tink collected one of the unused shelter tarps to finish the job. The sun reflected off the silvery material so that it almost looked like a small pond or lake, the way sunlight sparkles off the water's surface.

"We should say something," said Lainie, standing at the edge of the grave beside Tink. "Something to honor them."

No one spoke at first, and Adán once again felt the weight of glances being cast in his direction. They expected him to know what to do, what to say, but he didn't. He'd only been to one funeral before, his mother's, but he hadn't had to say anything.

He met Lainie's eyes and then Tink's, hoping they would remove this responsibility from him. Instead, they cast their eyes down. Fess fixed his gaze at the distant mountains, his expression severe like he was fighting back an emotion too powerful to handle. Dema looked directly into Adán's eyes. She smiled knowingly and gave a little nod of encouragement.

Adán cleared his throat and searched his mind for words that might be appropriate, but before he could speak, Jonah stepped forward.

"I've got something to say." He clasped his hands reverently in front of him. To Adán's surprise, he held a black book, a finger stuck into the pages.

Jonah opened his Bible and began to read. His voice was clear, unwavering, and it carried out across the barren sands.

"Lord, make me to know mine end, and the measure of my days, what it is; that I may know how frail I am. Hear my prayer, O Lord, and give ear to my cry; hold not thy peace at my tears: for I am a stranger with thee, and a sojourner, as all my fathers were. O spare me, that I may recover strength, before I go hence, and be no more."

Jonah closed the book without a sound. Reaching into the pocket of his uniform, he pulled out a bundle of gold crosses he had salvaged from some of the crew's personal effects, many like the one Jonah always wore around his neck. Dangling them by their chains over the grave, he said a quiet "Amen," then released them. They landed on top of the silvery tarp with faint clinks. A soft sniffle drifted into the air as Lainie struggled to keep her tears at bay.

Adán stood beside the pile of displaced earth from the grave and wrapped both his hands around his shovel. Then slowly, methodically, he began pushing the soil back into the hole. A cloud of dust rose up, but the gathered mourners did not retreat. They stood their ground, witnesses to this event, to the end of so many lives.

Once the hole was filled, Adán smoothed it out with the back of the shovel. Then Fess took both shovels and headed for the shuttle to put them away. Dema followed him. She needed to get back to Scott. Jonah stayed behind a little longer, staring at the finished grave. Adán felt like an intruder watching him, but Jonah did not seem to even notice his presence. The Bible still gripped in his hands, Jonah closed his eyes and bowed his head. He stood like that for a minute or two, then abruptly opened his eyes and marched off toward the shelter.

Adán felt the weight of someone's hand on his shoulder. It was Lainie. She gave him a wistful smile.

"You're doing a good job," she told him.

"Hmm?"

She gave his arm a gentle squeeze. "None of this is your responsibility, but we all appreciate what you're doing. Taking charge, giving us direction."

Adán gazed at the sand at his feet. Is that what he was doing? If so, it wasn't by choice.

"I'm just doing what any of you would do," he said, knowing as he said it how untrue it was. "Dryker's the commander, not me," he added. "When he's better—"

"Of course," said Lainie. "But in the meantime…"

Another smile, full of encouragement and gratitude. Then she turned and joined Tink, who waited nearby. They walked together to the shelter and disappeared inside.

Adán remained by the grave. Somehow it didn't seem right to walk away, to leave them alone out here. At least not yet. He felt the bitter cold creeping through his suit. He should get inside soon. Again, he listed off what else needed to be done today. The electrical systems. The temporary patch. Signaling the other shuttles again.

He thought of what Lainie had said, how it wasn't his responsibility, and she was right, but if he didn't step up, who would? He felt the sun gazing down on him, that unblinking eye that gave no warmth. He considered the landscape, a vast empty wilderness of crushed ginger, never changing, never moving, as if time didn't exist here. And, he realized, it didn't. Not in the way he'd always known time to function. On

Earth, time was a clock marking the passage of seconds and minutes and hours. It was a human construct, something people long ago invented to give order to their existence. To anticipate seasons. To observe the past.

Would mankind have created time had they lived on a planet like this where the sun never set? Where there were no seasons, no days, no years?

Adán noted the sound of his breathing against his visor, the rhythm of his lungs drawing and expelling breath. The cadence of his heart beating in his chest. Yes. One didn't need a clock or the sun and moon. One's own life marked time.

He looked once more on the grave, already invisible against the backdrop of sand, and understood in a way he never had before, how little time had been allotted to each of them. How precious each moment of it was.

He turned for the shelter where he would find Tink and remind him to get started on the wiring that had been damaged. So much to do, he thought to himself. So much to do, and so little time.

8

Using his E-Tab, Tink pulled up the shuttle's topographical image files, a holographic display assembled from Carpathia's most recent data of the planet surface. In addition to the mountains and giant fissure, there were several massive smooth areas that could be either vast deserts or oceans. The surface temperature never rose above ten degrees, so the probability of liquid water existing out in the open was unlikely.

But there was most definitely an aquifer, a layer of water-saturated soil below the planet surface. NASA had fitted the Carpathia's payload with a special bit for drilling wells and a processor for melting and purifying ice. Parts of the shuttle itself were also designed for the assembly of submersible pumps, as well as all-terrain vehicles, and other mechanical devices needed for survival.

Before turning in for the night (if that's what they could call it), Fess and Jonah had assembled the first of their two rovers.

"Tomorrow we'll need to explore the area in more detail," Adán explained. "Jonah, you could survey a spot to drill the well."

"Wherever we drill," said Jonah, "that's going to be our new home. And quite frankly, I'd rather not spend the rest of my life in the middle of a sand pit—or more accurately—dust pit."

"Aren't there any trees on this frickin' planet?" asked Fess, tightening the last screw on the rover's frame.

Tink shook his head. "I doubt we'll find anything like back home. According to the diagnostics, the gravity here is 1.2 times that of earth."

"No wonder I feel like hippo."

"It might affect what sort of plant life exists here—that is if there's water near enough to the surface."

Adán studied the holographic charts and schematics, but even with Tink's help, he had a difficult time deciphering them. Jonah was the guy for maps, but his eyes were drooping, and he'd been yawning for the past twenty minutes. They were all nearing exhaustion.

Tink turned off the holo and took the E-Tab back inside the shuttle. Once Jonah and Fess finished the second smaller rover's assembly, they headed for the shelter. Adán followed and found the interior large and inviting—and warm. Fess stripped off his gear, draped himself across his cot, and was out cold in minutes. Jonah insisted he couldn't sleep on an empty stomach, so he tore open a couple pouches of peaches and granola and settled onto his cot to read on his tablet.

Lainie, still suited up, grabbed a pillow and blanket. "I'm covering for Dema tonight," she said. "She deserves a good night's rest after sitting with Scott most of the day. Be sure to bring back some moon rocks." She waved at Adán before leaving the shelter.

Tink passed her on the way out, lugging an overstuffed red canvas pack behind him. "Night, Lainie," he said. She gave him a quick, playful smile and disappeared outside.

Adán waited until he was sure Lainie was far enough from the shelter not to hear him, then he asked Tink, "What's going on with you two?"

"What do you mean?" Tink replied, failing miserably to hide his embarrassment.

"C'mon. It's obvious to everyone you've got a thing for Lainie."

"It is? I mean, I guess—yeah."

"And she seems to have a thing for you too."

Tink's eyes lit up. "You think so?"

"What? Don't you know it?"

A look of doubt spread across Tink's face. "I've liked her since the beginning, and before departure I tried a few times to connect, you know? But she didn't seem interested."

"You mean she blew you off? That doesn't sound like something she'd do."

"No. She's too nice for that. More like skirted the issue. She was really good at avoiding the subject. But here, I figure I've got nothing to lose, right?" Tink smiled tentatively. "You think I have chance with her?"

Adán thought he definitely had a chance and told him so.

He noticed Tink struggling with the weight of the pack he carried, which, due to gravity, was heavier than it would have been on Earth.

"What's in that thing?" asked Adán, taking it from Tink.

"You mean besides food?" answered Tink. "How about the camera, extra comms, and—oh, maybe the most important thing—water. You shouldn't go out *there* without it."

"It'll freeze before I get a mile from the shuttle."

Tink grinned, pulling something silver and square from his pocket. He squeezed it and the sound of crinkling foil and a slight pop made Adán smile.

"Hand warmer. Should keep the water just above freezing for a couple of hours at least." Tink tossed the warmer into the pack, then closed it up again.

Adán switched on the portable Tab strapped to his wrist. Like the larger E-Tabs, it received and transmitted information from the shuttle.

"Ready?" asked Tink.

"Ready as I'll ever be."

Tink patted him on the shoulder and gave him a thumbs up. Then Adán headed out of the tent to where the rover stood waiting.

"Hold up!"

Just as Adán was securing Tink's pack to the rover's flat bed, Dema appeared at the shuttle hatch. She jogged across the open stretch of ground between them. She was out of breath by the time she reached them, gripping the handle of a square white box.

"Here," she told Adán. "Just in case."

"Thanks." Adán added the first aid kit to the red pack. "How's our commander doing?"

Dema gave a non-committal nod of her head. "Okay, I guess, but I wish I could get him out of there, away from all that dust. It can't be good on his lungs."

Dema stepped back from the rover, and Adán pressed the ignition button. The engine ran on compressed solar cells rather than liquid fuel, so there was no concern about getting stranded without a refill.

"I'll be back in an hour or two," he told Dema over the drone of the rover's motor.

"Be careful," she replied.

He squeezed the throttle, and the little rover lurched forward. He was moving—away from the Carpathia. Away from the last scrap of humanity Adán might ever see. The thought sloshed inside of him like a cup of half curdled milk. It made him a little sick. He couldn't help himself. He had to turn around and look. Take one last mental picture of the shuttle and—the thought struck him—of Dema.

A jagged sound, a sudden horrible sound like Adán had never heard before, ruptured the air. Loud enough to be heard over his comm, loud enough to drown out the hum of the rover. At first, he thought something had gone wrong with the motor. A belt had snapped, or Fess hadn't installed a gear right and it had jammed. Adán switched off the motor and listened. Then he turned to look over his shoulder at Dema. She stood stock still, her face drained of color. A second later—half a second—another sound came, this time human. A human scream that could only come from the most unimaginable kind of fear or pain. Then Dema was off, sprinting away from him. Away—towards the shelter.

Tink's voice shouted in Adán's comm. "Adán, you'd better get back here—quick!"

Adán unsnapped his safety harness and ran for the shelter. He found Fess outside in front on his hands and knees, a string of yellow bile dripping from his heaving mouth into the matching pool of it between his hands and a trail of blood behind him in the sand. Jonah lay on his back a few yards away, his eyes wide with fear. Neither wore their helmets. Dema dropped down beside him and took his shaking hands in hers. His palms, Adán noticed, were scuffed up pretty badly with patches of the orange dust caked in the bloody scratches.

He had crawled out, Adán realized. Crawled out on his hands and knees. Couldn't get out fast enough.

"What the hell happened?" shouted Adán. Tink ran up to him, his eyes wide with fear.

"I'd just gone outside, to keep a lookout, like you said. It was seconds. I was gone only seconds!"

Jonah pulled one of his hands free of Dema, pointing a finger at the shelter. It fell to Adán, then, to see what was inside, to find out what had scared the crap out of these guys. He listened for a few seconds, wondering if what had scared them was still inside. What could it be? They hadn't seen any animals. Not even the tiniest insect. And the shelter wasn't more than fifty feet from the rover, in full view. Adán hadn't seen anything go in. Maybe on the other side? The side he couldn't see from here?

He took a few hesitant steps, and then realized what that must look like to the others. He had to be confident. They expected him to be. He took a deep breath and marched around to the opposite side of the shelter, the one facing away from the shuttle and towards the desert. As soon as he rounded the corner, he pulled up short. His mind emptied out completely as if someone had punctured a hole in his brain and drained out all rational thought.

In the center of the shelter wall were three parallel tears running from top to bottom. The edges of the shelter material were shredded as if something had slashed through

71

it all at once very quickly, but what was that something? What—in the middle of an empty desert—could do this? Adán came closer, touching the frayed edge of one of the three slices. Something sharp, something large. A knife? Three knives?

Adán dropped his hand to his side and took several steps back until he could see the whole thing all at once. He knew what this looked like. He'd seen something like this before, but on a much smaller, almost insignificant scale. He knew without any doubt what had done this.

Claws.

Adán

They had spotted it quivering in a dark, wet doorway on the way home from school. The day's storm had paused, but the air was still frigid, and Adán and Saul's breaths formed lacy clouds in front of their faces. The shivering orange ball of fur peered up at Adán with two huge blue eyes. It was just a kitten, and its pathetic meow seemed to plead with him to save it.

Adán had never had a pet before. His father wouldn't allow it, but surely if he and Saul brought this little creature home, even Father would have to take pity on it. At least he would let Adán dry it and feed it, maybe give him a chance to find it a home if not let it stay in theirs. Adán's head swam with possibilities. He knelt down on the wet pavement and tried to coax the kitten out from the shadows, but still the little fellow shrank back, suspicious of the approaching boy.

"It's frightened," said Saul. "Just let it alone."

Adán ignored his older brother's advice.

"It's okay," he said to the kitten in as soothing a voice as he could. Sliding his backpack off his shoulder and setting it on the ground beside him, he reached out, cautiously gathering the kitten into his hands. The kitten resisted at first, wriggling to get free, but Adán quickly pulled it close and tucked it beneath his jacket.

Saul shook his head disapprovingly, but there was a hint of a smile on his face. "All right then," he said finally with a sigh, "let's get you and that *thing* home before it rains again."

Adán resisted the impulse to run the rest of the way home, not wanting to jostle the kitten too much. Even so, he was out of breath by the time they arrived. Their father was waiting for them on the porch steps.

"Donde has estado?" Father directed his question to Saul. He wasn't a tall man or broad, but as he stood there, dress sleeves rolled up to his elbows and tie hanging loosely around his neck, he was imposing just the same. "I said, where have you been? I told you to hurry."

It was then Adán remembered that today was the day his father had circled on the calendar in red marker. On finding the kitten, he had completely forgotten.

"We've waited months for this audition, Saul. I took off work early for this, I expected you to get him home on time. Adán," he said turning his glare on his younger son, "get your violin, and let's go."

Saul glanced down at Adán, and their eyes met. It was Adán's fault they were late. It had been *his* decision to rescue the kitten. He should take the blame, but it was Saul who spoke up first.

"We found something," he said. "I know we can't have pets, but we thought we could take care of it for a few days until we found a place for it. It was freezing."

His father glared at him from beneath thick black eyebrows. He was a serious man who expected his sons to take things seriously, too.

"There isn't time—" Father began, but Saul cut him off.

"If you would just listen—"

The slap came without warning. The sound of it sent a jolt through Adán as the weight of Father's hand jerked Saul's face to the side.

Adán blinked back tears. Father didn't understand. He would show him what he had brought. He would show him the kitten! Then he'd realize what they were trying to do.

Maybe the kitten sensed his nervousness. Maybe it was just scared. When Adán opened his coat, the kitten practically exploded out of it. It scurried right up Adán's chest and onto his face, its tiny, needle-sharp claws scoring three finger-length lines across his cheek. Then it bounded off Adán's face to the ground and skittered away around the corner of the house.

They weren't deep. Hardly even bled, though later he'd spent a good ten minutes staring at the three parallel scratches in the mirror. They did hurt a little, but the pain was nothing compared to the shame he'd felt under his father's glare, which expressed more satisfaction than anger.

"That's what you get," Father said, "for rescuing someone who doesn't want to be rescued."

AND THE WORD WAS...

The Official Blog of The Terrestrial Brotherhood

"And out of his mouth goeth a sharp sword, that with it he should smite the nations...and he treadeth the winepress of the fierceness and wrath of Almighty God." (Revelation 19:15 KJV)

O ye peoples of the Earth, hear ye the mouthpiece of the Lord. Yea, the world has been condemned. It stands before the judgment bar of God, for the blood of the innocent dead cry out to God from the dust. And the punishment shall be hell fire! And our punishment is just. The angel soundeth forth his trumpet! The horses of the Apocalypse ride down upon us! Let us humble ourselves before our Maker and accept his divine wrath, for we are unworthy creatures, less than the dust of the Earth.

Governments seek to circumvent the will of the Lord. They would send Adam's seed into the depths of the universe to inhabit a new planet. But I say, wo unto them who carry Earth's plague of wickedness to other worlds. We have destroyed our promised land with pollution, war, and greed. Let us not destroy any other planet. For the heavens are God's footstool.

Gather together, O ye house of Israel, and let not the wicked confound the righteous. Bring your children into your bosom and face the wrath of your God with humility and meekness. For his ways are just and merciful.

Amen.

Posted by Reverend Lucas T. Bigelow

9

Fess's pant leg had been sliced from hip to knee. Dema pulled the fabric back to expose a matching red gash underneath.

"What the hell did that?" Fess squealed.

Adán came around the shelter and found him holding tight to Dema's arm like a scared little boy who'd had a nightmare. On seeing Fess's bloody leg, a rush of alarm momentarily immobilized him. Whatever had slashed the shelter could easily have killed Fess or any of them, but he couldn't say that, couldn't cause a panic.

"I don't know," said Dema, examining the wound. "Didn't you see anything?"

"No!" cried Fess. "I was asleep, then something just cut me!"

By now Jonah had finished vomiting and had half crawled, half dragged himself to collapse on the ground beside Fess. He lay on his side with his head resting on his arm, his eyes closed.

Dema's eyes met Adán's, her expression fierce. She wanted the first aid kit.

"Tink," said Adán, "grab the kit off the rover, will you?"

Tink stood back staring at the gaping wound in Fess's leg. He didn't respond at first, like he hadn't heard Adán, but then he ran for the rover, snatched the kit's handle, and was back seconds later. By now, Dema had torn away the shredded fabric of Fess's uniform.

"You were still awake, weren't you, Jonah?" she asked. "What did you see?"

"Nothing," he said weakly.

Dema unlatched the kit's cover and rummaged through it with her clean hand. The other was smeared with Fess's blood. She found what she wanted: a surgical needle and thread.

"Tink, would you mind finding the antiseptic? It's in a brown vial." Dema carefully spread open Fess's wound and checked for debris. Tink dug in the kit for the bottle while Fess groaned.

"There's dust in here, and fibers from your uniform," continued Dema. "If I stitch you up without cleaning it properly, it could get infected. We don't know what sort of bacteria exist here. Adán?" Dema looked up at him again, and he made a conscientious effort to pull himself together. "I need to get him inside to the showers. I've got to rinse this out."

Fess cowered, his eyes squeezed shut. "No, Dema. It's gonna hurt."

Adán knelt beside Fess and patted his shoulder. "It'll be all right, kid. Dema's got a gentle touch."

Dema cast him a curious glance and gave him a little smile. Then she returned her focus to Fess.

"I'll try to be quick about it, okay?" she said. "In the shuttle, I've got some lidocaine. It'll numb you right up, I promise."

Adán started to slide his hand under Fess's arm to help lift him, but Dema stopped him. "Tink and I can manage," she said. "I need someone to stay with Jonah. Bring him in when he's strong enough to stand."

After Dema secured a couple of compresses around Fess's thigh to stem the bleeding, Adán helped Fess onto his feet, or at least to one foot. Then Fess put one arm around Dema's shoulders and the other around Tink. The going was awkward, but they managed to make it to the shuttle hatch without too much trouble.

Once they'd gone, Adán turned his attention to Jonah who hadn't shifted an inch from his spot in the sand. Adán was beginning to feel the bite of subzero through his suit. Jonah wasn't wearing his helmet and now risked getting frostbite without it.

"Jonah, I need to get you inside, buddy," Adán said. "It's too cold to stay out here for long."

Jonah didn't move. Adán patted his shoulder. Even through his own visor, the smell of vomit on Jonah's breath turned his stomach.

"At least let me get you back into the shelter," he added. "You can rest in there until you're up to walking back to the shuttle."

"I'm not going back in there!" The sudden urgency of Jonah's protest took Adán by surprise. Jonah peeled open his eyes. The desperate, confused look in them gave Adán chills. "There was nothing there," Jonah hissed, forcing out each syllable. "There was *nothing* there."

Adán broke away from Jonah's piercing gaze and scanned the horizon. If there had been something, someone should have seen it, shouldn't they? The shuttle's readings said it was more than a hundred miles to the nearest mountain. Except for the canyon a mile to the west, the remaining landscape was nearly flat in every direction. There was nowhere for an animal to hide, no way to sneak up on them unseen.

The attack had come from the far side of the shelter, away from the shuttle. He and Dema had been distracted, talking. And they were closer to the shuttle than the shelter. And Tink was in front near the door. So, it could be possible that something might have approached . . .

But from the size of the tears in the shelter wall, it was something big. Shouldn't they have seen it run off, at least? There was nothing around them but open terrain. Nowhere to hide.

There was *nothing* there?

"C'mon, Jonah, I'm getting you to the shuttle. I'm freezing my balls off out here."

The intensity of Jonah's stare relaxed slightly, and the corners of his lips lifted. "You're going to need those eventually," he said, his voice trembling. "I mean, that's why we're here, isn't it? To colonize a new world?"

"Yeah, but don't remind Dema and Lainie, all right? With five of us guys and only two of them, it'll go to their heads."

"I don't like those odds either," said Jonah, managing a forced chuckle. With some effort, he raised both arms, his hands drooping forward like wilted flower petals. Adán took them both in a firm grip and hoisted him to his feet. Jonah wobbled a bit and welcomed Adán's steadying arm around him. They started forward slowly.

"Jonah," said Adán cautiously, "you said you didn't see what attacked the shelter. Were you facing away from it? Were you asleep?"

Jonah moaned. "Sorry," he said, leaning more heavily against Adán. "I feel a little dizzy. No, I wasn't asleep. I was sitting at the table reading the greenhouse specs. The sooner we can grow our own food, the sooner we can stop eating that dehydrated crap."

"Tell me what happened."

Jonah paused as if trying to assemble his thoughts. "Fess was out like a light," he began. "At least I thought he was, but then he suddenly sat straight up. It startled me, so I turned to see what had happened. There was this look in his eyes—a mix of confusion and fear—you know, like someone who wakes up all disoriented. I think maybe he heard something I hadn't. He was right next to the wall. Anyway, this was all in half a second, and then there was this tearing sound, and these three rips just appeared, and Fess's leg opened up. And then he was screaming."

"What was it?" asked Adán.

"I don't know. Like I said, there was nothing there." Jonah looked at Adán as if pleading with him to confirm what he had just said, like he wasn't exactly sure about it himself. When Adán didn't say anything, Jonah continued. "I was so scared, it was all I could do to get myself out of there."

They were within two yards of the shuttle hatch now, and the closer they got the more relieved Adán felt. Once inside, maybe he could talk to Fess again. Maybe once he'd calmed down a bit, he would be able to think more clearly, tell Adán what he'd seen—or heard.

Just then, Tink appeared at the shuttle hatch. "Hey, Lainie sent me to tell you the good news," he said, though his eyes looked more worried than relieved. "Commander Dryker's awake."

10

Adán found Dema, Lainie, and Tink in the Quarters gathered around his cryo unit. Dema was intent on the monitor, while Lainie and Tink stood back a little, allowing her room to maneuver as necessary.

"How is he?" asked Adán. He came around the opposite side of the unit to face Dema. The first thing he noticed was Scott's color. His skin was no longer sallow but had some pink in it.

"His brain functions appear to have stabilized," said Dema. "His heart rate's good. A moment ago, I detected movement in the fingers."

Lainie spoke up from behind Adán. "I was watching him for Dema," she said, "and he moved. His hands twitched, and his mouth opened a little."

"When did that happen?" asked Adán.

"About ten, maybe fifteen minutes ago. I would have told you right away, but Dema asked me not to leave him alone for a moment. I let her know as soon as she came back."

"I saw Fess out cold on the common room floor," said Adán. "Is he going to be okay?"

"He'll be fine," said Dema. "I cleaned his wound and stitched him up. I gave him a pretty strong sedative. In fact,

I was going to send Tink back out to fetch his bedding. Fess will be out for at least eight hours. After that, he'll need to remain in bed for a few days. The wound's pretty deep."

"I'll go right now for the bedding," said Tink.

"Are you sure it's safe?" asked Lainie, sincere concern in her voice.

Tink gave her a reassuring smile. "Don't worry about me. If something sneaks up on me, I've got the moves." He took a couple of awkward karate chops at the air, and Lainie laughed a little. Then he left.

"Did you bring Jonah inside?" Dema asked Adán.

"Yeah, but the guy's confused. I mean, he described what happened, but it doesn't make sense. Anyway, I left him on a bench near Fess."

In the cryo unit, Scott Dryker's body jerked.

Dema peered at her E-Tab, now synced to the monitor. "I think he's coming around," she said.

As if responding on command, Scott swiveled his head from side to side, and a soft, low moan escaped his mouth. A moment later, his eyelids fluttered open. His unfocused gaze wandered aimlessly. Then he fixated on the flickering overhead light. Adán watched the recognition dawn in Scott's face as he slowly came to understand where he was. Then his eyes darted from the light to Dema's face.

"Scott, are you all right?" she asked him. "Can you hear me?"

The commander's eyes widened in astonishment. He blinked hard, and on seeing Dema once more, his expression froze. He shifted his face to the side and found Adán. When he saw Lainie, a look Adán couldn't quite describe came over him. Was it disbelief? Or panic? Maybe a little of both.

Scott's body jerked again. His arms began flailing, and he shouted incoherently. Adán grabbed one of his arms, trying to hold him still, but Scott thrashed too violently to control, like some wild animal trapped in a cage. Dema reacted quickly. She keyed in a sequence of numbers on the monitor and almost immediately Scott's body relaxed. His eyes, however, remained fearful. He opened his mouth as if to speak, but all that came out was a series of inarticulate sounds.

"You're okay, Scott," Dema said. "I've just given you a small dose of Demerol. You had a rough time coming out of cryo, but there have been no other complications. You'll feel some muscle cramping and a little disorientation at first, but it'll pass. You're all right, Scott. You're alive."

Scott squeezed his eyes shut. His lips quivered as he tried to speak again. "H-how m-many—"

Dema slid her hand up to Scott's forehead, smoothing his hair back from his face. "How many?" she asked. "How many what?"

Scott swallowed. Adán noticed how dry his lips looked.

"He's thirsty," said Adán. Rather than ask Lainie to go for water, he went himself. In the common room, Tink had returned and was gently rolling the sleeping Fess onto one of the mattresses from the shelter.

"How is he?" asked Adán, filling a cup at the aqua mixer.

"Heavy." Tink grunted as he shifted Fess into place and pulled a blanket over him. Then he grabbed a second blanket and draped it over Jonah, who had laid his head on the table and fallen asleep.

Adán wondered again at the strange circumstances of Fess's injury, how something big enough to cause it could attack and retreat without being seen. He wondered, too, if the attack on the shelter was related to the damage on the shuttle.

The cup filled too quickly, and he poured a little out.

"How's Dryker?" asked Tink.

"Awake now," said Adán. "Trying to talk."

"Good."

"Did you see anything out there just now?"

"No. Course, I didn't really want to. I got Fess's stuff as quick as I could and hustled right back." Tink sat down at one of the tables. "What do you think did it?"

Adán still held the cup beneath the faucet. A single drop fell into it, sending tiny ripples across its surface. "I don't know," he said.

"Do you think—" Tink rubbed his thumb across his bottom lip. "Do you think maybe it was the same thing that damaged the shuttle?"

"Maybe."

Adán waited for Tink to say something else, but instead he laid back on the bench, stuffing a rolled-up towel beneath his head, and turned on his tablet.

When Adán returned to the Quarters with the water, Scott's eyes were closed again.

"He fell asleep," Dema said, looking up with an uneasy smile. "Don't worry. He's really weak and needs to rest. He'll probably wake up starving in a few hours."

"Jonah's out, too. Maybe we should all get some sleep."

Lainie stood nearby, arms folded defensively across her chest. She looked on the verge of tears. Dema must have noticed, too, because she slid a comforting arm around her shoulder.

"You're exhausted, Lainie," she said. "I think we should all stay in the shuttle tonight. We'll make room."

"Agreed," said Adán. "I'll have Tink remove another table."

"Tink's back?" asked Lainie, hope in her voice.

"Yeah."

Lainie looked at Dema as if asking permission. Dema nodded. "Go on. Get some sleep."

Adán sensed something lingering underneath Dema's usual confidence. After what happened in the shelter, she was afraid—and Adán couldn't blame her. They were all afraid.

11

"So, where the hell *are* we?" Fess hobbled to a bench and lowered himself onto it, his injured leg jutting out in front of him, stiff from the layers of bandages Dema had wrapped around it. He accepted a steaming paper cup from Lainie, sipping it cautiously.

They'd all slept surprisingly well despite the events of the previous day. Even Adán had passed out the moment his head hit his pillow. Now the Carpathia's crew sat around one of the tables eating rehydrated scrambled eggs and drinking cocoa. Even Dema had momentarily left Dryker to join them.

Jonah stroked the cross around his neck. "We know this isn't Europa. So, how hard could it be to figure out what planet this *is*?"

They all looked to Tink, who had spent his three-hour watch isolated in the shuttle cabin studying data and records the rest of them could hardly decipher. He slid his tablet to the center of the table and switched it on.

"Computer, display image."

A three-dimensional holo of the planet appeared, rotating a foot above the tablet, a floating ginger-colored orb with dark jagged lines across its surface.

"This image is being projected from the shuttle's sensors and data banks," Tink explained, "in a holographic form intended to give us a realistic impression of what this planet looks like."

Adán stood back from the table, letting the steam from his cup warm his face. From this vantage point, he could see the holo and the faces of most of the crew. They looked worried but hopeful.

"It kind of looks like Mars," said Lainie. "Are we on Mars?"

"Naw, man. It looks more like Io, one of Jupiter's other moons." Fess set down his drink. The brown liquid sloshed, and a little spilled over the rim onto the table. "Maybe we just landed on the wrong moon?"

Jonah retrieved a cloth rag from a drawer and handed it to Fess, who used it to swipe up the spill. "We couldn't survive on Io," said Jonah. "Its atmosphere is mostly sulfur dioxide. If we'd landed there, we'd all be dead."

Tink pressed a fingertip against his tablet screen, and the holo enlarged, the landscape details becoming clearer. "We're not on Mars or Io, or any planet in our solar system," he said.

Everyone shifted uncomfortably.

Out of the solar system? Impossible, thought Adán. The program they'd all been a part of for two years specifically stated that they would be colonizing Europa. A coalition of international governmental space agencies had established the Europa Project to train and transport a team of qualified colonists to Jupiter's moon to dig wells, build greenhouses and power sources, in essence, lay the foundation of a society where humans could exist. It was Star Trek in real life, humans boldly going where no one had gone before.

But they hadn't landed on Europa or any planet anywhere near Earth. So, where were they—and how did they get there?

Tink pulled up a long list of running data beside the planet's image, pointing out various equations and numbers.

"The planet we're on now is, as you already know, tidal locked. It has a similar atmosphere, temperature, and gravitational pull to Earth and occupies the same habitable distance from its sun as Earth does to ours. It has water, though whatever liquid water exists here is likely located beneath a frozen crust. That's what these dark spots might be." He pointed out several shaded areas on the holo.

"What about those lines?" Fess said.

"Fissures in the planet surface, some several miles deep."

"Rivers?" asked Lainie.

"Maybe at one time," replied Tink. "Or they could have resulted from massive quakes. The rest of the planet is pretty much desert."

"Duh," said Jonah. "As if we didn't already know that."

Dema hadn't said anything yet. She stood near the open door to the Quarters, keeping an eye on Scott who had been sound asleep in Adán's cryo unit since the previous night.

"If we're not in our solar system," she ventured, "then are you saying we don't know where we are?"

Tink released a slow breath as if preparing to deliver bad news. "We're on Gliese 581g."

Fess's lips parted, and he blinked in confusion. "Gliese five-eighty—what?"

"581g," repeated Tink.

"That's an odd name for a planet," said Lainie.

"Actually," continued Tink, "Gliese is the name of the star, or the sun. There are six planets orbiting this particular star, and this one happens to be 581g. It was discovered by Stephen S. Vogt of the Lick-Carnegie Exoplanet Survey in 2010 and is sometimes referred to as Zarmina."

"Okay," said Dema, "so why are we here on Zarmina instead of Europa? It doesn't make sense."

"Boy, did we miss our target," said Jonah with a sardonic laugh.

Fess snapped his head up. "You don't *miss* landing on a planet. NASA must have sent us here on purpose."

"But why?" asked Lainie.

Adán didn't have an answer, and by the silence in the room, he suspected none of them did. Jonah swallowed the last of his cocoa and set his cup noisily on the table.

"I have an idea," he said through a half grin, "but you won't want to hear it."

Lainie began to collect the now empty food trays while Dema came farther into the room and sat down.

"Just say it, Jonah," said Dema. "I think we're all open to suggestions at this point."

Jonah pointed to the holo. "Our supposed mission was to establish a colony on Europa so that larger populations could be transported there from Earth over time, but what if that was all a lie? What if there was never any intention of transporting anyone?"

"That's bull," Fess scoffed, but Adán wanted to hear more.

Jonah continued. "Think of the missing mix tanks, our space suits. What if they knew from the very start that we were going a lot farther than they let on?"

"How far are we talking about exactly?" asked Dema.

Tink tapped on the tablet and new figures appeared in the holo. "You're not going to like this, but Gliese is just under twenty-one light years from Earth."

The room fell silent as everyone tried to process this new detail. Adán tried to calculate the distance in his head but couldn't.

"But the cryo was set for three years..." said Fess, his voice trailing off in disbelief.

"Clearly, we've traveled longer than that," answered Jonah. "What? Twenty? Thirty years?"

"More, actually," said Tink.

Lainie dropped the empty trays into the recycle bin. "How much more?" she asked.

"In 2024," Tink answered, "NASA's Clipper spacecraft began its mission to study Europa and arrived in just under six years. In 2026, Space X traveled 40,000 kilometers (25,000 miles) per hour to reach Mars. The Carpathia's speed is comparable to Space X, which should have delivered us to Europa in three years' time, or at least that's what we were told."

Jonah huffed impatiently. "We all know our space flight history, Seoung. Get on with it."

Tink slid his finger across his tablet, and the holo of the planet disappeared, replaced by more equations. "At that speed, it would have taken us over 600,000 years to reach Gliese."

"What?" Fess shouted. "That's impossible!"

Tink held up a defensive hand. "Yes. Yes, it is impossible."

The crew let out collective sighs of relief. Adán felt a sheen of sweat forming above his brows. What was Tink doing, messing with them like that?

Tink went on. "I've calculated the Carpathia's fuel capacity and usage, the amount of power we've generated and consumed, and a bunch of other data from the shuttle's internal flight reports. Taking acceleration into account, I estimate that we've been traveling at 30,000 kilometers—per second. That's one tenth the speed of light, which makes us the fastest space vehicle in human history."

Adán tried to swallow, but his mouth had suddenly gone dry. NASA had hidden more from them than just their destination.

"So, at that speed, realistically," said Dema, but she didn't finish her sentence.

Tink nodded. "It took us two hundred and twenty years to get here."

The expressions on everyone's faces matched the shock that Adán felt. Two hundred and twenty years? He thought of Saul, his father, the friends he left behind. No, he couldn't grapple with the thought of what this meant. But if it was true, if Tink and Jonah were right, he had only one question: *Why?*

"It could be a mistake," suggested Dema. "A systems malfunction. Tink?"

"Possible, I suppose," Tink replied, "but highly improbable."

No one responded. It was clear by the fear and confusion on their faces that the crew felt overwhelmed by this development.

Adán broke into the silence. "I know this information isn't what we expected to hear, but until we search the archives and further study the mission data," he said, "we can't know anything for certain."

Jonah cut in. "What's there to know? All the hype about relocating the human race on Europa was a cover up. Massive scale colonization was not only impractical, it was impossible."

"What does that mean?" asked Lainie. "NASA, the government, the world lied to everyone on Earth and sent a fleet of shuttles twenty light years away, for what reason?"

Fess, in his growing agitation, shouted. "No reason! There's *no* reason! This is all a bunch of bull shit! I say we get this shuttle back online and hightail it home."

The tension in the room was palpable. Adán didn't know what else to say. He was just as confused, felt just as betrayed as everyone else. Fess had good reason to feel frustrated, to doubt the reality of their situation. And what if Dema was right? What if this was all some big mistake?

"There's no point in speculating," Adán said, trying to quell the crew's fears. "We're just getting ourselves worked up for nothing. Better we focus on what we know, and get our jobs done as best we can."

He gave Fess a gentle pat on his shoulder, adding a smile for good measure.

Fess nodded nervously. "Yeah. Yeah, okay. Get our jobs done."

Already Adán noticed the pressure in the room dissipating, and most of the others began talking about greenhouses and wells, but Jonah remained seated at the table, shoulders hunched over his hands clasped around his cross. As Adán's eyes met his, he saw in them a sort of resignation, as if he had accepted a truth known only to him. They shared that look for a moment until Adán finally broke away, joining the others in their conversation. Yet the weight of Jonah's eyes and the probability they carried stayed with him like a bad dream.

NEW YORK TIMES

NATIONS HIT BY RECORD HIGH HEAT WAVE

By Darnell Archer

Over the past several weeks, cities around the United States have been experiencing record high temperatures. Los Angeles, California, for example, hit 118 degrees in August, surpassing its previous record of 113 in September 2010, while New York reached 110, beating its previous high of 103, also in 2010.

Until recently, experts have believed temperatures across the nation had reached their peak as numbers began to level off in recent years. Yet a sudden surge in solar radiation levels, as reported by the National Oceanic and Atmospheric Administration, is being blamed for the current rising heat.

The U.S. is not the only nation facing oven-like temperatures. Governments across the African continent, Australia, Central America, and even Europe have expressed growing concern.

"If this heat wave does not subside soon," said Kwame Gbeho, Ghana's Secretary of Agriculture, in a recent press conference, "we will face the worst drought in our nation's history."

Efforts are underway in both the United States and India to adapt desalinization technology on a massive scale in preparation for such disasters around the world, but not everyone is confident such measures will make a big enough impact should temperatures continue to rise, as some are predicting.

12

The rover bumped along the uneven Gliesen terrain. Though the surface was covered in several inches of dust, the ground beneath it was rocky and pocked with thousands of small craters. Adán held tight to the steering mechanism, but his gloves made it difficult to grip, and his hand slid off whenever they hit an especially deep hole. As a result, they traveled at a speed far less than the rover's capacity, dragging out the trip longer than what might otherwise be necessary.

Once Tink had verified which planet they were actually on, he and Adán decided it was time to scout out the area. Adán's first attempt had been interrupted by the strange attack on the shelter, which had left them all shaken and scared, but when nothing of note occurred over the next twenty-four hours, Adán decided they had better get back outside and take a look around.

They drove east for fifteen minutes, covering the three-mile distance from the shuttle's scanners, and they were soon out of sight of the Carpathia. The dry, barren plain reminded Adán of a documentary he'd seen once on the Arctic tundra, only the land here was orange instead of white. There was no mistaking the Zarmina's landscape for Earth.

"So, what exactly are we looking for again?" asked Adán.

Intent on the holo image in front of him, Tink didn't respond.

"Tink, there's nothing out here, and yet you're watching that thing like it's the season finale of *Games of Thrones*."

Tink cracked a smile. "I'm looking for water, for one thing, heat signatures for another. Even the slightest variation in temperature could suggest the presence of life—and where there's life, there's water."

"I thought it was the other way around, 'Where there's water, there's life.' At least that's what I remember being told."

"Microorganisms. You're talking about microscopic forms of life. I'm not interested in those right now. I'm looking for something—bigger."

Adán's hand slipped again. "We're out here freezing our butts off looking for—for what, Tink? Something we can't even see?"

Tink grinned. "Exactly."

They continued driving for another half hour toward the mountains, which appeared as distant as ever. Except for a breeze disturbing the top layer of dust, all around them lay an unaltered barren desert. Adán took his foot off the accelerator, and the rover cruised to a gentle stop.

"What do you think?" Tink asked, finally glancing up from the holo.

"What do I think about what?" replied Adán. Despite the fact that they had a clear view in every direction for miles around, he couldn't shake the uneasy feeling in his gut that something might pounce on them at any moment.

"About everything," said Tink. "Those mountains, the ice, all this freakin' dust."

"Well, for the mountains to be so far and look so huge," said Adán, "they've got to be a helluva lot bigger than we thought."

"Yeah. Like Olympus Mons on Mars. Did you know it's the biggest mountain in the whole Solar System? Well, *our* Solar System anyway. Fourteen miles high. Mount Everest is just under three miles, just to give you an idea."

"So, I guess reaching those mountains by rover is out of the question."

"Maybe," said Tink. "But it would take a long time. I'm guessing a few days at least."

They stared at the jagged range on the horizon. One crest stood out much higher than the others, a prominent peak with a cup-shaped summit.

"Do you think anyone's given that a name?" asked Tink.

"Who would have? No one's seen it but us."

"Then we should give it a name, don't you think?"

"Sure," said Adán. "Why not? Do you have something in mind?"

"It reminds me of that Disney movie, you know, the old one with the music."

"*Fantasia*?"

"Yeah, *Fantasia*." Tink's eyes lit up. "There's this massive mountain and a village nestled at its base. The sun goes down, and all these spirits and demons come up out of the ground and start dancing around. And the mountain? It's the devil, this massive black demon with wings. That mountain reminds me of that demon."

"Night on Bald Mountain."

"That's right. I remember now. How did you know?"

Adán shrugged. "My dad was a music professor. I must have watched *Fantasia* a hundred times as a kid. The demon from the film was based on Chernobog, a Slavic black god."

"Chernobog. I like it," said Tink. "Let's call it Chernobog Mons."

"Chernobog Mons it is." Adán thought it sounded funny, but it didn't seem right to laugh. By putting a name to it, the mountain seemed more alive somehow, and as the vast shadows that ringed it spread across the land, it was as if the mountain were acknowledging its title. Adán wondered if they had done something they would eventually regret.

They continued forward, though Adán was beginning to wonder if they'd spot anything worth seeing. If there was any life on this planet, any flora or fauna like what they called it during training, it wasn't anywhere near where they'd landed.

He was just about to tell Tink to turn back when something caught his eye, a thick black line cutting across the entire horizon.

"What is that?" he asked. He noticed, too, that the terrain had changed a little. Instead of just dust and craters, there were baseball-sized chunks of dirt scattered around. The closer they got to that line, the more chunks there were. Soon the rover was bouncing and bumping along even worse than on the craters, and the chunks had gotten bigger. They were now as big as basketballs. The line on the horizon grew bigger, too.

Tink whistled. "It's the canyon."

The rover came to a stop twenty yards from its edge, though Adán had never seen any canyon like this before. The stones were too large and too numerous now to maneuver the rover any closer. Adán and Tink got out and picked their way through the mine field of jagged boulders, some of which were as tall as their thighs, toward the edge of the canyon. When they got close, Adán dropped to his knees and crawled forward until his fingertips were level with the very edge, and he cautiously peered down into the depths of it. The walls were several shades darker than the planet surface, a warm cinnamon color, and dropped straight down for what seemed like miles. It reminded him of the Grand Canyon, only bigger. He'd gone there several times with his family when he was younger and had always been in awe of it. His mother had taken a panorama view from the North Rim which hung on his bedroom wall, a wide expanse of layered oranges, beiges, browns in curving, sloping canyon walls that seemed to carry your gaze either straight up to heaven, or straight down to the Colorado River below. He had never felt afraid when he was there, but here, kneeling at this vast snake-like pit that was so deep he could see no bottom to it, he felt something prick deep inside his gut. His heart rate sped up, and his breath came faster. His stomach clenched.

"You ever see anything like this?" said Tink who stood just behind him. He whistled long and low to emphasize his amazement. "Any guess how wide it is?"

Adán lifted his eyes to look at the opposite cliff far off in the distance. "I don't know," said Adán. "The Grand Canyon is ten miles across in some places."

"This is way wider than the Grand Canyon, wouldn't you say?"

"You been there?" asked Adán.

"Yeah, once. About two years ago… I mean, before I was recruited."

Tink leaned over Adán a little to look down into the canyon. "I can't see anything down there. Grand Canyon's a mile deep, right?"

"I think so."

Tink shook his head. "Geez. This is no Grand Canyon. This is like, I don't know, like the whole planet just broke open or something. Should we give this a name, too?"

Adán didn't reply, and Tink didn't offer any suggestions. They just stood there without saying anything more.

They stared a while longer before Tink finally broke Adán's trance. "We should get back," he said. "We'll have to explore in the opposite direction tomorrow. Maybe we'll find something more hospitable to human life that way."

Adán slowly crawled back away from the canyon's edge until he felt the tightness in his gut relax. Only then did he get back on his feet. He climbed into the rover beside Tink, but he couldn't shake the feeling he'd had at the canyon.

"You all right?" asked Tink.

"Yeah," said Adán. "Why?"

"You look pale as a sheet, and you're all sweaty."

Adán lifted his visor to wipe the perspiration off his lip and forehead. He did feel a little light-headed, and a finger of nausea crept up his esophagus. He leaned forward and put his face against his knees.

"I actually don't feel so good," he said.

Suddenly, it hit him. Adán swung his body out of the rover and barely got his helmet off before heaving onto the ground. His stomach convulsed violently, spewing out whatever remained of his meals that day. The sour smell of it made Adán feel even sicker, and he retched again. When he was done, he leaned back and closed his eyes. He felt weak, and his arms and legs trembled.

"What brought that on?" asked Tink, half laughing, though there was a strong undercurrent of worry in his voice. "Do you need anything? What can I do?"

Adán drew in a deep breath. He was grateful for the cold air that filled his lungs and soothed his stomach. He opened his eyes and took one last look at that black gash of the canyon. Then he closed them again and pulled on his helmet, dropping the visor down.

"I think you'd better drive," he said.

13

By the time they got back to the Carpathia, Adán was feeling almost back to normal. The only sign that he had been sick at all was the lingering burning at the back of his throat. Though he had rinsed his mouth with water and even swallowed some, the taste of vomit persisted.

"I'm going inside and get something to eat," he told Tink, who slowed the rover so Adán could hop off.

"You sure about that? My mom always said you should wait twenty-four hours after puking before eating or drinking anything."

"Yeah, my mom said that, too. But it's not like I've got the flu or anything. I mean, the sanitation team back home made doubly sure there wasn't a germ in sight when we went into cryo. And from the looks of this landscape, I doubt there's anything here I could've picked up."

"So, what happened?"

Adán shrugged. "I dunno. I guess looking down into that canyon sent my head spinning for a second, that's all. Like motion sickness or something, but I'm better now."

"Positive?"

"Positive."

"All right then. I'm going to clean up the rover and get it ready for tomorrow. The drive shaft's grinding a little. I think some grit got into the gears. I don't want it seizing up on us."

"Yeah, that's all we'd need is to get stranded miles out from the shuttle."

"Exactly."

Tink and the rover headed toward the back of the shuttle and the rear cargo bay where the rover's spare parts and tools were kept. When Adán entered the shuttle, he was surprised to find Scott Dryker awake and hunched over one of the tables, sipping from a warm cup of cocoa and a blanket draped over his shoulders. It was the first time since before the shuttle's departure that Adán had seen their Mission Commander sitting upright. He had forgotten how big Scott was, easily six feet, with an intimidating athletic build that was evident even through the blue jumper he wore.

Fess nodded to Adán as he came in. The rest of the crew stood silently around Scott in a ragged semi-circle. Dema had been very clear about what to do once the commander awoke. Don't aggravate him. Don't ask too many questions or reveal too much information. At least not right away. He'd been in a coma, and he was likely to feel a bit out of sorts for a while.

Scott shakily set his cup on the table, a thick tendril of steam snaking into the air. When he lifted his eyes, everyone else looked away.

"This is crazy," said Scott. "You don't have to ignore me. No matter what Dema told you. I'm fine. Really."

Fess glanced at the others as if asking for permission to speak. "You're okay then?" he asked.

"Yeah, I guess. Have a hell of a headache, but otherwise I'm no worse for wear. You guys act like I came back from the dead or something."

"You did," said Jonah.

"Jonah," snapped Dema.

"Well, I don't see why we have to walk on eggshells around him," Jonah replied. "I mean, look at him. He's not brain damaged. His limbs are all functioning properly. If he says he's fine, he's fine."

Fess spoke next. "Jonah's right. We've got a mission to accomplish. Now that the commander is in a position to command, we should get on with it."

"I agree," said Scott. He stood up and let the blanket fall to the floor, but he wobbled and grasped the edge of the table to steady himself. "I expect to be briefed on what happened while I was out."

"The ship was damaged," said Fess.

"I can see that," said Scott. "All that crap in the Quarters isn't pixie dust. What caused the breach?"

Fess glanced at Adán. "We don't know exactly."

"You don't know—exactly?"

"Something punctured the hull," offered Jonah. "Possibly during landing or just after."

"And the rest of the crew?"

Lainie hesitated, but then spoke up. "They were already dead when we got here."

"I suspect they were dead before we passed the Moon," said Dema.

"How so?" Scott's tone was skeptical.

Dema refilled Scott's cup. "They'd been dead for years. They were all but mummified."

"Impossible."

"You didn't see them."

"I don't have to. The Carpathia's cryo system is the most advanced in the world. I initiated the sequences myself after liftoff."

"That's right," said Jonah. "You're the Mission Commander. You piloted the shuttle out of orbit and verified cryo stabilization before putting yourself under."

"And when I went down," countered Scott, "everyone was fine. All systems stable."

Adán had been standing aside, listening to the conversation, surprised no one had brought up the most important question of all.

"Did you check our coordinates, too?" he asked, stepping forward into the circle.

Scott noticed him for the first time. "Coordinates? Yes, of course. Three years to Europa."

"The coordinates were changed," said Adán.

"Changed?" asked Scott. "By whom?"

"That's what we want to know. We're twenty light years from earth on a planet called Gliese 581g."

Scott's jaw muscles tightened. At first Adán wondered if Scott doubted him, but then the commander's gaze wavered, and he looked down at the table. His hands, clasped in front of him, tensed and relaxed over and over like he was considering his next move. Finally, Scott placed his palms on the table, looking from one team member to the other.

"Well, wherever the hell we are, we have a mission to accomplish, and we're going to do it right. Fuentes, has anyone tried to hail the rest of the fleet, or are we the only ones on this goddamned sand pit?"

That's it? thought Adán. *We tell him we're twenty light years off course, and he just accepts it and moves on. Odd.*

Adán responded to Scott's question in an official tone. "We've sent dozens of hails since we awoke, but we haven't gotten any responses—yet."

"I see," said Scott. "Well, keep sending them. Until we hear from someone, we'll have to assume we're it. Where's Seoung?"

"In the cargo bay, maintaining the rovers," said Adán.

"I need a full report of everything's that's been done in my absence, and I mean everything. I want to know what you all ate, drank, and crapped—you understand me?"

Scott looked at Fess, taking in the bandage around his leg. "What the hell happened to you?"

Fess glanced nervously at the others before responding. "I was attacked."

"Attacked? By who?"

"Not by who," said Lainie. "By what. And we don't know."

"It doesn't matter right now," interrupted Dema. "Commander Dryker's got enough to worry about. He needs to rest—"

"Tell me." Scott's voice was firm, insistent. So Dema, clearly against her better judgement, filled him in on the story. When she had finished, Scott sat in silence for a while as if digesting all the information he'd been given.

"So, we're not on Europa," he said. "Most of the crew is dead. And something, we don't know what, destroyed the shelter. All right. Put up another shelter."

"But Scott—" Dema protested.

"I said put up another shelter. Got that? Or are you and I going to have issues?"

Adán glanced at Dema hoping to share some unspoken comment on Scott's call to action, but the moment his eyes met hers, she looked away, fixing her gaze on her tablet instead.

"Sarkissian," said Scott in a voice that was more demanding than it needed to be, "I want an updated bio scan on everyone—stat."

Dema visibly bristled at the sound of her name. Lainie placed a hand on Dema's shoulder in a show of support. "She performed complex scans on all of us when we came out of cryo."

Scott did not even acknowledge Lainie. He kept a stern eye on Dema until she lifted her gaze to him. "I'll take care of it, Commander Dryker," she said.

"But it's only been three days," Lainie started, but Scott cut her a look that immediately silenced her.

"I'm going to review and update the logs," he said. "I don't want to be disturbed. And just so we're all on the same page, whatever happened over the past couple of days is of no significance." He aimed his glare directly at Adán. "I'm in charge now, and we're going to do things according to mission protocol. By the book. Is that clear?"

No one responded.

"Is that clear?" Scott repeated.

"Yes, sir," said Jonah with just the slightest hint of contempt. Lainie, Fess, and Dema followed with hesitant "Yes, sirs" as well. Dryker's dislike of Adán was pretty evident, and he wondered why the commander had a grudge against him. Adán had done nothing but try to keep the mission going despite being short three quarters of their crew and being attacked by some unseen indigenous creature. It wasn't personal, Adán reasoned. Dryker needed to regain his authority.

"Yes, sir," Adán said.

Scott headed for the cockpit. When he stumbled, Dema instinctively reached toward him to help, but he pushed her hand away and made the rest of the way on his own.

Fess

My name is Raymond, but I don't think anyone here knows that or cares. They dubbed me The Professor, Fess for short, but it wasn't meant as a compliment. They know I'm not supposed to be here. They know it took serious brains to do what I did.

Like a lot of the team, I'm bright. Smarter than your average high school graduate. Funny, the ad for colonists said nothing about intelligence being a prerequisite. In fact, NASA made a big point that the selection process would be anonymous, random. Anyone from any walk of life could get lucky, but those of us on the final ticket figured out the truth pretty quick. There was nothing random about it.

The balance between races was the first giveaway. I mean, think about it. The American population is made up of 76% white, 18% Hispanic, 13% black, 6% Asian, and a smattering of "other". Due to the laws of probability then, a truly random selection would mean the list of finalists should break down very close to these numbers. Instead, there is a very discernible even number of races represented here. And there's a pretty obvious 50/50 ratio of men to women.

Then, to really ice the cake, all of us—I mean *all* of us— are brilliant. Some more than others, of course, but it doesn't take much sleuthing to figure out that every team member either has an advanced degree at a young age or has excelled in his/her field in some other extraordinary way. I'm the exception, of course, since my expertise can't be found on any public database.

My question is: Why didn't NASA just recruit these guys instead of going through a façade of random selection? My guess is it had something to do with public opinion. Get the country all excited about throwing their names into the hat for a chance to be the first. The thing spread through social media like a California wildfire. By the time the names were announced, the whole damn country, the whole damn world, was on board.

Maybe it also had to do with funding. The application cost a pretty penny, not so expensive as to exclude the middle class, but expensive enough to dissuade the "undesirables". I imagine that was the first culling. They say more than a million applications were submitted, non-refundable. That's a chunk of change.

Clearly, the teams were selected for their intellect, their DNA, gender, race. I mean, c'mon. We're space colonists, right? NASA expects us to breed, to populate Europa with the human species. Though it's not written in the protocol, it's pretty obvious, and I don't think there's a guy in the entire program averse to that idea. So why the secrecy? Why the smokescreen? Money—check. Public support—check. There's got to be something else, something I'm missing.

In any case, I count myself lucky to be here not because I'm one of them, not because I fit in—but because I'm not, and I don't. I'm better. I'm more.

I beat the system.

I'm a hack, see? I didn't even make the first cut. I dropped out of high school, so maybe that was it. Steve Jobs was an average student and a college drop out. Zuckerberg. Gates. Dorsey. They were too smart for school, and so am I, but on paper, that doesn't look so good.

Maybe they'd already reached their quota of egotistic young black studs and didn't need anymore. No matter. I wanted on the team, and when Raymond "Fess" Duchene wants something, he gets it.

The hack wasn't easy, but in the end, my name was on the list. Not the front list, mind you. That would have been too obvious. I placed myself on the backup crew. Then I waited, and when the time was right, I fixed the blood test results for some guy named Trey something-or-other, gave him a positive for the latest mutation of Covid, and got him bumped.

So now here I am, training with the best of them. Yeah, so I'm a little younger than the rest of the crew. Hoping my future "soul mate" won't care about that when the time comes to pair up and propagate. In the meantime, I'm here and that other guy isn't. That's what matters. And if NASA has any suspicions that their system isn't as crack proof as they thought, they haven't said anything to me about it. In a week, I'm heading into space to see a new world and leaving this shitty one behind once and for all.

14

Tink was just securing the rover when Adán found him.

"I thought you were gonna grab dinner and take a nap," said Tink, cinching the safety strap around the rover's rear wheel.

"I was," said Adán, "but Commander Dryker had something else in mind."

"Scott? You mean he's up?"

"Yeah, he's up all right and slinging orders like hash. He wants us to erect the other shelter." He pointed to the thick silver log tucked under his arm.

"After what happened to Fess?"

"He doesn't buy it. And why should he? He was in La La Land during all the excitement. Now he's here and in charge, and he wants things to be done by the book." Adán framed the words with fingered quotation marks.

Tink chuckled. "Sounds like Dryker."

"Anyway, Jonah and Lainie are placing the stakes now. We decided to move it closer to the shuttle, twenty yards directly ahead of the nose. That way whoever's on post can have a clearer view of it."

"Computer, close the storage bay hatch, please," said Tink into his comm. In response, the eight-foot metal panels began to move on massive hydraulic hinges, controlled from the ship's hub. Had the electrical damage affected this part of the grid, opening them manually would have been challenging. Not impossible, but the hatches weighed several hundred pounds apiece and would have required several of the crew to heft them.

"So, how is he—Scott?" asked Tink, brushing a layer of dust from his gloves.

Adán shrugged. "Says he's got a whopper of a headache. Seems a bit wobbly on his feet, but he's as ornery as ever."

"In other words, he's back to normal."

The two of them headed over to where the new shelter's metal skeleton now stood. Adán unrolled the silver tarp and handed Jonah, Lainie, and Tink each a corner.

"Secure the corners first, then we'll raise the support beams," said Adán, "just like before."

"You know I'm not sleeping in this thing," said Jonah. "I don't care what Dryker says. He can bullwhip me for all I care."

"No one blames you for that." Adán adjusted his helmet. "I think we all feel the same, but it's been more than twenty-four hours since—I don't even know what to call what happened—since the incident, and it's been quiet since then. If it makes Dryker happy, we should at least make a good show of it."

"I'm sleeping in the shuttle with Fess. Period."

"I'll stay in the shelter," Lainie volunteered, attaching her corner, "as long as someone else stays out here too."

"Scott will be out here for sure. And Dema."

"I will, too," said Tink.

"All right," said Adán. "That makes five of us. I'll take the first watch tonight."

"Dryker might claim that for himself," said Jonah.

"He's still pretty weak," said Adán. "Dema's going to insist he get a good night's rest, and you know how persuasive she can be."

"I'll take second watch," said Tink. "I could use the time to study the schematics for the grid, and I want to look at the transmissions again. I spotted what I think may be a glitch in the program. Might explain why we haven't heard from anyone. I think I fixed it, but I want to make sure."

With the four corners firmly fastened, the crew worked together to hoist the inner framework, locking the beams and supports into place. The experience reminded Adán of an old-fashioned barn raising. They would soon be constructing greenhouses in the same manner.

"Okay," he said. "I'll report to Scott and then bring out the heater and comm. Lainie, Tink, can you help with the cots and bedding? Jonah, I'll tell Scott that Fess has to stay in the shuttle until his wound has healed. Dema doesn't want any chance of infection anyway, and he shouldn't stay alone."

"Thanks," said Jonah, relieved.

By midnight Ephemeris Time (ET), everyone was settled. Scott, having little energy remaining after his initial tirade, quickly agreed to all of Adán's suggestions and was the first to fall asleep in the new shelter. Lainie, Dema, and Tink soon followed suit. Adán retreated to the shuttle cockpit. Just as he had anticipated, from its windows he had a clear view of the shelter and much of the surrounding terrain. Nothing could approach within miles without his seeing it. Just to be on the safe side, however, he had erected a motion detector on the far side of the shelter, the side he couldn't see even from the cockpit. If anything moved within range, it would trigger a signal on his E-Tab.

Adán tapped on the overhead console, and a list of diagnostics appeared on the screen, the same information Tink had been studying when they'd first awoke. Beyond the screen, through the shuttle's windshield, Gliese's barren landscape lay like a vast sea of orange. The planet couldn't all be like this, Adán thought. Earth had deserts and plains and mountains and forests. If an alien visitor were to land in the middle of Iraq, he might mistake the planet to be a barren wasteland. Only after traveling hundreds of miles would the alien begin to see the true nature of Earth. It could be the same for Gliese. This was supposed to be the most Earth-like of any of the planets. There had to be more.

Adán passed the first hour easily, playing "Survive" on his E-Tab, a simulation from training that the crew members had turned into a game. When he grew bored, he read from a paperback copy of Stephen Crane's *The Open Boat and Other Stories,* one of the many books rescued from the dead crew's personal stores. In three hours, Tink's alarm would wake him to start his watch, but Adán didn't even make it to two.

He dreamed of Victoria Beach. It was his favorite summer retreat when he was a kid, a narrow strip of sand between two stone breakers stretching out into the sea like knobby gray fingers. He and his family spent just about every Friday there during the hottest weeks of the year. Adán and Saul had passed the time hunting for sand crabs and feeding the anemones that clung to the rocks. Sometimes his mother would buy a loaf of stale bread from the dollar store, and they'd break off little pieces to throw to the gulls. Adán never tired of watching the flock of white and gray birds sprint toward their snacks. He always felt a little sorry for the younger birds, the ones that were small and still mostly gray, and would make a point to toss plenty of bread where they could reach it before the adults could snatch it away. Once, he held out a piece for nearly ten minutes before one gull got up enough courage to pluck it off his palm.

When the days grew late and the tide started to come in, his mother would announce it was time to pack up and go. Adán still remembered the last time she waved to him from the car. He was on his boogie board out past the cresting waves. As he sat there watching her, he noticed as if for the first time the graceful curve of the shore, how it bowed inward like a giant letter 'C'. The waves rolled into it in gentle white coils, licked the dark, wet sand with their wide flat tongues, and then retreated back beneath the next set of waves. It reminded Adán of a picture he'd seen once of an ancient Mayan king sitting atop his throne surrounded by row after row of bowing subjects. The waves bowed to the shore in unceasing veneration.

If he had known then that he'd never see the ocean again, that his mother would die before the next summer, he might have lingered there a little longer. Instead, he had paddled forward, caught a wave, and raced to shore where he hopped up and ran to the car without even looking back to say good-bye.

The memory gave him a nauseated feeling, like when you wish so desperately for the chance to correct some wrong, but you know you can't. So, he was grateful when something

118

woke him from the dream. At first, he felt relieved, and then the regret, the isolation descended on him once again.

The slow, steady *beep* seemed unnecessarily loud in the empty cockpit, and it sent Adán's heart racing. He sat up, cursing himself for falling asleep.

The signal remained steady. Adán peered out the cockpit windows, worried that the motion detector had picked up on something. Yet he saw nothing but the vast orange desert and the still silver shelter. Confused, he glanced down at the E-Tab. The signal wasn't coming from there at all. It came from the cockpit itself—from the communications panel.

It was an incoming hail, a signal from another ship. Someone was trying to communicate with them!

Adán blinked hard. After three days of sending out signals and getting nothing in return, this was a relief. More than a relief. It was a miracle.

"Computer," he said, "receiver on."

A holo image appeared several inches above the built-in pad in the control panel. The NASA logo appeared, followed by a string of words blinking against a blue background:

INCOMING TRANSMISSION 027111:
ENSIGN HAILING CARPATHIA—PLEASE RESPOND

Ensign. The fleet's flagship and first shuttle to leave Earth. Adán reached for the 'Accept' button on the controls, but then hesitated. Only the shuttle commander was supposed to receive transmissions. For a moment, he considered comm-ing the shelter, but it would take several minutes at least to get Dryker up and in here, and by then it might be too late. The signal might be cut off. He would first respond to the hail, he decided, and then comm Dryker.

He typed in the command:

CARPATHIA ACKNOWLEDGES ENSIGN

A few moments passed, and then more words appeared beneath his message:

THIS IS COMMANDER EDWARD PARKS OF THE U.S.S. ENSIGN.

PLEASE ACTIVATE VISUAL AND AUDITORY TRANSMISSION.

Adán grabbed his E-Tab and quickly switched it on. He spoke into the mic. "Tink!" he hissed. "Tink, wake up!"

He heard a crackling noise come from his speaker and then Tink's tired voice.

"Did I sleep through my alarm?" Pause. "Wait, I've got another hour. What's this about, Adán?"

"Tink, we're being hailed."

Another pause.

"Are you serious?" asked Tink.

"You'd better get Dryker up here pronto."

"Sure. Right. Give us a minute."

Adán turned his attention back to the holo transmission. He typed in the code Tink had showed him earlier, hoping he got it right.

An image of a man appeared on the screen. An older man in his late thirties, Adán guessed, dark skinned with a long, thin bearded face and a broad chest and shoulders. Adán peered at the image, hardly believing his eyes. No one that old had boarded any of the shuttles. All the crews had been young, most no more than twenty-three or twenty-four. In the prime of their lives.

So, what was a middle-aged male doing hailing him from Ensign?

15

Adán punched the transmission key, hoping whoever was sending that message was capable of receiving one as well. The light in the console switched on, indicating that the camera was recording.

"This is fleet shuttle Carpathia responding to your transmission," said Adán. "I repeat, this is fleet shuttle Carpathia. Your hail has been received, but the signal is erratic. Can you hear me? Over."

The holo image of the man flickered and then disappeared. Adán panicked. What happened? Had he done something wrong? Cut off the lines of communication somehow? But no. The image reappeared, clearer this time. The static was gone.

"Sorry," said the man, and now Adán could make out the early signs of wrinkles around his eyes and a touch of gray in his hair. "I adjusted the frequency to target your incoming signal. Is that better?"

"Yes," said Adán, relieved. "Much better. Thanks for answering our hails. We've been trying to reach you for three days."

The man's forehead crinkled in confusion.

"We haven't received any incoming. You answered *our* hail. We've been sending these out periodically for years, but honestly, we gave up hope of getting a response a long time ago. I can't believe you're out there."

Years?

"Who are you?" Adán asked.

The man's eyebrows rose curiously. "I'm the captain of the fleet shuttle Ensign. Who are you?"

"You're Ensign's captain?"

"Yes. Captain Edward Parks."

Eddie Parks? It couldn't be. Eddie and Adán were the same age when they left Earth. Impossible.

"But you're...you're older."

Parks' expression was somber. "Are you Commander Dryker?" he asked.

"No. I'm Mission Specialist Adán Fuentes."

"I see," said Commander Parks. "I need to speak directly to your commanding officer."

Adán looked out the shuttle window. There was no sign yet of Scott or Tink.

"Our commander is unavailable at the moment, but we're trying to locate him. Can you hang on a few minutes?"

"Of course."

Adán couldn't believe it. He was speaking to Commander Eddie Parks of the Ensign, but Eddie had aged at least a decade, maybe two. Unless this wasn't really Eddie. And what did he mean he hadn't received their hails?

"Are you on Gliese 581g?" asked Adán.

"Yes," replied Commander Parks. "I'm transmitting our coordinates to you now."

"What about the rest of the fleet, the other shuttles? Are they with you?"

There was a pause before Parks spoke again. "We were unable to rendezvous with any of the other shuttle crews. It took us a while, but we eventually pinpointed the distress signals of three. We sent rescue teams, but when we arrived, we found the crews all dead. We assumed the Carpathia had met the same fate, but your location was simply too far for us to investigate. We only have one rover that runs on limited battery cells."

"Too far? You mean you've known our location all along?"

"You're more than two hundred miles away from us, and our hails were never answered—until now."

Adán thought about what Tink had said, about a glitch that may have blocked incoming transmissions from the fleet. And Parks said the Ensign hadn't received theirs. Seemed Tink was successful in fixing the problem.

"What about your shuttle?" Adán asked.

"The Ensign suffered significant damage when we landed. We couldn't take off again. And as the years have gone by, we've dismantled much of the hardware to use for other things."

Again that word—years.

"How long ago did you land?"

"We reached our present location fifteen years ago," said Parks. "Listen Specialist Fuentes, I really would like to speak to your commanding officer."

Adán leaned back in the pilot's seat. Fifteen years. So, Parks and the Ensign's crew, no doubt, had aged normally in that time while the Carpathia's crew had stayed in cryo and had hardly aged at all.

Parks spoke again, his tone solemn. "Fuentes, is your cargo intact?"

"Cargo?"

"Your embryos. Did any of them survive?"

"Embryos? What embryos?"

"You haven't watched the vids?"

Vids? Embryos? What was he talking about? Through the window, Adán finally caught a glimpse of Tink and Scott leaving the shelter. It didn't look good though. Scott was leaning heavily on Tink for support, and they were moving at a snail's pace. Adán waved for them to hurry.

"Captain Dryker is on his way," Adán told Parks. "Hang on, all right?"

The interior of the shuttle was dark, but when Tink and Scott entered the hatch, the overhead lights detected motion and flickered on. Jonah moaned as the unexpected light brought an abrupt end to his sleep.

"Who turned on the lights?" he grumbled, blocking his eyes with his raised elbow. "Isn't there some way to keep those things off?"

"Sorry," said Adán, opening the cockpit door to let Dryker through. "Go back to sleep."

Jonah grabbed the edge of his blanket with both hands and tugged it up over his head. Fess hadn't stirred. He was laying on his stomach, half his face buried in his pillow. Adán was pretty sure he was drooling.

Tink delivered a trembling Scott into the copilot's chair in the cockpit. They closed the door behind them. Like all of them, Scott wore his assigned white pajamas with the NASA logo below the left shoulder. His skin had a pale, clammy pallor.

"What's going on?" he asked.

"A transmission came through from one of the other shuttles," Adán explained.

"Which one?"

"The Ensign." Adán took a minute to quickly bring Tink and Dryker up to speed on his conversation with Commander Parks thus far, carefully explaining the time that had passed and Parks' age. When he was done, Scott re-opened communications.

"Commander Parks, I'm Commander Dryker. Mission Specialist Fuentes here has briefed me about your situation."

"Yes," said Parks. "I was just asking if you had viewed the vids. Dryker, you were to run the NASA control vids on waking."

Dryker cast a questioning glance at Adán and then Tink, who shook his head. "I've been in the archives searching for stuff on the electrical systems. I didn't look for anything else."

Parker explained. "Only the Mission Commander has access to them. Dryker, you should have the code."

Adán thought Dryker appeared confused at first, but then he nodded as if remembering something important. "I, uh, was incapacitated," he said. "But I'll view them now. Seoung, is the connection to the main viewer functioning?"

"Yeah, I think so."

"Pull it up."

After a bit of fidgeting with the control panel, a separate screen on the cockpit wall lit up. Scott punched a series of numbers into the keyboard, and the NASA logo appeared.

"It's up," said Scott.

Parks cleared his throat. "As I was explaining to your fellow crew member, the Ensign reached the rendezvous sector fifteen years ago. Unfortunately, our shuttle had to make an emergency landing and was damaged beyond repair. We discovered too late that one of our crewmembers was a mole for the Earthside terrorist group Terrestrial Brotherhood. He destroyed most of our cargo and tried to sabotage the mission, but we took him down. We believe the same thing happened to each of the other ships. That's why they didn't make it."

Sabotage? The idea that someone would intentionally kill the shuttle crews turned Adán's stomach. He thought of his own crew, most of whom were lying dead beneath the sands of Gliese. He thought, too, of the gash in the shuttle's side. Had the Carpathia been sabotaged as well?

"So, these vids explain all that?" asked Commander Dryker.

"Well, not quite. They do explain why we are where we are and what we are expected to do now that we're here. They do not provide any alternatives should our original mission be compromised, which it has.

"You will need to view the vids before we can proceed. We'll continue this conversation tomorrow and see if we can't form a strategy to rendezvous. Until then, Parks out."

After Parks' face faded away, Scott, Tink, and Adán sat in silence, staring at the blank screen.

"I have a feeling," said Tink, "our mission is not what we thought it was."

Scott keyed in a second code. On the main viewer screen, the NASA logo vanished, and a new face appeared, one which Adán and the others knew well. General Travis Berkeley was age-worn with deep grooves sprouting from the corners of his lips and eyes, evidence of countless battles both won and lost, and years of commanding soldiers. He had been called out of retirement to head up the Planetary Colonization program. Despite his gruff exterior, he had been surprisingly kind and patient with his young crew members. He spoke now with a solemn expression on his face and a voice that was steady but somehow sad.

He spoke slowly and with authority:

"If you are viewing this video stream then you and your crew have arrived at your destination, which, you may have already discovered is not Europa. You may feel betrayed, believing you were lied to, tricked. Let me assure you this deception was born out of necessity. Should the world discover our true intentions, there would be anarchy and chaos on our hands. When faced with certain annihilation, human beings are capable of the worst kinds of inhumanity.

"To maintain worldwide peace, NASA, the International Space Council, and NGIS crafted the plan to send the shuttle fleet to Europa as the first phase of a long-term colonization program. The world population believed the process of colonization would take place over the course of decades, an entire generation, and that it was a unified international journey into a new future.

"This, unfortunately, simply isn't true."

Commander Berkeley sighed and swiped his fingertips across his perspiring forehead.

"The Earth will not survive decades. It won't survive two years. Our scientists calculate that due to significant solar radiation levels, the hole in our ozone layer will soon break

128

wide open, and when it does, temperatures on Earth will rise by a hundred degrees, possibly twice that, in a matter of days. All life on this planet will die, and all liquid water will be vaporized. By the time you view this vid, everything I have just described to you will have happened long ago."

Adán gripped the armrest of the pilot's seat. Heat rose from deep inside of him, making every inch of his skin burn. He had already begun to guess there was some dire reason they'd been sent to Gliese, but the General had more to tell, and waiting for it felt like that horrible moment at the top of a rollercoaster just before the final drop.

"You are probably wondering why we did not send you to Europa," the General continued. "We had to take into consideration the reactions of the populace to whatever plan we promoted. Europa was, quite frankly, plausible. There has been talk of sending colonists to Europa for years, but the truth is Europa's inhospitable climate would require more resources to construct a viable colony than we have time to gather. We needed a planet with a life-sustaining atmosphere and water, with temperatures comparable to Earth. Somewhere humans could survive without a dome or other construct that could get damaged or worn out over time, resulting in yet another catastrophic extinction. The nearest such planet is Gliese 581g, twenty million light years from earth. The world's top engineers and scientists have been working around the clock to design spacecraft capable of traveling that distance at a speed never before achieved."

So Tink had been right in his calculations, and his brilliance astounded Adán. Yet the confirmation that they were so far from home, without even the remotest chance of returning, left him feeling gutted.

129

"Your mission is as you were initially instructed—to dig a well, construct greenhouses and plant food, and to build a colony with whatever resources are at your disposal. Yet there is one additional responsibility of which you are not yet aware.

"Each shuttle has been equipped with a special compartment located in your laboratory. Inside you will find five thousand frozen zygotes, fertilized animal eggs. Not all species are represented. That would have been an impossible task, but our scientists have selected a diverse population and divided them among the twelve shuttles.

"In addition, your shuttle carries one thousand *human* embryos, carefully selected from fertility centers all over the world to represent the most genetically healthy and racially diverse population possible. There is an equal ratio of male to female, and of one ethnicity to another. These are the survivors of the human race.

"Once the initial colony is sustainable, it will be your responsibility to establish life on your new planet. We have provided each shuttle with three incubation vessels for developing the zygotes into viable fetuses. Your BIO squad is trained in their use.

"Your primary objective, above all others, is to restore the human race. Expect that this will take generations to achieve, centuries if not millennia. Whether the mission is ultimately successful rests solely on you. Our future is in your hands.

"Berkeley out."

THE NEW YORK TIMES

THE WORLD MOURNS THE DEATHS OF BEACON'S CREW

Written by Yemeni Bastien
11:22am

All twenty-four members of the shuttle Beacon's crew died this morning in what insiders are calling the worst disaster in NASA history. The crew had been placed in their cryo units to undergo psychological evaluations when a massive electrical surge pulsed through the monitors, which were connected to each member's head and chest. The surge was the equivalent of more than 2000 volts, the same as the electric chair.

Investigators released a statement hours after the tragedy revealing that the American-based extremist group known as The Terrestrial Brotherhood has claimed responsibility for the deaths. Lucas Bigelow, the group's leader, has threatened similar attacks on the colonization program. "We suspect," said Nancy Foo, NASA's spokesperson, "that one or more of the terrorists infiltrated the crew, possibly months ago. Whoever was responsible managed to program the surge into the shuttle's system long before today,"

In a public response to Bigelow's threats, President Barrios stated that "The United States government and every government in the United Nations is committed to our ideals. Terrorists and extremist groups beware. We will remain undaunted in our quest to seek out new worlds where the human race might thrive, no matter the danger, no matter the opposition we might face. All possible precautions are being taken to ensure that a tragedy like the one we all experienced today will not happen again. I invoke the protection and blessings of Almighty God, in whose name this great nation was founded."

16

Commander Dryker drew a deep breath and let it out very slowly. "Specialist Fuentes," he said with resignation, "wake the crew."

Adán obediently went to the cockpit door, and as it slid open, the overhead lights in the common room flickered on again. He stepped over Fess, who was now groaning, and nudged Jonah with his toe.

"Jonah, get up," he said. "I need both of you awake—now."

Jonah snapped the blanket back from his face and squinted up at Adán. "What's going on?"

"We've been hailed. I need you to go get the girls."

Jonah was off his cot in a heartbeat. Tugging on his gear, he was out of the hatch in less than a minute and running for the shelter.

Fess sat up, rubbing his fists against his eyes. Scott came in with Tink behind. "Get up, Fess," Scott barked. And to Tink he said, "Is the main viewer functional?"

Tink shrugged. "I guess we'll know in a second." He waved his hand over a panel in the wall and a three-foot square section slid back revealing a flat screen nestled in the common room wall. To Adán's relief, the NASA logo immediately appeared. Whatever damage the electrical had acquired had not affected the viewer.

A few minutes later, Jonah returned with Lainie and Dema in tow. They stripped off their gear and settled onto the benches at the table.

"A few minutes ago," Scott began, "we received a hail from the Ensign."

This announcement elicited surprised gasps and questions from most of the crew.

"What? When?"

"What did they say?"

"Where are they?"

"What about the other shuttles?"

Scott held up his hands, and the crew went silent. They were all eager to hear what he had to say. "With the exception of the Ensign and ourselves, none of the other shuttles survived the landing."

As Scott explained about the transmission from Ensign, the fleet's sabotage and destruction, and the news about their mission, Adán considered what Parks had said about a mole. He studied the faces of his six fellow crewmates. Could one of them be responsible for the deaths of the others? No. It was impossible to imagine any one of them wanting to do to the Carpathia what had been done to the other shuttles.

He turned his attention back to Scott.

"The Ensign has established a colony about three hundred kilometers from here to the north. Commander Parks transmitted the coordinates. Seoung?"

Tink switched on his E-Tab, and a holo of Gliese appeared. The planet rotated until the mountain range came into view. Beyond that, a flat expanse. "The data indicates that this area is a freshwater sea, mostly frozen, but there is liquid water accessible via drilling. The Ensign's colony, New Earth," he said indicating a speck on the edge of the sea, "is situated here."

"What? Wait a minute," said Jonah, skeptically. "Do you mean they established a colony? In just a few days' time?"

Adán spoke up. "Not days. Years. Fifteen years, to be exact."

The crew went silent. The expressions on their faces took on a look of disbelief.

"I know that seems impossible," Adán continued, "but think of the circumstances of our awakening. Our ship was damaged. Most of our crew was dead. We suspected early on that things hadn't gone according to plan. Well, they hadn't. We probably landed about the same time as the Ensign, but we remained in cryo while they established New Earth."

"Weird," said Fess.

"There's a vid from NASA that you all need to see," said Scott. "After that, we need to reevaluate our current situation and objectives."

They viewed the vid, and everyone's reactions were what Adán had expected: stunned silence. Fess rubbed a nervous hand across his face. Lainie shifted noticeably closer to Tink. Jonah clutched the gold cross hanging around his neck. Berkeley's message was overwhelming, crushing, like an unexpected blow to the stomach. Their objective was not to prepare a place for future colonists to inhabit. There would be no other colonists but themselves—and the zygotes. Humans in embryonic form.

Finally, it was Jonah who spoke up. "Well, that was— interesting."

His comment seemed to jolt everyone out of their stupors. Fess cracked a nervous smile. "I'll say. Just when I thought things were going so well."

Tink chuckled. "Did you hear that? A thousand microscopic babies on board. What do you know? I'm a father!"

Lainie's face turned red, but she smiled too. Dema was unusually silent and sullen. The news seemed to have hit her the hardest.

Suddenly, Scott stood up. Though he held onto the back of a chair for support, he looked stronger than he had been before. His jaw was set, and he peered pointedly at each crew member before speaking. "This isn't some joke," he said. "Earth is gone, don't you get it?"

"We get it," said Jonah, reclining against the wall with an arm draped over one knee. "We are the proverbial Adams and Eves of the new world. Only I think we'll have it a little easier than they did, what with three incubators on board and all."

Scott pressed his lips into a thin, hard line. "We shouldn't have come here. They should never have sent us, any of us. This is all wrong."

He dragged hooked fingers through his hair. Adán could see the muscles clenching in Scott's face and arms. Their commander had not been himself since he woke from the coma, not that he was ever a particularly likable fellow, but he seemed agitated, on edge. Adán reached out and touched Scott's shoulder. Scott jerked back.

"Easy," said Adán. "It's okay. This is crazy, I know. The rest of us have had a couple more days than you to get used to the idea. I think we're all in shock, but we have to stay focused and figure out what needs to be done next."

"Don't you think I know that?" snapped Scott. He straightened himself and took a deep breath, regaining some self-control. Adán thought he actually looked like a commander now.

"All right," Scott said with an authoritative tone. "All right. So, we need to rendezvous with the Ensign. That's our priority now. Fuentes, can the Ensign's crew send someone to collect us?"

"Negative," said Adán. "The Ensign is no longer flight worthy. She was damaged on landing and has since been salvaged for parts. They do have a rover, but it runs on battery, not solar like ours. It wouldn't make it the whole way, and it certainly couldn't carry all of us if it did."

"So, we'll have to get to them somehow," said Scott. "We've got our two rovers. It'll be a tight squeeze, but we should be able to fit all seven of us."

Fess huffed. "And do what? Drive a couple hundred miles clutching crates of frozen embryos on our laps? Who knows how long it would take to drive that far, or even if the rovers are capable of carrying that much weight that distance."

"Fess is right," said Jonah. "We'd have to take enough food and water for all of us. It's just not feasible."

"We'll make two trips then," said Scott. "Three if we have to."

"No," said Adán. He knew Scott didn't like him interfering, but he had to speak up. "The rovers are no good. There's a mountain range between us, and we have no idea if there's a pass through them. We have incubators and thousands of embryos. We have to fly."

Scott's face went red. "Fly! You want us to fly—with a damaged shuttle!"

"We can repair the breach. We have the materials."

"But not the crew! Or have you forgotten that the tech team is lying dead out there!"

"We've got Fess. He can do it."

Suddenly, all eyes were on Fess. He laughed nervously. "Yeah, I installed the temporary patch, but you're asking for a major repair job! Maybe I could've done it before, with help, but I can hardly walk right now let alone heft those parts. It's a job meant for three sets of able-bodied hands."

Adán understood Fess's hesitation, but there was no other alternative. "Fess, you know how to read the specs and are far more experienced with the physical design of the ship than any of the rest of us. That's why you were recruited, right? We'll help you if you tell us what to do. We just need to know, can you repair the shuttle?"

"Yeah, but . . ."

"But what?" asked Scott.

"If it's not done right, not perfect, we could take off okay, but once we reach a certain altitude and speed—she could come apart. And then we'd all be dead."

Adán glanced expectantly at Fess. Everyone did. They had planned to repair the shuttle eventually, but everything was put on hold when Fess was injured. Now there was no more time to lose.

"Shit," said Fess, resignedly. "Yes, I can repair the shuttle. At least I'll do my best."

"Good," said Scott. "We'll proceed with those repairs first thing in the morning. Dema, as the remaining MED squad member, you're in charge of the, uh, cargo. Take inventory to see if any were damaged and report back to me."

For the first time since watching the vid, Dema raised her eyes from the floor.

"Scott, I can't—"

"The cargo will be your primary responsibility from now on."

"But you heard General Berkeley," Dema protested. "The BIO squad had the proper training. Really, I could be more useful doing anything else. I could teach Lainie—"

Scott's reply was sharp. "You're the only one here with any medical training at all, Sarkissian. They're yours, is that clear?"

Adán expected Dema to wilt under Scott's glare, but she glared right back at him with equal intensity. "Yes, Commander," she said through clenched teeth.

Adán couldn't believe it. Maybe Dema was the only one even remotely qualified to manage the zygotes, but he didn't like the way Scott talked to her. While he was comatose, the rest of them had worked as a team. Under the circumstances, none of them were treated better than any other. Scott had changed all that.

"Dryker," said Adán, "if Dema doesn't feel equipped to handle the zygotes, any one of us could do it. Me, Lainie—"

"You'll refer to me as Commander," Scott said, cutting him off. "Maybe the rest of you are NGIS recruits, but my authority comes straight from NASA."

"You know, *Commander*, if you hadn't noticed, most of your crew is dead. We're on a remote planet in the middle of nowhere, and the very leaders that gave you your authority to begin with ceased to exist centuries ago. So, what makes you think you can bully Dema or any of us?"

Scott whipped around with his hands up, and for a second, Adán thought he might take a swing at him. "You're out of line, Fuentes!" said Scott with restrained fury. "You got a little taste of power while I was out, and now you don't want to give it up, is that it?"

"No, *Sir*. That's not it at all."

"Then back off, or there will be one less member on this crew."

"Are you threatening me, Dryker?"

Dema quickly stepped in front of Scott, placing a hand against his chest. "No one's trying to undermine your authority here, Scott. We're all under a lot of stress. Like you said before, we need to stay focused, keep to protocol. Now that we know about the Ensign, the question is what do we do next?"

Scott squeezed his fists at his sides, but he backed off. There was a long, uneasy pause before he spoke again.

"Seoung, it's your watch. Keep the lines of communication open with the Ensign."

Tink nodded.

Scott continued. "Get as much intel from Parks as you can. I want to know what to expect when we arrive."

"What about me?" asked Adán.

Scott gave him a cocky sneer. "You? I don't know, Fuentes. Why don't you grab a brush and scrub down the toilets? The rest of you, back to sleep. We all need our rest."

Tink disappeared into the cockpit. The women headed back to the tent while Fess and Jonah settled into their cots.

140

Scott, however, stomped off toward the Quarters. Before he reached the door, Dema took him by the arm. Though they were at the far end of the common room and their voices were low, Adán could just make out what was said between them.

"You shouldn't treat Adán that way, Scott. He's gone over and beyond for this crew."

"Over and beyond?" hissed Scott. "He's done exactly what any of us would be expected to do. Not more, not less. I'm Commander. He needs to remember that. And what is it with you two anyway?"

"What do you mean?"

"You know what I mean." Scott's voice changed. He spoke more gently now, although Adán sensed an underlying edge. "You used to look at me the way you've been looking at him."

Scott stroked Dema's cheek with the backs of his fingers. Dema made no move to stop him, but her body visibly stiffened at his touch. Scott must have noticed, too, because he drew his hand back and smirked. "That's what I thought," he said, and then disappeared through the door to the Quarters.

Dema remained frozen in place. Adán wondered if she had forgotten he was there, but then she turned and looked at him. Their eyes locked for one brief moment before Dema broke their gaze and hurried out of the shuttle.

Once she had left, Adán stood numbly, staring at the closed hatch. Beside him, Jonah pulled his blanket to his chin. "Is it just me," he said, "or is our commander cracked?"

Lainie

It was a cold day in Boise when I rolled out of bed and slid my feet into my slippers, which lay parallel to each other on the floor. First day of college, and I was nervous as hell.

After showering and finishing off my customary breakfast smoothie (OJ with bananas and kale), I kissed my mom goodbye and hurried out the door. Class started in an hour, but it would take ten minutes to reach campus and another thirty to find a parking space, not to mention the trek from my car to the classroom. I wasn't even sure yet which building it was in.

I had just reached Boulder Hall when my cell phone rang.

Dang. Nearly forgot to turn off the ringer. The professor would have loved that.

I slipped my phone from the back pocket of my jeans, glanced at the screen, and froze. The phone kept ringing, but my hand would not respond.

Northrop.

The call went to voice mail.

It wasn't that I didn't want to take the call. It's that I hadn't expected to hear from them. Not really. I hadn't even told my parents I'd applied. They probably would have tried to talk me out of it anyway. Who'd want their kid flying off into space for who knew how many years? So, I had filled out the online form and hit send, and then promptly forgot all about it.

Though not completely.

In the back of my mind, I had imagined what space travel would be like. I'd been to California and seen the shuttle Endeavor at the Space Museum in Los Angeles, and I'd been kind of a geek about the planets and astronauts as a kid. Secretly, I dreamed of going up there someday, but I doubted if I'd ever really get the chance. How many astronauts were there anyway? Most came out of the military or had years of education and experience in engineering and science. I was a botanist. Well, that would be my major, anyway. I was good with plants. Had a greenhouse in the backyard where I grew exotic fruit that normally wouldn't thrive in Idaho's climate. My eleventh-grade science project about growing drought-tolerant plants to help end the famine in Sudan and Somalia had won first place. I'd even earned a scholarship from Action Against Hunger, and the newspaper had run the story with my picture.

I had mentioned that in my essay to NASA and NGIS. I'd also talked about how I envisioned using a green house on Europa to regulate temperature and moisture, yet would focus on developing crops like lima beans, corn, quinoa, and okra that could be easily sustainable in a cold, dry climate.

I felt rather silly afterwards. Surely NASA had plenty of botanical engineers on their colonization staff, though the ad did specify applicants should be between eighteen and twenty-five, and I would be nineteen soon.

The truth was, I wanted to go. It wasn't as much about space as it was about leaving. Leaving Boise, leaving school, leaving home. I'd felt stifled for years, trapped in my middle-class suburban life, trapped in a family who expected things of me I never expected of myself. Maybe that's what had drawn me to Tom.

Tom wasn't the kind of boy I could take home to my parents. He was slicked haired, tatted, and quite frankly smelled of weed half the time. But he was good to me. Treated me like I mattered. Unlike my father, whose eyes would wander when I'd try to explain the significance of hydroponics to third world nations, Tom listened with intensity.

"That's brilliant," he would say. "You're brilliant. And beautiful."

We'd gotten serious last year. He'd dropped out of school and was working at an auto shop, doing pretty well for himself, actually. When I'd asked him about college, he'd replied, "What could college teach me that I can't learn right here?"

I admired that about him. He wasn't beholden to anyone or anything but his own dreams. Yet my parents expected me to go to college, and I needed a degree to someday get a job in my field of interest.

"Why?" Tom had asked me one day from underneath a Ford pick-up. His denim-clad legs jutted out from under the chassis, one knee bent, the clang of metal-on-metal echoing through the garage. "Why not join up with that organization you go on and on about? Go to Africa? Plant those seeds? Make a difference?"

I had explained to him, of course, that college was necessary. That I intended to get a doctorate if I could. Ten years of school. But Tom's questions had plagued me. How many people would die of starvation in the next ten years?

At dinner that night, I had brought it up to my father. I didn't mention Tom. My parents didn't know about him yet.

"I could volunteer," I had said. "For a couple of years."

School could be postponed, I reasoned while my dad slowly consumed his steak and mashed potatoes. He'd grown up the son of a farmer. Surely, he would understand.

And he did understand. Farming, he said, was no way to live. He'd escaped from all that, gotten his degree in accounting, earned a respectable living as a tax auditor. College was the best route for me. My mind was made for science. He expected great things from me. I'd make him proud.

The conversation ended, and Dad excused himself from the table and headed to the living room to watch the news. That was it then. The decision had been made.

I broke up with Tom the next day via text. He tried to call me, but I blocked his number. It would be too hard to hear his voice. I just couldn't bear it. He even came by the house once asking for me, but my mother sent him away. And when she asked me who he was, I said he was a mechanic with news about my car.

I never saw or spoke to Tom again, but I dreamed of him every night, imagining the hurt and disappointment in his face. Sometimes, I cried myself to sleep all while reassuring myself it was for the best.

I realized I'd been holding my breath. My chest burned as I forced myself to breathe. I listened to the voice message from Northrop Grumman.

Then I listened to it again.

I turned around and raced back to my car, my class all but forgotten. There was no question about it now. I'd have to tell my parents because I'd be leaving for Florida—tomorrow.

17

The night passed in relative peace and quiet. Adán wondered how many of the crew actually got much sleep after finally hearing from the Ensign's commander and viewing the NASA vid. He almost wished he could have taken first watch again instead of Tink, so he'd have an excuse to stay awake. As it was, for the next several hours he lay on his cot counting the stitches in the tent seams.

At 6:00am ET, they all dutifully rose, showered, and breakfasted on hash browned potatoes, scrambled eggs, and peaches. At least that's what the packages said, and the rehydrated piles of mush at least somewhat resembled the menu.

After breakfast, Tink helped Fess make a list of supplies they would need to repair the hull breach. Fess could hobble around now, and though he flinched at every step, he insisted that he was fine. Tink would work on the grid while the rest of them gathered and took inventory of needed materials, then hopefully they'd begin repairs the next day.

Meanwhile, Adán filled Scott in on his and Tink's visit to the gorge, not that there was much to tell, but Scott wanted to know every detail—the changes in terrain, the distance of the mountains, the width and depth of the canyon. Lainie and

Jonah were assigned clean up duty in the Quarters. They'd located the vac and were making multiple trips outside to dump it.

When Jonah came in complaining that Lainie had broken a seal on the vac motor, and Scott left to see what was going on, Adán decided to check on Dema in the lab.

Next to the waste collection compartment, the lab was the smallest room on the shuttle. The narrow space ran along the port side, adjacent to the common room. It contained equipment and supplies needed for the BIO and SCI teams to evaluate samples, including a sophisticated computer system, microscope, and an assortment of tools, most of which Adán couldn't put a name to.

As Adán approached the sensor, the lab door slid open, and he stepped inside. Dema's hair was twisted into a loose knot at the nape of her neck, but several wavy strands of it had come free and bobbed against her shoulders. In the bright light of the lab, he could see the natural red highlights in it.

The specimen drawers were each two feet long and fifteen inches deep. Each was its own case with a handle and energy pack, should they need to be relocated. One entire wall was nothing but these cases, one of which had been pulled out and set on the counter. Dema leaned over it with an E-Tab in her hand, her eyebrows knit together in a serious expression.

"Everything all right?" Adán asked.

Dema gasped in surprise. "God, Adán! You scared me," she said, holding a hand to her chest.

"Sorry," he said. He couldn't help but smile when he saw the shock on her face. "You seem a bit preoccupied."

Adán glanced over Dema's shoulder at the dozens of glass vials embedded in thick protective foam. Thin white wisps coiled into the air, and Adán could feel the cold on his face. "How are the zygotes?"

"Not good, actually," said Dema, turning back to the vials. "The collision must have been very forceful because many of the specimens near the back of the drawers, the ones closest to the ship's hull, have shattered. Fortunately, I'd say at least two thirds of the animal embryos survived."

"And the humans?"

Dema glanced back at Adán before looking at her tablet. "They didn't fare so well. Look here." She entered a code onto the screen, and a holo of the incubation's power grid appeared above it. A large section of it was red. "The electrical damage was more extensive than we thought. Human sectors A, B are offline."

"But sectors C, D and E are okay?"

Dema hesitated before answering. "Mostly, but altogether, I'd say less than thirty percent of the embryos remain viable."

"Thirty percent," said Adán. "That's not too bad, is it? I mean we started off with a thousand, right? That means we've still got three hundred or so human embryos left."

"Yes, but the purpose of having so many was to create a large gene pool so that as they grew and matured into adulthood, they'd pair off." Dema's voice grew tense. "Remember that we started with twelve thousand embryos dispersed among all the shuttles. Our remaining embryos include an imbalanced ratio of male to female, and of ethnicities. And that's not the only problem," added Dema. "The BIO-specialist team are all dead, Adán. I'm a medic, not an embryologist. I have no idea how to cultivate a human embryo."

Adán didn't know how to respond to that. Their mission, apparently, was to save and replenish the human race. The concern Dema was raising was clear: Could they accomplish that task without those who were trained to do so?

"There's the shuttle data base," suggested Adán. "Supposedly it contains pretty much everything ever published. Makes Google look like finger painting. Tink accessed the shuttle diagnostics there. Surely NASA must have included a tutorial on fetus incubation, or something."

But Dema was not reassured, and her frustration seemed to be mounting. "I don't know how you can be so cavalier about this. Every single vial contains a *life*," she said, gesturing to the many closed and open drawers. "These are not just blobs of cells, Adán. Each one holds unlimited potential. Will it grow up to be the next Mozart or Monét? Will it be the man or woman who finally discovers a cure for cancer, or invents the next leap in technology? Will it experience sorrow, joy, love? When one fetus, one child, dies, it's not just that one life snuffed out, but hundreds, thousands. Entire potential civilizations."

Adán hadn't thought of it that way before, but he said nothing and let Dema continue.

"Did you know that of the one hundred and thirty passengers aboard the Mayflower, only thirty-seven are known to have had descendants? But do you know how many of those descendants were alive in the United States when we launched? Thirty-five million. About one tenth of the country's entire population. All from just a handful of survivors."

Dema reverently waved a palm over the open drawer in front of her, as if the vials it housed were the most precious of relics. But her eyes, Adán noted, were full of pain.

"I don't think I can do this, Adán," she said, looking at him anxiously. "I don't *want* to do this. The responsibility is too great for someone like me."

He could see what she meant, how each tiny zygote contained more potential than any of them could ever imagine. This was the purpose of their mission then, to guard these lives with their own and to give each one the chance to exist. Dema was right. The responsibility was huge.

"Well," said Adán, forcing a smile, "when we rendezvous with the Ensign, we'll hand these vials over to them. We'll just have to trust that they'll know what to do with them."

Dema went silent. She looked at Adán intently. "What if there is no rendezvous?" she asked with a sense of desperation. "What if we never see any other humans again?"

An unexpected voice from behind them answered. "Then I guess we'll have to propagate the species the old-fashioned way." Scott Dryker stood in the lab doorway, his arms folded across his chest and a satisfied smirk on his face.

Dema guided the specimen drawer back into its place in the wall and switched off the holo. "That's not in the protocol, Scott," she said, avoiding his stare.

"How do you know what's not in the protocol?" he asked. "How do any of us really know? Think about it. There were twenty-four of us, a dozen men and a dozen women of mixed races."

"We were selected at random," said Adán,

"Random, my ass! You know as well as I do there's nothing random about any of this. The sooner you accept that, the sooner we can get down to the real objective of this mission." Scott smoothed his hand over Dema's hair. She flinched at his touch.

"Don't," she said in a harsh whisper.

"What's the matter, Dem?" Scott said. "You used to like when I did that."

Dema's eyes flickered to Adán just long enough for him to see the shame in them before she set her gaze squarely on Dryker.

"That was a long time ago, Scott," she said sharply, shoving his hand away. "Two hundred and twenty years, to be exact."

Dema pushed past Scott and exited the lab. Adán started after her, but Scott braced an arm in the doorway, blocking his path. Scott's expression wasn't playful anymore. His grin had vanished, and he looked at Adán with a pointed glare.

"I'm the Commander of this shuttle," he said. "Alpha male. That means I get first pickings. You got that?"

Adán nodded. "Yeah," he said, "I got that."

Scott lowered his arm. His grin returned. "And don't you forget it."

18

After a long day of cleaning out the Quarters and preparing materials for the repair, the clocks all claimed it was once again time to sleep. Adán wondered if his internal clock would ever adjust to the lack of darkness. He felt tired, yes, but his brain told him it was still the middle of the day. He felt like a new baby, with its days and nights all mixed up.

Lainie had created an organized, if not rough, schedule for using the showers, eating meals, guard shifts, and sleeping. It helped to have markers throughout the day to create at least some semblance of time passing.

Adán finished his plate of what was supposed to be Pork Chow Mein but was really nothing more than indistinguishable clumps of protein suspended in a blob of reddish-brown jelly. It had tasted all right, though, sweet with a hint of soy sauce.

Scott, who had taken to eating alone at the farthest table from everyone else, dropped his tray into the recycle bin and stood to face the crew. "2200 hours E.T. Time to turn in." He clapped his hands together like an overly enthusiastic schoolteacher. "Hop to it."

No one moved. Adán imagined Tink, Dema, and the others were probably thinking the same thing he was. Now that they knew the location of the Ensign and the rest of the human race, they wanted to get underway as quickly as possible. Adán was wired, and he suspected everyone felt the same. They were anxious to get the repairs done, even if it meant working around the clock.

"What are you all doing?" demanded Scott, a displeased frown creasing his face. "You're all to head to the shelter! Pronto!"

"Pronto?" Fess snorted.

Scott's expression went rigid, but he did not immediately respond.

Lainie was the first to stand. Disposing of her tray, she started into her gear. "I don't know about the rest of you, but I plan on using my E-Tab to access the audio archives and listen to some Marty Robbins for a while."

"Marty who?" retorted Jonah.

Lainie clicked her visor into place. "I wouldn't expect *you* to have heard of him."

Tink was the next on his feet. "I'll come with you," he said, failing to hide a happy grin. "You can introduce me and old Marty anytime."

"Subtle," said Jonah with a sarcastic chuckle. Tink responded with a not-so-playful punch to Jonah's shoulder.

Lainie and Tink headed outside. As the hatch closed behind them, Adán caught a brief glimpse of Tink reaching for Lainie's hand, and it made him smile. Good for Tink.

Adán stood up and reached for his gear. Dema did the same. Jonah and Fess, however, remained where they sat.

Scott leaned over the table between them and dug his fists into it. "What about the two of you?"

"We're not tired," said Jonah.

"Did I ask you if you were tired?"

Dema held her gloves at the ready, but Adán could tell she was stalling, hesitant to leave. "Scott, c'mon. Fess's leg hasn't healed yet."

Scott ignored her. "I gave an order. Your job is to follow it, comprendé?"

"Bullshit," Fess mumbled under his breath. Scott turned on him.

"What did you say to me?"

Fess seemed to cower at first but then gathered his courage to answer. "You let us stay in here last night. What's the big deal?"

"What is this?" Scott didn't shout, but his composure was being strained to the limits. Adán could sense it in the tautness of his neck, the mocking tone in his voice, and the way he kept rubbing his temples.

"I get it. You're scared, is that it? Scared that some invisible monster's gonna eat you in your sleep."

"With all due respect, Commander," said Jonah, "despite what you think, what happened to us out there was real."

Scott glared at Jonah and Fess with an amused loathing. "All right. Fine. We'll try this a different way." Then into his comm Scott said, "Seoung, this is Commander Dryker. Come back in here, will you?"

A minute later, Tink reappeared at the hatch, alone.

"These two delinquents are reluctant to return to the shelter," Scott told him. "You and Fuentes here are going to assist them. Each of you grab a cot and bed roll and take them back to the shelter. Now. I'm taking first watch in the cockpit. I expect to see all of you marching across the sand in ten seconds."

Scott gave them all a firm eye, daring them to defy him, then he turned for the cockpit. Adán felt a wave of relief at hearing the cockpit door shut tight behind him.

"What's up his butt?" Tink asked.

Jonah snickered. "About a gallon of planet dust and a healthy dose of conceit, I'd say."

"His hands were shaking," noted Fess. "You see that?"

Adán had seen it too. "Dema, what did his bio scan show? Is he okay?"

"Technically, yes," she replied cautiously. "But he's not recovering as quickly as the rest of us did. He's really weak and keeps complaining of headaches. I'm pretty sure it's just the after-effects of the cryo and coma, but I still need to keep an eye him for a while, if he'll let me. He's as stubborn as a rock."

"So, what are we going to do?" asked Adán. "Fess, Jonah?"

Jonah glared at Adán. "We're *not* sleeping out there," he said matter-of-factly. Adán knew he meant it.

"Hey," said Tink. "If you all stayed in here tonight, that'd be fine by me."

Fess laughed. "Yeah, remember our comms are always listening, Romeo."

Tink's face turned red.

"I know how you feel, Jonah," said Adán. "But we'll all be out there with you. Come on, guys. Lainie's waiting for us—*all* of us," he added with a smirk for Tink's benefit.

"I'm going to run one last diagnostic on the *cargo*," said Dema, "and then I'll join you."

"Sure," said Adán, wishing he could think of some reason to stay behind with her, but he couldn't. So, he quickly geared up and then grabbed Jonah's cot while Tink picked up Fess's.

Adán was reaching for the hatch release when suddenly a thunderous, metallic *clang* sounded throughout the shuttle. The sound blasted a rush of adrenalin through Adán's veins, and his heart exploded into high gear. The crew all froze, their wide eyes fixed on each other.

No one spoke.

The noise came again, loud and sharp. "What's going on out there?" whispered Tink.

Fess swallowed hard. "Sounds like someone's smacking the shuttle with a crowbar or something."

The third time, the shuttle rattled as a tremor reverberated through its framework. Adán felt it through the soles of his shoes. Something had definitely struck the shuttle.

"Meteorites?" he suggested.

A collective, if not guarded, wave of relief washed over the crew, though they all remained fixed to their spots like petrified trees.

"Yeah, meteorites fell all the time on Earth," offered Tink. "The moon, too. That's what made all those craters."

They all listened silently for a moment, waiting.

There was harsh *thump* against the roof of the shuttle, followed by another and another. They came at precise intervals of three seconds apart. Adán counted, and with each *thump* his heart rammed harder against his rib cage.

The door to the cockpit flew open. Adán had to admit Scott looked like a commander, tall and confident. Not like how Adán felt at the moment.

"Are you hearing that?" Scott asked.

"Yeah, we hear it," hissed Jonah. "Now shut up!"

The thumping went on and on, sending waves of movement through the shuttle hull.

"What the hell is that?" asked Fess in a tight whisper.

"Not meteorites," said Adán. "Too regular."

Everyone stared at the ceiling as if they expected something to break through.

Tink gripped the edge of the table so tightly his knuckles had gone white. "A sandstorm?"

"Yeah," said Fess. "Has to be."

"Of course, it's a sandstorm," Scott said. "What else would it be?"

"The monster." Jonah clutched his cross in a fist.

When the thumping finally stopped, they all remained rigid for several minutes, but nothing else followed. Adán could hear himself breathing.

"There's no monster," said Scott, running trembling fingers through his hair.

"Creature, animal, alien, or devil," said Jonah. "Call it whatever you want, but it's out there, which means I'm staying in here."

Scott bore down on Jonah as if he was ready to take him apart, but Tink quickly moved between them and snatched up his E-Tab from the table. "Maybe something's out there, maybe not," he said, "but either way, we were right about the sandstorm. The wind velocity is steadily increasing. Adán, take a look outside and tell us what you see."

Adán hurried to the cockpit and peered out the window, which had been gathering a sheen of fine dust. Tomorrow he would need to clean it off again.

In the distance, something was moving. He was tired, exhausted now. Adán pinched his eyes trying to clear his field of vision, then he looked again. There was definitely something out there, a shadow stretching across the entire horizon as far as he could see in either direction. Each passing second, it rose higher into the air as well.

Adán tapped on the control panel and brought up the atmospheric readings. The air pressure was dropping, as was the temperature, but what caught his attention was the wind speed. Normally at near zero, the numbers were rapidly increasing. 40 mph. 45. 52. 67.

In the distance but approaching fast was what he now realized was a massive wall of sand.

"A storm!" he shouted, rushing back into the common room. "A gale-force sandstorm headed right for us!"

19

"We have to get the equipment back in!" Tink was on his feet, shouting at Scott who stood with mouth agape against the wall. "Scott! Commander Dryker!"

Scott blinked, his eyes slowly focusing on Tink.

"Commander, that sandstorm will destroy everything! We need to retrieve the equipment immediately!"

Scott nodded, taking a deep breath. He was himself again, and ready to take charge. "Jonah!" he barked. "Get your gear on and help Tink!"

But Jonah wasn't going anywhere. He leaned back against the shuttle wall, pulling his knees up and wrapping his arms around them. "If you want it so bad, you go out and get it."

"Fess?" said Tink.

"Hello," said Fess, indicating his still bandaged leg. "Temporary cripple here."

"Cripple my ass," Scott shouted, grabbing him by the arm and thrusting him a little too forcefully toward the hatch. "You're no more a cripple than my left nut."

"Oh, so you're finally admitting a weakness," quipped Fess.

Fist raised, Scott closed the short distance between him and Fess in two seconds, but Adán was faster. He wedged himself between them, holding up his hands like a referee at a boxing match. "Come on, guys. We've got more important things to worry about right now than your pride."

"Or Dryker's balls," chided Jonah from the safety of the far side of the room.

"Oh, for God's sake," said Dema. "You're worse than a bunch of school kids!" In the time it had taken Scott to bark out his orders, she had suited up and reached the hatch. "Lainie's already out there. Comm her to start bringing in the equipment. I'm going out to help. If any of you boys are man enough to come along. . ."

Tink and Dema opened the hatch and slipped outside, quickly closing it behind them. As Adán helped Fess pull on his gear, Scott spoke into his comm. "Lainie, this is Commander Dryker."

A moment passed before Lainie responded.

"I'm here," she said.

"There's a helluva storm blowing our way. I need you to retrieve the generator. The rest of us are on our way to gather the remaining items."

Another pause. The signal was weak, broken by snaps and static.

"Roger that," said Lainie.

"You realize that we have no idea how strong this storm is going to get," said Adán. "It could destroy everything. We should take down the shelter before it gets shredded; it's the only one we've got left."

Scott nodded in agreement, then shifted his helmet into place. "Everyone suited?" he asked into the comm. "All right, then. Let's go!"

Scott led the charge out of the hatch. The moment the door opened, the wind crushed against them, as solid as a wrecking ball. Fine grit exploded into the shuttle. Adán switched on his comm. "Get that door closed!" he called to Fess, the last one out of the shuttle. Fess nodded that he understood.

The shadow that Adán had seen through the shuttle's windshield seemed as tall as a New York skyscraper and was approaching fast. "How long before that hits us?" he asked Tink, blinking through the sand blasting his visor.

Tink's voice came in gravelly over the comm. He peered closely at the Tab unit strapped to his forearm. "The readings estimate we've got less than ten minutes."

"Wind speed?" asked Scott.

"It just tipped eighty. The heart of that storm is probably twice that."

They leaned into the wind, pressing forward until they joined Tink, Dema, and Lainie who gawked helplessly at their shelter. The canvas whipped violently against its frames, like a frantic animal struggling to liberate itself from its bonds. One corner of it had already come loose and was flapping violently in erratic silver flourishes. The sound of it beating against itself was like the booms of a cannon.

"We can't get near that thing!" shouted Lainie. "It'll cut us!"

"The instruments!" said Tink. "The sand will destroy them, if they don't get blown away first!"

Scott scrutinized the shelter. "Cut the restraints," he said.

"What?" said Adán.

"I said, let it go!"

"But it's our last tent!"

Scott pulled his utility knife from his pocket and opened the blade. "The equipment is more important! But we can't reach it like this!" Then Scott cautiously approached the tethered corner opposite the wildly flapping corner. A second later, it flew up and began twisting haphazardly in the air.

"Cut the other two restraints!" Scott's voice sounded desperate, and Adán realized why. The loose part of the tent was now whipping around so ferociously that from where he was standing, if he got too close it would strike him. The wind was so strong now that Adán struggled to remain upright. Leaning his body fully into the wind, he moved slowly one step at a time until he reached one of the remaining secured ends of the tent with Tink beside him. Fess headed to meet Scott at the opposite corner.

"Hold on!" shouted Adán. The sandstorm had gotten so close that the sky overhead had deepened to a murky black. The sound of the storm was deafening. He could hardly hear himself in the comm. "We've got to cut them at the same time!"

"What?" shouted Fess.

"The same time! Or else the free end will snap back, and one of us might get injured!"

In unison, Fess and Adán set their blades to the restraints and began to saw at them. With the rest of the tent straining against them, the thick straps pulled taut, twisting and popping like snapping turtles. At one point, the edge of the strap bit into Adán's glove, slicing clean through it like a razor. He jerked his hand back, the skin on the inside of his index finger burned from the sudden friction.

"You all right?" asked Tink.

"Yeah," said Adán. But Fess, unaware of what had happened to Adán, continued cutting. His knife severed the last strands of the strap, and the third corner of the tent broke free. Coming up from the ground, it struck Fess with such force that he flew back, hitting the ground with an audible grunt.

The massive silver canvas now held on by a single strap. Adán gazed up at it, undulating and spinning, a silver flame reaching thirty feet into the air. It dipped and lashed out like a cobra striking its prey, only to rise again each time. The generator, radio transmitter, and other heavy equipment lay toppled onto their sides at the base of the snake. The cots, blankets, and lighter weight items flew off one by one like desperate birds. One folding chair spiraled directly toward Dema, who dove out of the way just in time.

"Get back!" Adán shouted into the comm. "Everyone back to the shuttle!"

Adán guessed that the wind speed topped a hundred miles an hour. Sand struck him from all sides and tore into his gear. Instead of obeying Adán, Tink lunged forward, throwing his arms around the remote transmitter. Above him, the silver snake curled and danced. A table toppled to its side, skidded a few yards, and then toppled again. It rolled over and over like a child's toy and continued rolling until it was out of sight completely. Adán caught sight of Scott hefting the heating unit onto his shoulders. His back bowed with the weight, and his progress toward the shuttle was slow.

Suddenly, the tent, which had been snapping at the air, dipped down and coiled itself around Scott's chest. In half a second, he was tangled in it. Then the tent whipped back up toward the sky, taking Scott with it.

Scott

Stay down! Stay down, you little turd!

The kid is skinny and wriggles like a worm under my hand which has him pinned by the neck against the locker room bench.

"Get off me!" he shouts from his gut.

That's what I like to see. Some fight in them. The more they resist, the greater the thrill.

I push harder, and he squeals.

Because I'm behind him, he can't reach his arms back far enough to grab me, though he tries. His arms flail in the air, and his feet scuffle against the floor trying to get purchase. His skin is slick with moisture fresh from the shower, his bare ass white as whipped cream.

I had first spotted him from the field during football practice at the beginning of the term. He wore green silk shorts and a yellow tank. Running along the track in those beat-up sneakers of his, some off brand I'd never seen before, he looked like a corn stalk with legs. Glasses, too, strapped to his face by a latex band. Nerdsville if I ever saw one.

I nudged my friend Alex and nodded toward the kid on the track. I guessed tenth grade. Alex grinned and shook his head.

I was wrong about the kid's age because he turned up in my trig class. New student transfer, from Wisconsin the teacher said, and could we make him feel welcome. Turned out he was a brainiac, like me. Difference was I didn't shout it out to the world, you know? He and I were assigned the same study group, and I'd be lying if I said I wasn't impressed. He must have noticed what I could do as well because he tried to talk to me after school once.

"Hey, Scott, isn't it? Scott Dryker?"

When I didn't look at him, he continued. "I'm Corey, from Trigonometry."

I was heading toward the parking lot where Alex and the others were waiting at the car. Fridays we always go to Vincenzo's after school, grab a pizza and some coke, laugh off the shit of the week.

I hitched my backpack onto my shoulder and walked faster.

"Well, okay," I heard Corey's voice behind me. "I guess I'll catch you later."

In class on Monday, he acted as if that little scene had never happened. When I sat down across from him at the study table, he said, "Hi, Scott."

There were four other students with us, and we had work to do.

"Hey," I said back. That seemed to satisfy the kid because he smiled and nodded. I guess he thought he was making some kind of headway with me.

I admit that he seemed a decent guy. He was always helping the other kids when they got stuck on a problem. A couple of times even I got stumped. He'd patiently explain each step of the problem, how to work the equation, until I figured out the answer myself. The kid was smart. Smarter than me. Smarter than anyone I knew.

Over the next few weeks, I learned a little about Corey from bits and pieces of conversation that came up during the lull between lecture and study group. He was an accelerated student, so I'd been right about his being younger after all. And he'd been picked on most of his life. Things had gotten so bad at his old school, his parents had decided to move and start him fresh here. His dream was to get into Cal Tech and study physics. I was pretty sure he'd get in without a hitch. They'd probably beg him to enroll.

Once, Corey got to class early and was waiting for me by the door. Before I went in, he handed me a sheet of paper printed in colored ink. It was a flier for Jet Propulsion Lab's annual day for the public. I'd been once when I was kid, saw one of the Mars landers before it launched, took a tour of the engineering labs where they actually build the deep space probes.

"I was wondering," said Corey hesitantly, "if you and I—if maybe we could go together? I mean, I am from Wisconsin. What have I ever seen?"

I said yeah, sounded like fun. I'd pick him up Saturday at nine and we'd check it out. He smiled eagerly and then went into class. I folded up the flier and stuck it in my back pocket.

We never did get to JPL. We didn't even get to Saturday.

Corey ran laps after school a couple days a week. I saw him sometimes during practice. Most of the time I ignored him, but since that first day he'd shown up, Alex and the other guys had made it a point to notice him every time.

"Look," Alex would say. "There's little dweeb again." Or "What's he playing at? He's so skinny, how does he keep his pants up?"

Wednesday, the day after Corey'd given me the flier, Alex and I and the rest of the team were heading to the showers after practice. Corey had spent the whole last hour running laps around us, and I spotted him getting out of one of the stalls just as we entered the locker room.

Alex immediately zoned in on him.

"Hey, scarecrow? Better hurry. You shouldn't be in here with the big boys." He gestured toward his own dick and laughed.

Corey went red in the face. He reached for one of the towels on the rack, but Alex moved too quickly, snatching it away.

"No, you don't," he said, spinning it into a rat's tail.

Corey's jaw clenched. "Give me the towel."

In response, Alex snapped the towel at Corey. I could tell by the way he flinched that it had stung.

"Give him the damn towel," I said, forcing myself to laugh. This was Alex after all, and by now some of the other guys were watching, some hooting with laughter at the naked skinny kid.

They didn't mean anything by it. They were just being stupid. I was certain Alex would eventually lose interest and let him alone, but Corey's eyes shifted from him to me.

"Scott?" That was all he said. He was questioning why I was just standing there, as if he expected me to take his side. And frankly, I wish I could say I'd considered it. Even for a second.

Alex turned to me with a fake look of surprise. "What? This kid knows you?"

This next part has played itself over and over in my brain so often that I can tell you exactly how many moles Corey had on his back, and that the metal brace holding the bench was loose, that the air smelled so thickly of human sweat and testosterone that it stuck in the back of my throat.

I can still feel the texture of Corey's neck bones under my palm, those raised hard lumps underneath his soft, slick skin. I can still hear his gasping, terrified breath so close to my ear when he realized I could hurt him. I could kill him.

I had moved quickly, grabbing him by the back of his neck and shoving him face down against the bench. He was much more fragile than I had imagined, not just thin but weak, like a child. His arms had no muscle tone, though his legs were lean and strong from running.

He struggled violently as I held him down, such an easy feat.

Stay down. Stay down you little turd.

I hissed the words in his ear. I wanted to tell him it was for his own good, that once he'd given in, endured their ribbing a little, they'd soon lose interest and leave him alone. But he was a fighter, I could see that. He was the kind of kid who'd only make things worse for himself in the end.

So, I intervened.

He stopped flailing and went limp. I squeezed his neck harder, but not hard enough to do any damage. I reached out my free hand toward Alex, and he handed me the towel.

When I let go, Corey slowly got up, but he didn't look at me. His eyes were on the floor, and his face was a mess of snot and tears.

I tossed him the towel, and he caught it.

Alex laughed some more, and then he and the others turned away, heading for the showers. I wanted to make sure Corey was okay, to tell him he shouldn't mess with these guys, but I didn't want to damage my standing with them. So instead, I turned my back to Corey and followed my team.

Corey wasn't in the locker room anymore when I got out of the shower and got dressed. And he wasn't in class on Thursday or Friday. I didn't know his number, so I couldn't call him. And I didn't know where he lived. Otherwise, I would have still picked him up for JPL on Saturday, and I would have explained, apologized. But we'd never gotten the chance to exchange info.

When I heard the rumor going around campus the following week, I didn't believe it at first. A student had offed himself. One of our own. But no one seemed to know his name. Only the other kids in our study group noticed Corey's empty seat and made the connection, but the others didn't talk about it. We weren't really friends, so why would we?

I heard there was a memorial on campus. I didn't attend. And the family had a private service before his body was sent back to Wisconsin to be buried in the family plot. I never met his parents. I never even knew if Corey had brothers or sisters. I never asked. In fact, I knew pretty much nothing about him. Nothing except that he wanted to go to Cal Tech, that he liked to run, that he was really smart and probably could have changed the world.

I wish I could say I quit the football team, that things changed between me and the guys, that I never picked on anyone else again. But things didn't change, except for the hate expanding inside me – hate for myself and for the human race. Humans are weak, either weak in body or weak in character. Either way, every time I wake up in the middle of the night, the image of Corey's face in my head reminds me what a piece of shit I am – that we all are.

20

Adán stopped cutting. Only a narrow strip of cloth remained. Once it was severed, the tent would fly off never to be seen again. Scott could be carried miles before landing in a deadly collision. He had to get Scott down.

"Tink!" shouted Adán. "Help me!"

"But the transmitter!" Tink called back. He hesitated only for a moment, but then set down the metal box. The wind instantly pushed at it, shifting its position in the sand. Tink hurried to Adán's side.

Adán heard Dema, Fess, and Lainie calling out to him in his comm, but he didn't have a moment to spare to respond to them. They were clear of the tent, standing far enough away to avoid injury. He hoped they wouldn't try anything stupid. He and Tink alone would take the risk.

"Hold it here!" Adán jabbed a finger at the corner of the tent still attached. Tink obeyed, gripping the fabric with his gloved hands. Adán grasped the canvas several feet above Tink. Then he began to pull it, gradually drawing the fabric toward him. It was like trying to haul an anchor up from the ocean floor, the effort requiring every ounce of strength he could muster. He wasn't sure his plan would work. He was battling a storm that at any moment could snatch him up and carry him off.

"Get me down!" Scott screamed, his voice piercing through Adán's comm.

"I'm trying! Just hold on!" Adán kept pulling, but he made little headway with the wind pulling so hard in the opposite direction. "Scott, use your hands! Try to climb down!"

Scott started hand-over-hand down the column of living canvas. The distance between Scott and Adán slowly began to shrink. The sand pelted Adán so hard now that he could feel it through his gear.

"The rest of you get inside!" he called out. "It's too dangerous out here!"

Fess grabbed the heating unit that Scott had dropped and made his way toward the shuttle. Tink held tight to the tent behind Adán.

"Tink! I've got it! Go on!"

"You don't have it," said Tink. "I'm not leaving!"

"But you have to—" Suddenly, a powerful gust tried to rip the silver tarp from Adán's hands. The knuckle in his pinky finger snapped in a stabbing flare of excruciating pain, but he did not let go. Scott flipped around in the air, as helpless as a marionette on strings, though he was a good eight feet closer to the ground than he had been minutes before.

Adán tried to hold tighter to the fabric, but the pain in his hand throbbed ruthlessly and had robbed it of its strength.

"Scott!" he shouted. "You're going to have to let go!"

"Let go? Are you insane? This wind will blow me away like a kite!"

"Curl up into a ball! Wrap your arms around your knees and drop to the ground!"

Adán heard Tink's voice. "This strap is tearing! When it rips all the way, that tarp is taking you with it, Scott!"

"Scott, you've got to let go now!"

He did. Scott released the fabric and pulled his knees to his chest. He fell like a stone to the sand below. He hit the ground, his limbs sprawling out in every direction. Then, getting to his hands and knees, he scurried away like a bug just as the tarp tore free from its strap. The silver snake curled and whipped like a flag in a hurricane and then vanished into the darkening sky.

Adán, his back to the wind, dropped to his knees beside Scott. "You all right?" he asked. "Can you get up?"

Scott collapsed into the sand, moaning. Adán felt a wave of relief. Their commander was dazed, possibly even hurt, but he was alive. A few yards off, Tink fought against the storm's assault. He clutched the transmitter case to his chest and staggered forward one step at a time. The sky was so dark now and the sand so thick that the shuttle looked like nothing more than a broad mass of shadow.

Adán slid one of his arms beneath Scott's shoulder and hoisted the barely conscious commander into a sitting position. "Dryker, listen to me! We've got to get back to the shuttle or we'll die out here! Get up, Commander! On your feet!"

Scott moaned again, but Adán felt his muscles stiffen as he attempted to get his legs under him. With a bit of effort on both their parts, Scott was soon standing, though he leaned much of his weight against Adán. Adán looked back at Tink, who hadn't made as much progress as he'd hoped.

"Tink, drop it!" Adán shouted.

Tink shook his head furiously. "If the main transmitter ever fails, we'll need it to communicate with the other shuttles! They'll never find us without it!"

Tink's words came back to Adán broken and staccato. He tapped on his earpiece. He thought the storm must have damaged his comm. "Tink? Can you hear me?"

This time Adán heard only static. He looked back to the shuttle, a mere ten yards away. Dema and Fess, clinging to each other, were scrabbling for the hatch lever. Adán looked back at Tink, half that distance behind him. He'd get Scott to safety, he decided, and come back for Tink.

"I'll be back to help you in a second!" he said, though he couldn't be sure if Tink had heard him, then he trudged forward with Scott in tow.

The two minutes or so that it took for him to hand Scott over to Dema and Fess felt like hours. He was exhausted and in pain, but Adán turned and headed back out for Tink, now on his knees hunched over the transmitter just four or five yards away.

He had just reached him when Adán saw it—a dark mass rising up from the ground behind Tink. "What the hell is that?" he said more to himself than to anyone else.

Dema's voice crackled over the comm. "Adán, do you read me? Scott's okay. A bit stunned but okay. Fess is with him in the common room now. Do you have Tink and Lainie?"

Lainie. Adán had forgotten all about her. But Tink. . .

"There's something out here!" said Adán.

There was a pause before Dema's voice returned. "Adán, get out of there. The sensors are picking up something solid, something big!"

He reached Tink and pulled him to his feet. Together, with the transmitter still clutched in Tink's arms, they staggered toward the shuttle, which they could now barely make out through the thick haze of sand.

"Lainie!" Adán waited a moment for a reply. "Lainie, do you read me?" He shook his head. "The storm's interfering with the frequency!"

"She was carrying the generator," said Dema, her words nearly impossible to make out through the static. "She was closer to the shuttle than we were. You should see her!"

Adán and Tink continued trudging forward. Then just to right of the shuttle hatch, they spotted something square and black half buried in the sand at their feet. It was the generator tipped onto its side, but there was no sign of Lainie.

21

"Where the hell is she?" shouted Tink into his comm.

Adán felt the urge to call out her name again, but she wouldn't have heard it over the storm anyway. "With all this sand," he said, "she probably went right past us! Maybe she lost her bearings!"

The hatch slid open, and Dema emerged in full gear.

"What are you doing?" Adán shouted. "Get back inside!"

"I'm not leaving Lainie out here alone!" said Dema. "And neither would you or Tink!"

Adán nodded. Dema was right of course, but the storm was on top of them. Every second longer they remained outside increased the chance that one of them would get lost, injured—or killed.

"If we split up," said Dema, "we'll cover more ground!"

There were good reasons to reject Dema's suggestion, but Adán couldn't argue with finding Lainie as quickly as possible. Before he could agree or disagree however, Dema had already ducked under the shuttle.

As Tink and Adán headed back out into the wind, the two of them followed the shuttle's body down toward the tail. Adán kept his hand against the hull, using it as a guide.

"I can't see anything!" he shouted. Shielding his eyes with his arm did no good. "We have to turn back!"

"No!" shouted Tink. "No! I'm not leaving her!"

"We have no choice!"

Adán reached for Tink's arm hoping to coax him back toward the hatch, but Tink shook him off. "I'm going to find her, Adán!"

Suddenly and without warning, the wind ceased. Not tapered off, but abruptly stopped, as if it had just blown itself out. When it did, the sand and grit that had been swirling around in the air dropped straight down, raining on the Carpathia's crew like hailstones. A moment later, the sun was again visible, and the terrain for miles all around was flat and still.

Adán froze in place, stunned by the abrupt end to the storm, expecting it to pick up again just as quickly. When it didn't, Adán and Tink brushed the remnants of soil from their uniforms and helmets.

Adán pulled his helmet off. It had cracked in the gale, and his mouth was full of sand. He could feel the grit on his teeth and spit out what he could.

"I think it's over," he said, clipping the comm to his collar.

"Yeah," replied Tink. "Bizarre the way it just stopped like that. At least now that we have a clearer visual, we'll spot Lainie—or she'll spot us."

"She's only been out in it a few minutes," said Dema through the comm, which seemed to be working better now. "She couldn't have gone far."

"We'll find her," said Adán, more to reassure himself than the others.

"Lainie!" called Dema. She joined Tink and Adán back on their side of the shuttle. She had removed her helmet as well despite the bitter cold. Though the storm had died, Lainie still had not responded to their comm hails.

"Do you see that?" asked Adán, pointing to something in the near distance.

"What?" asked Dema.

"That bump, heap or whatever. The landscape is completely flat, but the ground is raised a little there."

The lump in the soil was about ten yards off the shuttle's port side, nowhere near the hatch at all. Dema took two hesitant steps toward it and then burst into a sprint. Seconds later she and Adán were on their knees scooping away armfuls of dirt.

Adán shouted into his comm, hoping the crew inside the shuttle could hear him all right. "Scott! Fess! We found her! We found Lainie!"

Dema brushed the thick layer of dust from Lainie's face. Grit caked the corners of her eyes which were partially open and staring blankly toward the sky. Dema scraped more dust away from Lainie's throat and abdomen, her hands only hesitating briefly when the sand turned wet and red with blood.

"She isn't breathing!" shouted Dema, pressing two fingers against the side of Lainie's throat. Then she bent forward, sealing her mouth around Lainie's, and gave her two deep breaths. More red grit slipped off Lainie's chest as it rose and fell. Adán realized that the ground beneath and surrounding Lainie was completely saturated in blood.

Dema placed her hands on Lainie's chest and pushed, grunting with the effort. She pushed three, four times, and then growled impatiently.

"I can't do it this way!" she shouted. She reached for the utility knife at her waist and used it to cut through Lainie's uniform.

"What are you doing?" asked Adán. "She'll freeze out here!"

"I can't compress her heart through all this fabric!"

Adán spoke into his comm again. "Lainie's hurt! I need blankets and warmers, stat!"

Dema reached for the ragged edges of Lainie's suit and tore it open. Lainie's breasts and ribcage were now exposed to the frigid air. Adán paused just long enough to take in the jagged wound in her stomach before looking away. That's when he realized Tink was standing behind him, his face contorted with disbelief.

Adán listened to the whoosh of air as Dema breathed into Lainie's mouth again, and the dull thumping of the chest compressions. At one point, a distinct crack of a rib cut through the sound of Dema's heavy breathing.

"Come on, Lainie," she said over and over. "Come on!"

Dema continued CPR while Fess appeared at the shuttle hatch. He half ran half limped across the sand, delivering the requested items. Adán unfolded the vellum blanket and covered Lainie's body with it. A layer of sweat had formed along Dema's forehead, and she was breathing hard. She'd been at Lainie for almost ten minutes by now. Adán, Fess, and Tink looked on.

"Dema," said Adán after another minute. "It's time to stop."

She ignored him. Her hands, coated in blood, compressed Lainie's chest again and again. Lainie's eyes, caked with sand, remained fixed on the sky. The gash in her body gaped open, but blood no longer gushed out of it. She had long since bled out.

"Dema," Adán said again. "She's gone." He placed a hand on Dema's shoulder, but she lurched back and swung her bloodied arm at him. Adán jumped back, just avoiding the blow.

Dema's expression was ferocious, crazed. Adán realized that her hands were not the only part of her that were bloody. The entire front of her, including her arms and face, were covered with it, which made her appear more animal-like than human. If someone had stumbled upon her like that hovering over Lainie's battered body, they might have thought Dema had feasted upon it.

Adán's stomach churned, and he forced the bile back down his throat. It was all a horrible nightmare, Lainie lying in the blood-soaked sand, Dema desperately trying to resuscitate her. He wished someone would wake him.

Dema dropped her arms to her side and let out an exhausted breath. She knelt there in the sand for a few moments longer, and then slowly stood, defeated.

"We can't leave her out here—like this," she said, her voice hoarse.

Adán nodded. "We'll bury her with the others."

He turned to Tink who hadn't moved from where he'd been standing before. His gaze was still fixed on Lainie's body, only now his face was wet with tears.

"Tink?" Adán asked.

Tink answered with an abrupt nod. "We'll bury her," he repeated. "With the others."

"Fess, maybe you should take Dema back to the shuttle."

"No," Dema said. "No, I'm fine. I'll go alone."

Adán watched Dema walk back toward the shuttle. When she reached the hatch, she didn't go in, however. Instead, she placed a hand on the side of the shuttle as if to steady herself. Adán ran after her.

"Dema, let me help you."

"I don't need help," she said.

Her comm hung around her neck, her mouth exposed to the frosty air. Adán switched his off. Whatever they were about to say to each other need not be heard by the others.

"There was nothing you could have done for Lainie," Adán said, slipping an arm around Dema. He was afraid she might faint or burst into tears, but she did neither. She just stood there with her head down, her hair hanging like a curtain from it. "You can't blame yourself, Dema," he said. "You tried—"

"That's right," Dema said, a sharp edge to her voice. "I tried. I tried and failed."

"The damage was—" Adán swallowed, not wanting to say what he had to "—extensive."

Dema raised her head and faced him. Her cheeks glistened. "You don't get it, do you?" she said. "Lainie was my responsibility. They were *all* my responsibility! I've let everyone down."

Adán gently squeezed Dema, trying to comfort her. "That's not true, Dema. You're part of a team. We all are. We all share the responsibility for each other. Whatever happened to them—it was an accident."

Dema took a step back from him, breaking his hold on her.

"An accident? You don't really believe that, do you? Did you see what that thing did to her? When I did CPR, when I compressed her chest, blood and muscle and tissue fell out of her! Something fell into my hands. I think it was part of her liver, and I—I tried to put it back in. Her whole body was sliced to ribbons!"

Dema looked into Adán's face, willing him to understand her. "Whatever did that to Lainie was no accident, Adán. Whatever tore open the tent and Fess's leg was no accident. There's something out here. Something real. Something— intentional."

AND THE WORD WAS...

The Official Blog of The Terrestrial Brotherhood

"For this city hath been to me as a provocation of mine anger and of my fury from the day that they built it even unto this day; that I should remove it from before my face." *(Jeremiah 32:31 KJV)*

The Devil's media has been slandering The Brotherhood, accusing us of murdering innocents on board the space shuttle Beacon, but we say there were no innocent among the dead.

Were the inhabitants of Jericho innocent when God commanded the Israelites to destroy them? Were Sodom and Gomorrah innocent when fires rained down from Heaven upon them? Were the Philistines innocent when Samson used his God-endowed strength to topple the columns of the temple down upon their heads?

In the Beginning, God placed Adam as Lord over the whole Earth. The seed of Adam has failed his mission. He must face the consequences. Should he attempt to run and hide from the face of God, as did Jonah of old, he shall not succeed. God will find him and throw him into the depths of the sea.

Beware, O ye who attempt to thwart the will of God! Ye cannot, ye will not prevail!

Amen.

Posted by Reverend Lucas T. Bigelow

22

Adán turned back to the vast, empty wasteland of Gliese, taking in the nothingness of it all. He observed Tink, Fess, Scott, Dema, and Jonah standing over Lainie's body, her blood an incongruent contrast to the otherwise unbroken sea of orange dust. They had all gathered beside her to say their goodbyes and were still coated in the storm's dust, looking like otherworldly ghosts. That's what they were, thought Adán, ghosts of a world and a people that had long ago ceased to exist. If what he had just witnessed in Lainie's death hadn't been so—so real, Adán might have convinced himself that everything—this planet, the shuttle, the monster—were nothing more than wisps of memory, like the impression of light left behind after someone looks at an object and closes his eyes, seeing it still against the backs of the eyelids.

But no. This was all too real. The dust. The fear. The blood.

Adán moved closer to Tink. "Let's lay her with the others," he said.

Tink shook his head. "No. I changed my mind.," he said. "She deserves better than a mass grave."

Adán knew how Tink had felt about Lainie. He could understand why he wanted her to have a proper burial. He gazed around, scouting for a good location and realized to his dismay that every location was the same as the next.

"Here," said Tink. "We'll just bury her right here."

"I'll go grab a shovel," offered Fess, who limped off toward the storage bay. He returned a few minutes later with two in hand, one of which Adán took. Despite the splint that Dema had placed on his broken finger, he felt it was his duty to lay Lainie to rest.

Adán's shovel bit into the loose soil. It was like digging in a child's sandbox, no resistance at all. It took no more than ten minutes to make a hole deep enough for Lainie's body. Adán and Fess stuck their shovels upright in the sand and started to reach for Lainie, but Tink got to her first, giving them both a ferocious look that claimed her for his own.

Tink squatted and slid his arms under her body. Then with some effort, he lifted her. When he stumbled, Scott hurried forward to help. Together, they walked the few feet to the open grave where Tink dropped to his knees with Lainie in his arms. Scott stepped away, but Tink stayed there for several minutes, staring at Lainie's face, still caked in dust. Then he kissed her lips and gently lowered her body into the shallow hole.

"Jonah?" Tink asked. "Would you say something?"

Jonah had brought his Bible with him, like before. "By faith," he began, but his voice caught. He paused, then started again. "By faith Abel offered unto God a more excellent sacrifice than Cain, by which he obtained witness that he was righteous, God testifying of his gifts: and by it he being dead yet speaketh." He took in a long, slow breath and expelled it. "Amen."

Fess grasped the handle of his shovel and began scooping the displaced sand over Lainie's body. Adán knew he should help again, but for some reason, he couldn't. He just couldn't. Fortunately, the others didn't seem to expect him to. Jonah took the second shovel and helped Fess finish the job.

Tink remained on his knees until they had finished. The sand was smooth as if no one lay beneath it. The fact that there was no evidence of Lainie remaining disturbed Adán like nothing ever had before. It seemed so final, as if Lainie had not just died and was buried, but that she had vanished from existence. That was why, he realized, people on earth left grave markers behind—their names etched in brass or granite to outlive generations to come, a solid tangible marker as evidence that someone once lived and still existed there, in that very spot.

But there was no grave marker for Lainie or for the rest of Carpathia's crew. Even if they tried to place something, it would be blown away or covered over with the next sandstorm. It didn't seem right, leaving her here to be swallowed up by the emptiness, but what else could they do?

After a while, Tink finally got to his feet. Without speaking a word, he turned and trudged across the dust to the Carpathia. Fess gave Adán a quick glance, then followed, along with Dema and Scott.

Jonah gathered up both shovels. "I hate to add to the solemnity of the moment," he said, hoisting them across his shoulders, "but someone's gotta say it."

"Say what?" asked Adán.

"This wouldn't have happened if it weren't for our fearless commander and his reckless orders. He hasn't been the same since he woke from that coma."

Adán couldn't disagree, but he didn't feel like saying so. He just wished Jonah would say what he had to say and leave him be.

"I have something to confess," Jonah continued. "When we went through the crew's storage boxes, when we gathered up the pictures and stuff to bury with them, I did something I shouldn't have."

Adán waited. He wasn't in the mood for conversation or for Jonah relieving his conscience, but he didn't want to be rude. So, he let Jonah continue.

"Once I was alone in the Quarters, well, alone with our comatose commander, I opened his box."

"You did what?" This was not anything close to what Adán expected to hear. "Trespassing personal property is a breach of regulations, Jonah. You could get court-martialed for that."

Jonah smirked. "Here? Right." But then he grew more serious. "Don't you want to know what I found? Nothing. Dryker's box was empty."

"So what?" said Adán, though he had to admit the revelation felt wrong somehow. Odd.

"Who travels to a new planet empty-handed?" Jonah said. "If I were a betting man, which I'm not, I'd lay it all on Dryker being the mole."

Jonah adjusted the weight of the shovels and headed across the sand toward the cargo bay, leaving Adán alone.

He should leave too, follow the others into the shuttle, but he hesitated. He rolled Jonah's confession around in his mind, but he didn't have space in his head for that just then. He had just buried Lainie and wished he could leave some symbol behind to claim this spot for her. He recalled something Saul had told him once, that in some cultures it is—*was*—taboo to name the dead, to speak their names out loud. Yet that didn't seem right, silencing their memories like that. No, it wasn't right.

"Lainie," Adán said in a whisper. Then he took a deep breath and threw his head back, shouting. "Lainie!"

His throat felt tight, but he tried again. He pushed the air out from deep inside of him, screaming her name over and over so that whatever was out there—whatever took her from them—would know she still existed and always would.

Jonah

The murmur of prayers hummed in Jonah's ears like a hive of bees. His instinct was to swat them away, but he knew it would do no good. Sundays were his least favorite of the week, but his father was the local minister and insisted on dragging his son out to every meeting.

At eight years of age, Jonah was bored by his father's sermons and the prayer rituals that followed. Still, he tried to find something to talk to God about, to help pass the time.

"I traded some Pokémon cards," he said one Sunday, rubbing his ear. "Got a really good one, but Mom said I had to give it back. Said it was unfair. What do you think?"

Jonah paused a moment and listened. His dad had always said that God spoke to people through scripture and prayer, but no matter how hard he tried, Jonah never heard anything but that annoying hum of other people's voices.

But today was different. He had something more important than Pokémon, or winning tomorrow's bike race with Harry, or whether or not he'd get that new Nintendo system for Christmas this year.

"God?" Jonah whispered. He didn't want anyone else to hear him. "Please bring Mommy home from the hospital. She's been there a long time, and I miss her."

He shifted in his seat. The old lady to his left glanced down at him disapprovingly.

"God, if you make Mommy better, I'll clean my room every day before bed. I'll help Daddy with the baby so Mommy can rest. Or maybe you want something else instead?"

He'd thought about it all morning.

Harry one time offered to water the lawn in exchange for Jonah's new Hot Wheel. He thought it was a good deal at the time and gave it up. Harry watered the grass the next morning, but the day after that, the task fell to Jonah again. He felt cheated, but a deal was a deal.

No, if he was going to make a deal with God, it had to be a good one. Something God would really want.

"I'll give you my soul," he said. "Just bring Mommy home soon."

The truth was Jonah wasn't really sure what a soul was. His dad called it spirit, but what was that? He guessed it was whatever made him alive. Because dead people's spirits went to heaven, or sometimes hell. A soul, Jonah thought, must be the same thing then.

Only, if he gave it away, would that mean he would die?

That's what Daddy was afraid of, Jonah knew. He was afraid Mommy would die, that her soul would go to heaven and leave him here on Earth all alone. The baby came too early. Too fast. It made Mommy sick. And Daddy was worried. He'd been at the hospital for two days.

But today was Sunday, and he said the congregation needed him. And he needed to pray.

"I'll give you my soul," repeated Jonah in a whisper, "if you let Mommy's spirit stay."

Father's sermon was short. He and the people prayed. He gave them the Last Supper. Then he and Jonah drove back to the hospital.

Daddy left Jonah sitting in a vinyl chair in the hall so he could talk to the doctor in private. He was gone a long time, so long that Jonah nodded off for a while.

He was awakened by someone gently shaking his shoulder.

"Jonah," said Daddy. Jonah blinked open his eyes and saw his father's face. He was smiling, but his eyes and cheeks were wet with tears. How can someone smile and cry at the same time, Jonah wondered?

"Mommy's going to be okay," said Daddy. "She's getting better. Our prayers are working."

Then he paused, rolled his bottom lip in between his teeth. He pinched his eyes, but he could not stop more tears from coming.

"But your little sister," Daddy said, his voice breaking. "The baby didn't make it."

Jonah wasn't sure what his father meant, and his confusion must have shown on his face because Daddy took Jonah's hands in both of his own and spoke again.

"The baby died, Jonah. Her soul has gone to heaven."

No. That couldn't be, Jonah thought. He'd offered God a trade, a good trade. His soul for Mommy's, but God didn't take him. He took his sister instead.

His father, still wearing his minister's collar, knelt in front of Jonah and laid his head in his lap.

That wasn't a fair trade, Jonah was thinking. It wasn't what he'd asked for. Then again, had he prayed for the baby? He wasn't sure. All that humming around him, the woman glaring at him. Had he asked God to save his sister? He tried to remember what he had said exactly. He had asked God to make his mother well again. He had offered his soul for hers.

But no, he had forgotten to pray for the baby. A loophole is what Harry would call it. When Harry had watered the grass, he had not watered the flowers. When Jonah pointed it out, Harry had said, "but I didn't offer to water the flowers. I only said I'd water the grass. And I did. It's a loophole."

God had found a loophole in Jonah's prayer. Again, he felt cheated, but he couldn't really blame God, could he? Jonah was the one who'd offered the deal. Jonah was the one who forgot about the baby. It was his fault then that the baby died.

His father took the seat beside him and buried his face in his hands. His shoulders shook as he wept. As Jonah watched his father come apart, he felt something deep inside him, a tight, hot burning making its way from his stomach up through his chest and throat until it reached his eyes. It consumed him, this burning, this pain.

The first tears fell onto his hands clasped across his knees, and Jonah vowed to himself that he'd never let God find a loophole in his prayers again.

23

Adán stripped off his gear and tossed his dusty outerwear into the laundry bin. It was almost inconceivable that even here, in this god forsaken outpost, they had to deal with the same drudgery as on Earth: washing laundry, cleaning the head, keeping the inside of the shuttle free from the ever-present orange dust. He entered the head, relieved himself, and took a shower—two more oddly mundane tasks. Standing in the spray of tepid water, he became aware of the fact that the skin on his face, particularly the lower parts of his cheeks and chin, burned like someone had held a lighter to it. The sand had scraped away much of the top layer of skin, leaving it raw.

The stream of water was replaced with a warm gust of air, drying his body in seconds. Then he dressed and entered the common room. Apparently, Tink had sequestered himself in the cockpit, probably throwing himself into studying more schematics. Adán would give him some time alone, to grieve in his own way. Fess and Jonah sat together at a table, Jonah's arm around Fess talking in hushed, reassuring tones. They made brief eye contact with Adán as he entered, but otherwise they left him to himself. He didn't see Scott but guessed he was back in the Quarters as usual. He was the only one of the crew who bothered going in there anymore. Adán couldn't imagine why he would want to, except that it was the only place left in the shuttle where someone could be alone.

And then there was Dema. He was more worried about her than about Fess or Scott or even Tink. He thought about those first hours after waking, how desperate Dema had been to find someone, anyone still alive. And when she'd found Scott—well, she had hesitated, but then she threw herself into saving him. If it weren't for her, he would never have made it. Then there was Fess, the way she mothered him and looked after him better than any real doctor might have. Adán couldn't imagine what she was feeling right now, after fighting so hard to save Lainie.

He found her in the lab, scrutinizing the zygote data— punching numbers into her E-Tab. She didn't even glance up when he came in.

"I have work to do, Adán," she said.

Adán closed the door behind him, so they were alone in the confined lab. "Dema—"

"Some of the damaged zygotes might still be salvageable," she cut him off, swiping a finger hastily across the screen. "If we could just get them to the colony—"

"Dema."

She had washed her hands, and the outerwear that had been splattered with Lainie's blood was gone. He hadn't seen it in the laundry. She'd probably tossed it in the incinerator instead, but the smell of dust and blood were still faintly present around her. Or maybe it was just in his mind.

"Adán, I know you mean well," Dema said, "but I need— *want*—to be alone right now."

He might have believed her if the tremor in her voice hadn't betrayed her.

"I'm not going anywhere," he said.

She raised her eyes to him, narrowed and accusing. "Why, Adán? So, you can taunt me like Scott, or judge me like Jonah? You know, I didn't ask for this responsibility." She swept a hand in the direction of the specimen drawers. "I'm doing the best I can, you know? This is the future of the human race. They're all that matter, Adán. *We* don't matter at all. *I* don't matter."

As she said the last few words, her voice broke, and for a fleeting moment, Adán caught a glistening in her eyes before she turned away.

"Of course, you matter, Dema," he said. "Without you, these embryos wouldn't stand a chance. None of us would. Fess and Dryker—"

"I don't give a damn about Scott Dryker!" she snapped with such vehemence that it took Adán by surprise. Then just as quickly, her face, which was enraged a second earlier morphed into a look of despair. Her eyes reached out to him, pleading.

"I tried to save her," she whispered.

Adán didn't know what to say. He stepped closer to her, expecting her to turn away, to retreat, but she didn't. He was right in front of her now, with only inches separating them. He could feel her warmth, hear her breathing. She looked— vulnerable.

Adán raised his hand to Dema's face, tracing it with his fingertips. Her skin was so smooth, satiny like a rose petal. He half expected her to back away from him, or to push his hand aside, but instead she closed her eyes and tipped her head until her cheek rested in his palm.

"It's okay, Dema," he said softly. "You did everything you could. Everything."

A tear slid down her cheek, moistening Adán's hand. He slid it forward, combing his fingers through her hair. If he were to admit the truth, he had longed to do that ever since he first saw her at the NASA orientation. She was in the line next to his, and they reached the sign-in table at the same time. As she bent over to log in her name, she turned to glance at him, tossing her hair casually over her shoulder. And she had smiled. At that moment, something inside of him fluttered. The feeling had never left him, but he had done his best to ignore it—until now.

Dema's eyes opened, and she looked at him with the same intense gaze as always, as if she were thinking some deep thought about him or searching his face for answers to questions she dared not utter. Yet there was something else, and Adán couldn't decide if it was disbelief or fear...or a combination of both.

Her expression broke, and she began to cry. Adán curled his arms around her, drawing her close. He felt the small shudders of her body against his.

"Shhh. It's all right," he said, trying to console her, but it was no use. She clung to him, weeping into his shoulder.

When the crying had subsided a bit, Dema raised her head to look at Adán. Her face, wet with tears, glistened in the unnatural light of the lab. She began to lean closer as if to kiss him, but then shook her head. "No," she whispered. "This isn't—I can't—" She started to back away, but Adán held onto her. She did not resist.

He didn't know what came over him at that moment, but he pressed his lips to hers. They were so warm, so soft, and they parted, inviting him in. He obliged, and the electric pulse that rushed through him set every nerve on fire. He slid his hands down to Dema's waist and felt the curve of her body pressing against him. His lips slipped from her lips across her chin and down her throat. Dema tilted her head back with a gentle moan, succumbing to Adán's caresses.

Cautiously, he felt for the zipper at the front her jumper and began coaxing it down. He paused, waiting for Dema to stop him or slap him or just walk away, but she didn't. Her breathing was shallow and fast, and Adán felt her heart thumping wildly beneath his fingers. He tugged the zipper down further until the insides of her breasts were visible. When he touched them, she gave a shuddering gasp. He kissed her lips again, and she was kissing him back with abandon. He felt her arms around his shoulders, her hands in his hair. Then suddenly, those hands slipped down to Adán's chest, and Dema gently pushed him away.

"Stop, Adán," she pleaded, fresh tears cascading down her cheeks. "Please stop." She turned as if wanting to get away, yet her hands gripped his uniform as though she needed his support to remain standing. He held onto her.

"I'm sorry, Adán," she said.

"No, I'm sorry. I shouldn't have—"

"No, that's not it." She was gasping through the tears that now fell in steady streams. "I just—I can't..." Her face twisted in grief and confusion.

"You can't what, Dema?" asked Adán. "You can't be with me?"

The way she looked at him then shot daggers through him. "Why not? Is it because of Scott?"

She seemed to struggle against a surge of emotion that threatened to overwhelm her. Then she nodded fiercely.

"You love Scott, is that it?"

"No," she protested.

"You two were together before. I understand—"

"No, you don't understand, Adán," she insisted. "I hate Scott. I hate him!"

Now Adán was more confused than ever. "Why do you hate him, Dema? You can tell me. Did he hurt you?"

"No," she insisted, her eyes brimming with tears.

"Then what is it? Dema, please tell me. I need to understand."

She looked at him so intensely he felt it in his gut. "You can't understand," she said. "No one can." Then she abruptly pushed away from him, briskly drying her eyes on her sleeve.

"I'm sorry," she said again.

"Dema—"

She shook her head, refusing to meet his eyes again as she hurried past him and out of the lab.

Private email correspondence recovered from NASA computer data banks during the Congressional Tribunal Investigation

Attn: Megan A. Whitlock
From: Colonel Jane Foster

No doubt you've been informed about our little "situation." You also know that the fetus would never survive the cryo process, and I cannot guarantee the absence of complications for the mother should we attempt it. I'd like permission to replace her with an alternate.

Reply: Megan A. Whitlock

Two weeks before departure? The media would have a hey day with that. We can't allow things to get out of control again, jeopardize the mission again. If we lose public support, we could lose funding. Replacing her at this juncture isn't an option.

Comment: Colonel Jane Foster

She won't agree to the alternative.

Reply: Megan A. Whitlock

Don't give her a choice.

24

There would be no sleep for the Carpathia's crew tonight, not after losing Lainie. Adán thought about her, about the blood and the way her body had been slashed open—like the tent and Fess's leg. What could have done that? The storm was fierce, true, but what had cut her? Maybe it was the generator she'd been carrying. The metal box had sharp corners and edges. But if she had injured herself on it, so close to the shuttle, how had she ended up ten yards away only to bleed to death there? Could the wind have carried her that far?

Most of the crew sat numb and silent in the common room, the minutes ticking by on their E-Tabs' digital clocks while the world outside remained stagnant and still. Adán had once again volunteered to take watch in the cockpit, watching the atmospheric readings and keeping an eye out for transmissions from the Ensign.

In truth, he was exhausted and longed for sleep, but it would be three hours before Scott came to relieve him. He'd finished the Stephen Crane book he'd been reading. Maybe a movie would keep him awake.

He thumbed through the endless lists of film titles in the database, most of which did not appeal to him, though he did briefly consider delving into James Bond, but he really wasn't in the mood for a movie after all. Instead, he selected "Spring" by Vivaldi, his favorite music composition, and turned up the tablet's speakers.

As the urgent, jubilant voice of the violins cut through the cockpit's silence, Adán tried to play along with his recorder. Yet trying to keep up with the fervency of the violins with a cheap child's instrument frustrated him. What he wanted, what he should have had, was his violin.

Adán punched his finger against the 'stop' icon on his E-Tab, and in the silence that suddenly filled the cabin, he let his mind settle on his situation. He was on a faraway planet. Earth was long gone. All that remained of civilization were his handful of fellow crewmates, a few hundred embryos, and whatever information about culture and history the shuttle had stored in its databases. Like Vivaldi, Adán thought, glancing at the album cover on the tablet's screen. Thank God someone back on Earth had been smart enough to save Vivaldi.

Adán swiped a finger across the screen, and the cover disappeared, replaced by the library menu. The archives had thousands, millions of songs by every artist who had ever recorded anything. It had films, TV shows, even commercials. The shuttle's memory included books, newspapers, magazines, blog posts, websites. Adán skimmed countless lists, their titles a blur. When he got bored with that, he sought out more serious stuff: science studies from hundreds of publications in many different languages, government documents, religious manuscripts. It went on and on and on.

His mind drifted, and he thought of Dema, how she had reacted to him in the lab. Something other than Lainie was bothering her, something that weighed heavily on her mind. Whatever it was, it was an obstacle between them, a barrier Adán suspected he could never hurdle on his own. Was it that she didn't trust him enough to confide in him? He'd felt slighted when she'd pushed him away, but the more he thought about it the more he empathized. He had things too private to share with other people, didn't he? Things he wouldn't tell Dema. Then again, maybe if she'd let him in, if they took the time to really know each other—

It was Scott. Though she'd denied it, he knew it had to be Scott. He'd done something to her, something that had left a scar on her heart. Whatever had happened between them, Scott would get what was coming to him. Adán would see to that.

He kept scanning, but he was no longer interested in movies or music. He returned to the NASA emblem and clicked on it. This is where Tink had accessed the schematics for the shuttle, where Dryker had found the vids about their mission. He scrolled down the menu until he came to the very last link: RESTRICTED.

Restricted to whom, he wondered? He clicked on the link and, to his surprise, entered the portal without a hitch. He had expected a code request, like what Scott had entered for the official vids about their "new" mission, but no request appeared. So, he proceeded.

"That was easy," he said to himself with a little laugh. "Forgot your firewall, guys." But then again, it had to have been intentional, as though NASA *wanted* the information to be accessible. He had assumed there'd be safeguards in place, but there were none.

He scrolled through all kinds of official-looking documents: public announcements, contracts, letters, emails. Curious, he typed "Planetary Colonization Division" into the search bar, and a new file opened. He spent an hour browsing through the pages, following hyperlink after hyperlink, barely glancing at all the titles, until he came to a list of the shuttle fleet's crew registers. That caught his attention. Adán clicked on Carpathia's, and the names of all twenty-four team members appeared. He paused. Seeing them all listed there, seeing their photos beside each name, filled him with regret. They'd never had a chance, it seemed.

What the hell had happened? Commander Parks claimed it was sabotage, something to do with a terrorist group and a mole.

Adán decided that would be the next thing to research. With so much endless information stored in the Carpathia's memory, surely there must be something that could answer his questions. And why hadn't Dryker, the shuttle commander, searched for it already?

He looked at the clock. Scott would be showing up soon. He didn't have time to dive in now. Besides, he told himself, I've literally got all the time in the world.

He scanned the crew list again. They were all there: Dema, Jonah, Tink, Lainie...

Lainie.

Adán swallowed hard, forcing back a wave of emotion.

And there were the names of those who had died before: Alan, Jermaine, Sophie, and all the rest. Each was highlighted in blue. They were hyperlinked. Probably leading to their bios or their NASA applications.

Adán found his own name and tapped it, but instead of taking him to the expected text, a holo appeared.

"Damn," he said as the initial images started to play. Then he settled back into his seat to watch.

WIRED MAGAZINE

"WHERE TECH AND PSYCHOLOGY CONVERGE"

by Edgar Sanchez, Contributing Writer

Excerpt:

Researchers in Norway have successfully completed testing on the highly controversial Cognitive Outreach Project or COP, an advanced method of ESP. With COP, researchers utilize complex computer software to project a subject's brain activity to a platform outside the subject's body.

"We have thus far been able to form distinct three-dimensional images from the brain activity of five separate subjects," says Peder Vooler, COP's project coordinator. "It is very much like creating a hologram, which uses cameras and special lenses to transfer the likeness of an object from a computer to an outside location. COP, however, transfers the image that exists only in the mind of the subject."

When asked if COP is capable of transmitting more than just images, Vooler suggested the possibility of expanding the program's ability in the near future. "As technology improves," he said, "so does our understanding of the human mind, which contains within it not just images, which are directly associated with memories, but also impressions left behind by our five senses, dreams, hopes, fears, and desires. Will it be possible to somehow transfer these expressions of the human psyche outside of the body? Only time and technology will tell."

Vooler went on to explain that the ultimate objective of the project is to be able to hone COP's transference capability into corporeal energy.

"Imagine being able to fly an airplane, move heavy machinery, or fight forest fires by just thinking it. Until now, manipulating our physical world with the human mind has been stuff of science fiction. Yet in time, that's exactly what we hope to achieve."

25

Adán couldn't sleep that night. He wanted to tell Tink what he'd discovered, but he resisted the temptation to wake him. It could wait, he convinced himself.

During breakfast, he mulled over the hologram he'd seen, though it wasn't so much a hologram, a stationary three-dimensional image, as a movie. Yet it was even more than that. It was more than visual. It was—how could he explain it?—*omni*-dimensional. He had *felt* as much as seen. How that was even possible, he had no idea. He hoped maybe Tink would know.

A sharp "Fuentes!" pulled him out of his thoughts. There was a conversation going on, and it seemed his mental absence had been noticed.

Dryker was glaring at him.

"As I was saying," he barked, jutting a finger at the closed shuttle hatch, "the only thing I know for certain is that if that breach isn't repaired, we are all stuck here."

"I don't want to go out there," said Fess, huddled on his cot in the corner.

"You have no choice, Fess," said Scott. "You're the only one who can fix it."

So, they were talking about repairing the shuttle. Tink had repaired the electronics, now it was time to place a permanent patch on the hull. Adán glanced over at Dema, hoping for some clue as to what he'd missed in the discussion, but when his eyes found her, she looked away.

Jonah, sitting at the table, trimmed his nails with a pocketknife. "Fess isn't going," he said with calm resoluteness. "Neither of us are."

"If we don't repair the hull, we can't fly to New Earth," Scott insisted.

"Then we don't fly." It was the first thing Adán had heard Dema say all morning. She looked intensely at each crew member in succession. "We could drive the shuttle to the colony, on the landing wheels."

"That may be fine on the flat terrain," said Scott, "but it's not designed for long distances. And there's the canyon—"

"The canyon is in the opposite direction from New Earth," said Tink.

"The mountains then," said Scott. "We have no idea how steep they are or even if they're traversable at all."

"Then we'll get as far from here as we can," said Dema, "and we'll walk, or hike, the rest of the way."

"Over Chernobog Mons? Impossible." asked Tink, sighing. "Let me do a more thorough study of the range and see if I can find some way through it, a pass of some kind." He looked to Adán. "What do you think?" he asked. "You haven't said anything yet."

Scott wanted to fly the Carpathia to New Earth. It had been their original plan, the only way to transport all the surviving crew and the embryos at once. Other than the breach in the hull and the damage to the electrical system, which Tink had been working on since they'd awakened, the shuttle was in good shape. Adán carefully considered what to say.

"Commander Dryker's right," he said, which elicited protests from the others. He continued anyway. "We already talked about this."

"But that was before…" said Jonah.

Adán understood their reluctance, but he didn't see any viable alternative.

"Even if Tink finds a pass, how many trips would it take to get all our cargo there safely? What if the rovers break down? I know you're scared," he said. "We're all scared, but flying's our best bet."

"Lainie is dead, Adán!" Fess shouted. "Whatever killed her—"

"—is gone now," said Scott. "What happened to her, it was some crazy storm, right? But look at the instruments. The storm is gone."

Adán noticed how everyone's agitation was growing. Fess's eyes pleaded with their commander. He would not relent. "Did a storm slash through the tent? Leave this gash on my leg?"

Adán pressed his eyelids shut. He hated to contradict him, but he felt compelled to stick to facts. "We don't know what did that," he said.

Jonah folded his knife and slipped it into his hip pocket. "I'm with Fess," he said. "I won't go out there again. Thou shalt not tempt the Lord thy God."

Adán rose from the table and grabbed a comm and suit. "That's BS, Jonah, and you know it. I'll understand if *you* don't want to go out there," he told Fess, "But I for one want to get to the colony and am willing to do whatever it takes to get there. Like Scott said, we still have a mission to accomplish, and we can't do it here, can't do it alone. We have to deliver those embryos to New Earth, and we're gonna have to fly to do it."

Adán clipped the comm onto his visor and secured the gloves around his wrists. He'd talk to Tink about the holo later. There were more important things to take care of first.

Scott grabbed a second comm, but Adán stopped him. "No," he told him. "You're the commander. Keep an eye on the controls. If it looks like the wind's picking up, let us know so we can get inside before it gets dangerous."

"All right," said Scott with a nod.

Adán left the hatch, hoping though not expecting anyone to follow. If Fess wouldn't fix the breach, then he would sure as hell figure out how to do it himself.

Scott was right about the air being still. Not a breath of wind blew, not a puff of dust lifted from the ground. Except for the sound of his own breathing, the area around the shuttle was swathed in an eerie silence.

Adán made his way down the length of the shuttle until he reached the breach near its rear, the section where the cryo units were. Fess's temporary patch still held, and Adán wished it were enough to ensure structural integrity in the air, but he knew it wasn't. He would need a sheet of coated Nomex felt several yards long to cover the hole. He turned to head under the ship to the cargo holds when he spotted Fess coming toward him. In his arms was a roll of the material.

"I thought you might be needing this," said Fess sheepishly. He set the roll on the ground, spreading the sheet out. "Jonah said I didn't have to come, but you're right. We need to do something, to act. Why don't you hold this in place while I apply the adherent?"

Adán nodded, relieved Fess had changed his mind. "I'll get the step ladder out of the cargo bay," he said. "It would be helpful if Jonah would lend us a hand."

"You and I both know that ain't gonna happen," said Fess. "I'd give anything to stay inside, but you don't know what the hell you're doing. If I let you patch this thing, we'll all probably explode on takeoff."

They both laughed, which released some of the stress between them. Then Fess grew serious. "After what happened to Lainie, nothing's gonna get Jonah out of that shuttle again. He just won't admit he's scared."

"Aren't you scared?" asked Adán.

Fess forced a nervous smile. "Scared as shit."

Adán patted Fess on the shoulder. "I'll be back in a sec," he said, then hunched beneath the shuttle.

He returned a few minutes later and set up the ladder. Fess immediately began securing the edges of the fabric to the shuttle hull with magnetic clips. It took more than an hour to secure the entire strip in place, and another half hour to trim off the excess. Fess found several tubs of adherent in the cargo bay along with some paintbrushes. "Seems pretty basic, I know," said Fess, prying off the lid from the first tub, "but that's what it is. We apply this goop underneath the material all the way around the edges, so it bonds with the exterior of the shuttle. Then we apply two coats over the whole thing. As it dries, it'll harden into a shell, strong as a bowling ball. Then we weld the sheet of metal over that. The whole thing will need to be filed down to create as smooth a surface as possible. Once we're airborne, even the smallest irregularity can result in friction that could tear this whole thing right off. And if that happens, we're going down."

"How long will the entire process take?"

Fess dipped his brush into the viscous golden adherent that looked surprisingly like a bucket of honey. "We can apply the adherent today, but it needs time to dry. I'll do the welding tomorrow. Once we file it smooth, we can take off pretty quickly after that, as long as Tink makes sure all the systems are functional. Would be kind of a waste, wouldn't it, if we go through all this trouble only to have something go wrong with the controls?"

Fess spread a swath of gold beneath a section of Nomex. Adán grabbed the second brush and started at the opposite end of the breach. What if something did go wrong, he wondered? At this point, there were so many things that could happen, he couldn't even think of them all. What if the systems short-circuited? What if friction tore away the patch? What if they crashed? What if—?"

Adán knew only one thing for sure—there were way too many *what ifs*.

26

After the initial repairs on the breach had been completed, everyone gathered in the common room for a solemn meal of Cream of Chicken soup, or what Fess had christened Wallpaper Paste. Most of the cots and bedding had been blown away earlier in the storm, with the exception of Fess and Jonah's which, it was agreed, should be used by Fess whose leg was still healing, and Dema. The rest of the crew dragged in padding from the cryo units and made makeshift beds on the floor of the CR, except for Scott who slept in the same cryo unit in which he'd spent his coma—Adán's old unit.

"You all just cluster together in here like a bunch of chicks," said Scott before leaving for the Quarters. "Scared little chicks all gathered under their mama's wing." He gave a pointed glare at Adán as he left the room.

"What an asshole," said Fess, curling up on his cot.

Jonah, heading toward the cockpit for his watch, chimed in. "Dema, he's your fault, you know. You should have let him flatline when you had the chance."

"Shut up, Jonah," said Adán.

But Dema didn't respond. She was already lying still, a blanket rolled tightly around her. Adán wasn't sure if she was actually asleep, but either way, Jonah's comment was over the line. Tink was equally unresponsive. He hadn't touched his food and was the first to turn in, choosing to sleep beneath a table. Adán still wanted to ask him about the holo linked to his name, but other than his few comments earlier about repairing the shuttle, Tink had kept to himself all day. So Adán thought it best to leave him alone, at least for tonight. He needed time to deal with Lainie's death in his own way.

Despite feeling beyond exhausted, Adán wasn't ready to go to sleep quite yet. He cleaned up after dinner, started a load of laundry, and rummaged in the personals bin for a new book to read. He could have read anything from the shuttle archives via his tablet, but he still preferred the texture of real paper between his fingers.

Wanting a quiet place to read, Adán joined Jonah in the cockpit, slipping into the co-pilot's seat.

"Hey," Adán said, "mind if I sit in here and read a while?"

Jonah did not respond.

"Sorry about telling you to shut up back there. I didn't mean it."

Jonah remained silent, staring intently at the blank monitor as if it, not the window, provided some view to the world outside.

"Jonah," said Adán, "are you okay, buddy?"

Jonah rubbed the instrument panel with affection, like it was the body of a fine sports car. "What do you think it wants?" he asked in a quiet tone.

"You mean Dryker?" Adán said, thinking of Scott's parting shot a few minutes earlier. He gave a cynical *hmpf.* "Scott's off it," he said. "The coma screwed with his brain, that's what I think."

"No," said Jonah, still staring at the instruments. "Not Commander Dryker. The monster."

It occurred to Adán then that he hadn't thought much about how everything had affected Jonah—the attack on the shelter and Lainie's death. Everyone was affected of course, some more deeply than others, but it had been Jonah all along who refused to step outside the shuttle, who insisted there was something out there.

"It's coming for us whether we believe in it or not," said Jonah, eerily calm. "Well, I believe. I was raised on believing: God, angels, miracles, Jesus casting out evil spirits—all of it. My dad was a pastor, did you know that? He read this story once over the pulpit. Jesus asked his disciples who they thought he was. They told him he was the Son of God. And Jesus told them that it is well to believe, but the devils also believe and tremble."

"So, you think it's some kind of devil out there?" asked Adán.

"I don't know," said Jonah. Then he seemed to change his mind, a sort of resolve taking over his expression. He dragged his gaze from the instrument panel to Adán's eyes.

"Adán, do you think there's a possibility, however small, that God sent this—this *thing*—to finish what he started on earth?"

"What do you mean, Jonah? Finish what?"

"The Apocalypse." Jonah's eyes widened in fierce determination. His fist clenched, pressing into the armrest of his seat. "We escaped God's final judgment, but he's followed us here. He's taking us one at a time. Who can hide from God?"

Adán considered this a moment. If anyone beside Jonah had talked about God and devils and the Apocalypse, he wouldn't have taken them seriously. From the little he knew about church, the religious claimed everything good or bad was God's will. Adán didn't believe in any of it. He believed tragedies were either a consequence of bad decisions or caused by nature. Either way, they were out of anyone's control. That's what happened to Earth. Not some divine judgment. That's what he believed—what he wanted to believe.

"C'mon Jonah. Think about it. Why would God let an entire planet full of people die?" Adán asked. "What kind of a God would do that?"

"He did it before—with the flood."

"Yeah, I guess." Adán leaned forward in his chair, glaring purposefully at Jonah. He had to calm him down, get him to see reason, or else he'd be useless to the mission. The last thing the crew of the Carpathia needed was a lunatic on board.

"Still, if God did send the Apocalypse," suggested Adán, trying to put his thoughts into some logical pattern, "isn't it just as likely that he arranged for us to escape? I don't know a lot about the Bible, but if I'm not mistaken, God saved a handful of people from the flood to start the human race over again."

Jonah nodded uncertainly. "So, you're saying maybe we're like Noah's Ark?"

"Maybe."

Adán laid his elbows against his armrests and thumbed through the pages of his book. Tomorrow he and Fess would finish the repairs. Tink was supposed to input the coordinates

217

of New Earth into the shuttle's guidance system so they could test Carpathia's flight capability, if possible. To do that, they would need everyone, including Jonah, to be at the top of his game.

He gave Jonah's arm a gentle shove. "C'mon," he said. "I'm not tired. I'll take this watch. You get some sleep."

Jonah looked again at the instruments, then got to his feet. He started for the cockpit door, but as he reached for the handle, he paused.

"I like the idea of the Ark," he said. "Only there's one major difference."

"What's that?" asked Adán.

"Noah didn't have some invisible beast tearing his family to pieces."

"How's it look?"

Fess brushed his palm over the hardened patch, then tapped on it with his knuckle. "Good. Looks real good," he said. "You ready for phase two? Grab yourself a length of flashing."

Adán did as he was told, holding the strip of flexible metal in place along the edge of the patch. Fess dropped the welding shield over his eyes and lit the torch. The angry blue flame hissed like a viper.

"Avert your eyes," Fess told him.

Adán turned his face away from the shuttle and stared absently at the horizon, a scene that had become all too redundant over the past week since they had awakened from cryo. He was growing more and more anxious to join the colony at New Earth. Even if the terrain there was the same as here, at least there would be some structures and more faces to help break up the monotony.

"Once this is welded on," continued Fess, "we'll sand it all down and get out of here."

"I can't wait," said Adán.

A crackle sounded in his comm, followed by Dema's voice. "How is everything coming along, boys?"

"Morning, Dema," said Adán. "It's coming along fine. I think we'll be done here by noon."

Fess kept at the welding.

"All right then," said Dema. "I'll have lunch waiting for you—Mac & Cheese."

"Yum."

Dema laughed. "Listen, Adán, you got a minute?"

"Yeah, sure." By the tone in Dema's voice he could tell she wanted to talk alone. He heard the distinctive click in his earpiece signaling that she had switched frequencies. "Are we alone?" he asked.

"For now," Dema answered. "I just wanted to apologize for yesterday—in the lab."

After Lainie's death, Adán had found Dema in the lab intending to comfort her. Instead, he'd come onto her. He hadn't planned to let it get that far and had been too embarrassed to bring it up himself afterwards. In truth, he'd let the whole thing eat at him.

"I'm the one who should apologize," he said quickly. "I totally overstepped my bounds."

"No," Dema insisted. "That's what I wanted to tell you, Adán. I like you. I really like you, and under any other circumstances, I would have responded—differently. Losing

219

Lainie like that, I just wasn't ready. I let things get to me, but I'm fine now. I just don't want things to be weird between us."

Dema was fine? What did that mean? Did she want him to try again—wanted him to kiss her again? His mind reeled with the possibility.

"Well, anyway," continued Dema, "I've got to get back to the lab and finish those diagnostics. Tink's on watch this morning, so he'll be in soon. Oh, here he is now. I'll talk to you later."

Adán heard another click, and the frequency went quiet. Fess cast him a sly grin.

"What?" said Adán, but he couldn't help but smile back.

Fess continued welding. The process was slow going. After a while, Adán's mind started to wander back to Dema. He replayed in his mind those moments in the lab—her lips on his, the warmth of her breath on his skin, the smooth curve of her breasts. He wanted to be with her again, more than anything. Not that anything more could happen between them, not here where privacy was as scarce as the color green. But when they got to New Earth, maybe there they could be together. Maybe Dema would choose him to be her—the word *mate* seemed wrong, insensitive, but any other word for it seemed equally strange. And it didn't matter what they called it anyway. Dema was interested in *him*—not Scott. Boy, wouldn't Scott blow a gasket when he found out? The thought gave Adán pleasure, and he tried to imagine the look on Scott's face when Dema blew him off once and for all and chose him instead.

A loud crackle on the comm broke through Adán's thoughts. Tink's voice came on.

"Fess? Adán?"

"Hi Tink," said Adán. "Nice to hear from you. Did you get a good night's sleep?"

There was a long staticky pause as Adán waited for Tink to reply. When he did, there was a tight gravity in his voice.

"Guys, something's going on out there."

27

The hiss of the welder stopped. Fess pulled up his shield, and he and Adán looked at each other.

"Pressure's dropping," continued Tink. "Wind velocity is rising."

"Another storm?" asked Fess.

"Storm my ass," replied Adán, already coiling up the cord. "Let's get this inside!"

"What about the flashing?" Fess replied. "It's only half done. The wind—it'll rip it right off along with the patch."

Adán grumbled under his breath. "Damn it!" He uncoiled the cord, and Fess lit the torch again, holding it to the flashing.

"Hurry," said Adán, although it didn't need to be said. They both knew time was against them. Already, Adán could feel the temperature plummeting as the wind shot daggers of sand at them. In under a minute, Adán was struggling just to hold the loose flap of flashing in place.

"Fess! It's no use! We've got to get inside!" shouted Adán into his comm.

Fess's hands paused, but only for a moment before he went right back to the job. "It's nearly done!" he hollered over the howling wind. "Just a couple more feet, and it will be secure enough to withstand just about anything!"

"But Fess!"

Crackle.

"Guys!" shouted Tink. "There's—there's something on the monitor!"

Adán grabbed Fess's arm. "We've got to go!" He looked back at the shuttle's forward hatch trying to gauge how long it would take to reach it. Too long, he realized. They'd be fighting against the wind the whole way.

"Fess! The storage bay!"

The storage bay was on the opposite side of the shuttle but closer to where they stood than the hatch.

"A few more inches!" yelled Fess. "If this gets ripped off, there isn't enough material left to do it again! It has to be now!"

The few seconds it took for Fess to weld the last bit of flashing felt unbearably long. The moment the flame went out, Adán pulled Fess away. "Drop the welder! We'll recover it later if we can!"

Crackle. "Are you guys coming?" Tink sounded frantic.

"Negative," said Adán. "Wind's too strong. We're going to wait it out in the bay!"

Suddenly, Dema's voice came over the comm. "Adán! Fess! You need to take cover now! The monitors show a mass the size of the Statue of Liberty coming up behind you!"

Adán spun and peered through the pelting sand. "I don't see anything!"

Fess and Adán ducked under the belly of the shuttle, scurried up the ramp, and dove into the storage area. "Close the bay hatch! Close the bay hatch!" they both shouted.

Tink's voice again came over the comm, broken and staticky. "Computer, close cargo bay door number one," said Tink. "Stay clear, you guys."

To Adán's relief, the ramp retreated beneath the shuttle and the massive door panels began to move on their powerful hydraulic hinges, but slowly—too slowly.

"Are you in?" asked Dema.

"Yes! Yes, we're in!"

The space between the two door panels grew narrower, and Adán allowed himself to feel relieved. Through the gap, he watched the sand blow sideways in hurricane force winds. Too much of it slipped in, clawing at them.

Then suddenly everything shifted. The sand that had gotten trapped inside the bay, swirling like a cyclone, abruptly fled the compartment as if a giant vacuum had sucked it all out. And that's precisely what had happened. Along with the sand, several smaller objects—containers of hardware, tools, rolls of Nomex were instantly gone. Adán felt the strong tug of the vacuum sucking at his body, and he managed to grab hold of the rover, strapped securely to the floor. Fess, too, reach for a hand hold but his fingers clumsily slipped along the side of the compartment and failed to find purchase.

His body, legs first, shot toward the opening with the speed of a bullet. Without thinking, Adán let go of the rover and grasped Fess's hands with his own. Fess's legs were pulled through the opening, but Adán spread his feet apart at the last second, bracing them on either side of the door panels.

"Stop the hatch! Stop the hatch!" he screamed into his comm, but all that he heard in return was static. "Fess is in the way! Stop the hatch from closing!!!"

But the panels continued to close.

"Pull me in!" Fess screeched. "It's gonna cut me! Pull me in!"

Adán held onto Fess as if to his very life and pulled until his leg and arm muscles cramped, but the force pulling on Fess's legs was stronger. It was if something big, something inhumanly strong, had a hold of him.

"It's got me!" Fess screamed. "Adán, please! Please!"

Spittle flew from between Fess's trembling lips. His eyes, wide with terror, pleaded with Adán to save him. Adán had to make a decision: allow Fess to be crushed to death by the closing hatch—or let him go.

At the last possible second, just as the edges of the hatch touched Fess's gear, Adán loosened his fingers.

Fess was gone instantly, sucked out into the darkening storm with a gut-wrenching wail, but in that sliver of a moment when Adán released him, he saw his mistake in Fess's face. It wasn't shock or even fear that twisted his features. It was pain. In its basest, most primal form. Pain— and terror.

The panels came together with a loud *clang*, and Adán was thrust into utter blackness and a silence so severe that the only sound was his own breath filling and emptying his lungs. For a moment, fear penetrated every cell in his body, paralyzing him. Then, like a rope tossed to a man trapped in a well, the comm crackled to life.

"Adán! Fess!" Both Tink and Dema's voices came in loud and clear. "Are you all right?"

Adán's body shook so hard he could hardly find the strength to speak.

"I'm here," he managed.

"The storm, it's over." Tink's voice sounded relieved, joyous even. "Just like before. It hit nearly two hundred miles an hour and then, poof! Over just like that!" Strained laughter came through the comm. Laughter.

"Open the bay doors!" screamed Adán.

"What?"

"I said open the goddamn bay doors!"

Tink didn't deserve to be spoken to that way. How could he possibly know what had happened? But only a minute had passed. It might not be too late.

Tink called the order to the shuttle computer, and the doors separated with a metallic groan. Adán waited only as long as it took to shove his body through the gap. He tumbled to the ground below, his fall cushioned by the soft orange sand. He tried to stand, but his legs buckled beneath him. He tore off his helmet and scoured the landscape, now completely still. He searched for any sign of Fess—a lump of bloody soil, body parts, anything, but it was all flat and lifeless for miles in every direction.

"Fess!" He yelled before he realized he was shouting into his comm. He tore it from his face. "Fess!"

Suddenly, something had him round the shoulders. He flailed his arms trying to shake it off.

"Adán, hey! It's me!"

It took a few seconds for Adán's brain to register Tink's voice and then his face. He desperately grasped the front of Tink's uniform.

"Tink! Tink, it's Fess!" he hissed. "He got sucked out! We've got to find him!"

Tink nodded, blinking, trying to absorb what Adán was saying.

"Okay, Adán. Okay. We'll find him."

Tink left Adán and climbed into the storage bay. A minute later, Adán heard a motor start up and the heavy clumping of the rover coming down the ramp. It moved ever so slowly while time seemed to race past and through him. They had so little time.

"Get in," said Tink, pulling up beside Adán. "Let's go find Fess."

28

"There's nothing out here, Adán."

Tink and Adán had been driving for an hour in ever widening circles around the shuttle hoping to find even the smallest evidence that Fess was out there somewhere, but not only did they see nothing, the scanners saw nothing too.

"If he was anywhere near here," added Tink, "the scanners would have picked him up." He lifted his foot off the rover's accelerator and let it come to a slow stop.

"I know," said Adán. "I just can't believe he's gone. I mean where could he be? He couldn't have just vanished."

But that's exactly what had happened. Fess was gone, and that bothered Adán more than even Lainie's death because at least they knew Lainie was dead. With Fess, they didn't know anything. He could be lying miles off alive and needing help, but how far did they dare stray from the shuttle to look for him? They were already more than a mile off, far enough for the shuttle to look like a small speck behind them.

They continued on without speaking, adding one more ring to their circular path.

"I think we'd better get back," said Tink. "We've gotten out of range of the shuttle's comm."

"All right," Adán agreed reluctantly as Tink turned the rover back toward the Carpathia.

They drove in silence, Adán's mind reeling between Fess's pain-wracked face, Lainie's lacerated body, the slashed tent, the scars in the sand he'd seen by the shuttle wheels. He thought again of what Commander Parks had said about the Terrestrial Brotherhood and finding a mole on board the Ensign, but a human mole couldn't be responsible for the damage he'd seen. This was something bigger, something not human.

Tink's voice cut through Adán's meditation. "You okay, Adán? I mean, it's beyond awful about Fess, but from the looks of it, there's something else on your mind. Wanna talk about it?"

There was something Adán had wanted to talk with Tink about. He switched his comm to a private frequency.

"I found something," Adán began, "in the shuttle's database."

"You mean aside from a trillion really bad movies?" asked Tink.

But Adán was in no mood for joking. "For one thing," he continued, "I accessed NASA's records. Even the restricted stuff. I didn't have time to look at much, but it was easy. Too easy. Like we were meant to find it."

Tink kept his eyes on their path ahead, the shuttle slowly growing larger in the distance. "That makes sense, knowing what we know now. If Earth was destroyed, what would be the point of keeping anything off limits?"

Adán thought about Tink's comment, but it seemed more than that. NASA *wanted* them to read something, but what?

"When you combed through the archives, did you find anything—unusual?" asked Adán.

Tink shook his head. "I was focused more on schematics, checking for damage to the grid, learning how to run diagnostics. Why?"

"There was something else." Adán told Tink about accessing the crew register and how each name was linked to a holo. "But not just any kind of holos. These were stories, memories, segments from our lives. I watched mine for a while. I couldn't believe what I saw."

Tink slowed the rover to a complete stop and faced Adán with a serious expression, but he said nothing, just waited for Adán to go on. So, he did.

"The day I left for NASA, my brother Saul came home high. He'd been in trouble with drugs for years. I was hoping to say goodbye to him, but he was messed up. Then my dad came into the living room, shouting at him. 'Where is it?' he demanded. 'Where's your brother's violin?'"

Adán paused. Saying this out loud was one of the hardest things he'd ever done.

"Saul had sold it to buy drugs. Left the empty case behind, which is how I hadn't noticed. I was going to bring it with me—here."

Adán noticed a slight breeze picking up. The layer of dust on the ground began to shift.

"It hurt that he would do that, but I could've lived with it. But Saul got defensive and took a swing at my dad. Looked like he was ready to kill him. I was angry, so I called 911. The cops took him away in handcuffs, still high as a kite. That was last time I ever saw him."

Tink sat quietly for a few moments, then said, "That's rough, man. I'm sorry."

"It's been eating me up inside for a long time, the guilt of having called the cops on my own brother. And now that he's gone—everyone's gone…"

Adán hesitated, then continued. "But the thing is," he said, "I never told anyone what happened, but there it was right in front of my eyes. And I *felt* it, like I was living it all over again. It was so real, I could smell the cinnamon candle burning on the fireplace mantle. It was like I'd been—invaded."

"So, you're saying that your thoughts and feelings, your memories, were somehow stored in the shuttle's databanks?"

"That's exactly what I'm saying. And not just me—all of us. The whole crew. How is that possible?"

The breeze grew into a wind. "We gotta go," said Tink. The rover growled back to life and started forward. "It must have something to do with the patches. You know, the patches we wore during cryo that recorded our brain activity."

Adán gripped the hold bar. "Well, it recorded a lot more than just brain waves, I'm sure of that."

The rover hadn't gone far when a sudden gust of wind whipped icy pellets of sand against their visors. As the wind grew stronger, seeing more than a few feet ahead became more difficult.

"This isn't good," said Tink, referring to his wrist tab. "Wind velocity is steadily increasing. What is it with these crazy storms?"

Adán felt an undeniable sense of dread. "We need to get back quick. We can't stay out here, Tink."

A powerful squall of sand slammed into them, and the rover veered to the left, two of its wheels lifting a few inches off the ground before crashing back down again.

"I can't see a thing," Adán shouted to make himself heard over the roar of the wind. "I can't make out the shuttle anymore! We might miss it altogether! We'll have to follow the coordinates on your wrist tab."

"I can't even see the screen!" Tink replied. "We may have to just wait this out!"

The idea of staying out in the storm in the same conditions that had killed both Lainie and Fess made Adán shudder. He thought of what Jonah had told him, that the monster was God's way of finishing what he had started on Earth, but Adán did not believe in God—or monsters.

"We could set up a portable," suggested Tink, "protect us from this wind, at least! There's one in the ER kit on the back of the rover!"

They got off the rover and fought the wind to the back of it. Tink opened the metal box that contained all the equipment, tools, and survival items someone would need on a short journey away from the shuttle. The portable was a scaled-down shelter, just large enough for two, like a camping tent, only sturdier.

The wind had only grown stronger by now, so strong Adán had to hold his helmet on with one hand while unfolding the shelter with the other. He and Tink held tight to the canvas, which flapped in the gale like a panicked bird beating its wings in a desperate attempt to take flight. It was supposed to be a simple setup, easy enough for one person to manage. Yet even between the two of them, they couldn't hold it steady enough to secure it to the ground let alone stand it upright.

"It's no use," said Adán. "We can't do this without help."

Adán rolled the shelter into a thick ball and stuffed it back into the case. He and Tink stood together, grasping each other's arms now, trying to remain upright in the battering wind.

"We're a little closer than we were before," said Tink. "We might be in comm range now."

Adán switched his comm frequency back to open and hailed the shuttle. "Carpathia, this is Adán. Is anyone there? Situation has deteriorated. We can't get back on our own, can't get the shelter up. We're exposed. Over."

The comm crackled loudly. Interference from the storms had proved an ongoing challenge with communication.

"Dema here," said a female voice after a few agonizing moments of silence. "Adán, are you and Tink okay?"

"So far," he replied. "But unless this storm lets up soon, I'm not so sure how long we can last."

"Did you find Fess?"

"Negative. He's gone. Not a trace. I'm afraid the same thing might happen to us if we don't get back to you soon."

"The shuttle sensors are reading seventy-two mile an hour winds, and it's only increasing. Can't you get back on the rover?"

"Again negative. We can't make visual. It's so bad Tink can't even see the readings on his wrist tab anymore."

There was a pause which felt like forever to Adán. When Dema's voice came on again, he felt as though it was salvation itself.

"I'll rig a transmitter to the other rover. The guidance system will use audio signals to lead me to you and back. We can drive blind that way, but it's going to take me a few minutes to get the rover out of the storage bay. Can you hang on that long?"

"I don't think that's such a good idea, Dema. It's bad out here."

"I don't see any other way, Adán. You run the risk of dying out there in the storm or let me come get you. We can tether the rovers together, and you can follow me back that way. According to the sensors, you're not too far from here, a little more than half a mile. I'll be there in in a few minutes. Just hang on."

"Okay," Adán finally relented. "But let's keep this channel open. I want to make sure you're all right."

Dema snorted. "You want to make sure *I'm* all right? Give me a break," she said, but Adán could hear the smile in her voice. "I'm heading for the rover now. See you soon."

Adán turned to Tink. "You got all that?"

"Yeah."

"Good. I guess we just wait then."

They stood there, clutching the rover, when Adán noticed something different in the storm. "Hey," he told Tink, "I think the wind is shifting."

"Shifting?"

"I mean it's changing direction."

Sure enough, the sand blowing nearly horizontally before was now altered somehow. Adán squinted, trying to figure out what was different. It was difficult to see at all, but there was no mistaking it. The sand was blowing in two directions at once!

How was that possible? It couldn't be, yet Adán was seeing it with his own eyes. Blurs of sand collided and raced through and past each other, like a cyclone that couldn't make up its mind. And it wasn't blowing straight either, but in a circular pattern, spiraling up from the ground. The sand was compressing together, he realized. It was taking shape.

The mass of churning sand rose above the desert floor, coagulating into something not quite solid. Adán followed it with his eyes, watching it grow taller and wider until it eclipsed even the pale smear of sun left in the sky.

Beside him, Tink stood rigid, eyes fixed on the shape looming above them. As the storm whipped around and through it, the edges solidified into harsh three-dimensional curves that bulged out, forming what appeared to be lopsided appendages.

Adán took a step back. "Tink, is that...?"

One of the appendages, a thick stub of swirling sand, extended outward, lengthening, dividing into fingers—no, not fingers—claws.

"Run! Run!" Adán grabbed Tink by the arm and hurled him onto the rover. The motor hummed to life and shot forward as Adán threw himself into the passenger seat. Tink pressed his foot to the accelerator, quickly reaching the rover's top speed, which wasn't, Adán realized with horror, nearly fast enough.

The clawed arm of the sand monster swooped down on them, slipping beneath the rover and flinging it into the air with ease. The rover toppled end over end, throwing Adán and Tink free of it. They both hit the ground and rolled away from the crashing vehicle.

In his comm, he heard the sickening crack of a bone breaking and of Tink howling in sudden pain. Adán clambered to his feet, scanning the area around him. Tink lay ten feet away, writhing on the ground.

The wind relentlessly shoving at his back, Adán ran toward Tink, but the wind was too strong. He toppled forward, skidding face first into the ground. The sand beat mercilessly on him, pinning him helplessly in place. Adán watched in horror as the monster, for what else could he call it, bore down on him.

Suddenly, Tink was there grabbing him by the arm and hauling him to his feet. How he had managed to reach him, Adán couldn't begin to guess. Tink held one of his arms tight against his chest, the jagged fractured bone protruding from his forearm like the tooth of a wild animal. And there was blood. A lot of it.

"Get up!" Tink shouted. "Get up and run!"

Tink dragged Adán blindly through the storm toward what they hoped was the safety of the shuttle.

"Dema!" Adán screamed into his comm. "Dema, can you hear me?"

"I'm coming, Adán," said the familiar voice. "I'm maybe twenty yards away from you!"

"There's something out here! Something big!"

Through the swirling sand, Adán could just make out the dark outline of what must be the rover. He had allowed himself to feel a moment of hope when a virtual mountain of sand dropped down right in front of him. It was as dense as any solid wall, and he plowed into it before he could stop himself. The force of the impact broke Tink's hold on his arm. Tink continued to run, but to Adán's horror, he realized he had veered off in the wrong direction.

"Tink, get back here!"

Adán peered again at the rover's silhouette in the storm—safety, escape. Then he turned and took off after Tink, but the enormous wall of sand lifted and dropped in front of him again, effectively blocking his path and separating him from Tink. He couldn't even see him through it. Adán backed away from the barrier, his gaze following it to its origin: the creature itself. This block was part of its arm.

Suddenly, the arm shifted away from Adán, rolling like an enormous wave across the sand toward Tink as fast as the wind itself. As it did, Adán caught glimpses of his friend staggering blindly ahead.

"Tink!" Adán screamed. "Tink!" But it was no use. The connection between them had gone dead. Tink was alone.

The wall of swirling sand pushed forward, sweeping the surface of the ground with merciless efficiency. It reached Tink in seconds. Adán saw Tink shudder with the impact, and then the sand swallowed him up. And he was gone.

29

The storm breathed a final gasp and died out. The trillions of grains of sand that had been caught up in the maelstrom fell to earth like dry rain. The sound of it reminded Adán of the time when he was a boy when he lay awake half the night listening to hail pelting his roof.

The sand fell for five seconds. That was all. And then there was silence. Even the static in Adán's comm had ceased. Everything was still and deadly calm.

Adán's legs trembled as he took a hesitant step forward, and then another. Soon he was running, stumbling, and then crawling across the frozen sand to the spot where he had last seen his friend.

"Tink, where are you? Please come in! Tink!"

But there was no answer. Adán tore off his helmet and shouted Tink's name again and again. He scanned the horizon in every direction. Nothing. Nothing.

A few minutes later, Adán heard the rumble of the rover's engine coming toward him. Dema pulled up beside him.

"Adán, I've been calling you." She looked around. "Where's Tink?"

Adán tried to move, but his muscles refused to respond. If he could just bend a finger, scratch somewhere, anywhere, then he'd feel normal again, like maybe everything else wasn't so awful. Yet his body remained rigid, and he kept staring out toward where the storm—the monster—had scooped up Tink and…

He couldn't think about it anymore. If he did, he was going to be sick.

Finally, with more effort than he'd ever put into anything he ever had before, he twisted his right foot to the side. He forced his other foot to follow, and he turned away from the barren horizon that was Tink's vast grave.

"Did you bring the scanner?" he asked Dema.

"Yes, but—"

"Tink's gone." He took the scanner from Dema's hand and methodically waved it side to side, examining the landscape, searching for any sign of his friend. "It was here," he told Dema. "The monster is real. I saw it."

The scanner was useless. Adán slapped it repeatedly with the heal of his hand. "Damn it!" Then he threw it with all his might.

"The storm," he continued, breathlessly, "the sand swirled around it, and I saw its outline. It's big. Bigger than the shuttle. And it went after Tink." In his mind, he saw how the creature's massive limbs dropped in front of him, cutting him off from Tink, and then swept his friend away. It was all so—intentional, just as Dema had once said. Adán blinked, confusion muddling his brain. "It wanted him," he said. "But why?"

"I'm so sorry, Adán," said Dema. "I would have reached you sooner, but Scott tried to stop me. He'd been in the Quarters for hours. When he came out, I told him what was happening. He stood in the doorway, blocking me from leaving. I tried to push past—"

"Scott blocked you? Why would he do that?"

"I don't know. Maybe he didn't want me to get hurt. I managed to get past him, and he didn't come after me."

"Scott knew we were out here. He knew that thing was out here."

"I don't know, Adán. He was crazed about it. Kept saying we aren't supposed to be here."

"We're not supposed to be here? What the hell does that mean?"

Adán glared back at the shuttle. There had always been something different about Scott, something not quite right. Ever since he'd awaken from his coma, he'd been edgy and anxious. Adán thought about what Jonah had said—that the monster was sent by God, but what if God had nothing to do with it? What if this was something mankind had brought upon itself?

"Dema," said Adán, "do you remember what Commander Parks said about the other shuttles being sabotaged?"

"Yeah?"

"Give me your tab."

"What? Why?"

"Just give me your tab!" Dema pulled it from her pack and handed it to him. He clicked and scrolled frantically.

"It's all here," he said. "All of it. Newspaper articles, official documents. I saw this before, but I was rushing through, just skimming the surface, but I get it now. They wanted us to know."

"Know what? Adán, I don't under—"

"Just look at this."

She read the headline on the screen and then scanned through the story. "What am I seeing?"

Adán scrolled through more stories, more pages. "The Terrestrial Brotherhood claimed the human race had no right to try to escape God's punishment. They planted a mole on the Beacon and destroyed the entire crew."

"And Parks found a saboteur among his crew," said Dema.

"What if there was a mole on every shuttle? On the Carpathia?"

"No. That's not possible."

"What if that mole, that traitor, is *still* on the shuttle?"

"Still on the—Adán, there's only four of us left. If the saboteur was on the shuttle at all, he's probably dead."

"Maybe, but maybe not. Maybe we were all supposed to die but something went wrong. Some of us survived, and now whoever was responsible has to finish the job."

"I still don't see what you're—"

"It's Scott," said Adán. "The monster. That thing that killed Fess and Lainie and now Tink. It's Scott's mind, see? I don't know exactly how he's doing it, but I think the monster is connected to him somehow. Think about it. He was the last one to go into cryo and the last one awake. Tink said the hail transmitter had been turned off. He thought it was glitch, but what if it was done on purpose? To prevent communication. Isolate the shuttles. Jonah looked in Scott's storage box, and it was empty. Why would he bring anything with him if he knew he wouldn't be needing it? Then the first night we were attacked, when it tore the shelter, Scott had just woken up. And he's in there, in the Quarters, all the time.

241

With that machine, those patches. Is he still connecting to that thing? What does he do in there anyway?"

"Adán, this is all a bit far-fetched, don't you think? I mean, you're accusing our Mission Commander of murdering the whole crew!"

Adán shook his head. "I know it sounds crazy. Jonah warned me days ago, but—"

"Jonah? Since when do you believe anything Jonah says? He's a fanatic."

"Sometimes he makes sense. He's the one who first suggested that something's wrong with Scott, but I didn't take him seriously—until now."

"He's got some crazy ideas, Adán, but that doesn't make him right. If you're talking about religious zealots like the Terrestrial Brotherhood, maybe you should look at Jonah. Where is he, anyway?"

"I don't know. Wasn't he in the shuttle with you?"

"I haven't seen him since you left with Tink to find Fess."

"Get in the rover," said Adán.

"What about the other one?"

"We'll retrieve it later if we can. Right now, we've got to get back to the Carpathia. We need to find Jonah before Scott does."

OPINION by Nancy Orlov

From global warming to GMOs, the human race has indisputably damaged Mother Earth. After centuries of polluting the air, land, and seas, we have created a toxic environment that has caused an alarming rise in incurable cancers, has led to the extinction of countless animal and plant species, and has set humankind on a path from which there is no turning back. With the eminent cataclysmic destruction of what's left of the planet's rain forests, the earth will soon be unable to recycle its own atmosphere. At this rate, our air will cease to be breathable in less than fifty years, a single generation.

While governments around the world make promises they cannot keep and pass increasingly stringent regulations to restore our planet to a habitable state, the evidence proves that it is too late. Our planet is doomed. The question we ask is this: Do we have the right to curse any other planet with the presence of human life, setting it on the same course as Earth now travels?

NASA plans to colonize Europa, but will doing so simply multiply and proliferate Earth's problems? Some experts claim our

planet may face disaster sooner than
previously predicted. If so, we have brought
this crisis upon ourselves. To think we can
escape the consequences by spreading our
legacy of self-destruction is a crime
against humanity's future generations and
the entire universe.

30

As the rover neared the shuttle, Adán spotted a figure standing outside the hatch. It was Scott peering off into the desert. Orange dust coated his face and hair, as if he had been out there through the whole storm. Adán jumped off the shuttle while it was still moving.

"Adán, wait," warned Dema, but he ignored her. He strode up to Scott and without hesitation struck him across the jaw.

Scott stumbled back, almost losing his balance. A thin line of blood threaded its way from a nostril down to his lip. His tongue darted out of his mouth, tasting.

"What the—?"

Adán hit him again. Scott tried to block the blow, which he had expected to land on his face again. This time, however, the fist landed in his stomach. Air woofed out of him, and he wrapped a protective arm around his middle. Then, slowly, he straightened up, his face cringing from the pain.

Scott's brilliant blue eyes shifted until he was looking right at Adán. Adán couldn't tell if the emptiness in his face was from shock or indifference, but he didn't care anymore.

"You wanna fight me?" Scott jeered. His bloody lips curled into a taunting grin. Adán stood, his fists poised.

"If this is about Dema," Scott added, "she's not worth fighting over. You can have her." He spat a mouthful of blood onto the sand.

They stood staring at each other. Adán was lucky. He'd caught Scott by surprise. If he tried a third time, Scott would be ready for him. Keeping his eyes on Scott, he turned for the rover, which had come to a stop beside him. He unlatched the toolbox and snatched out a wrench. Eighteen inches long and made of solid steel, it had to have weighed five or six pounds. He gripped it so tightly his fingers ached.

Scott gaped, his face frozen in an expression of disbelief. He raised his hands, palms out.

"Hold on," he said. "I don't know what I did to piss you off, but we can talk about this, can't we?"

Adán hadn't notice before, but now he spotted Jonah standing at the base of the shuttle hatch.

"Do it," Jonah said, his voice as steady as ever. "Do it, Adán. He deserves it."

"So, she told you about us, right?" said Scott, arrogance and alarm rolling off him like sweat. "I screw a girl, and I deserve to get bludgeoned to death? It's not like I raped her, you know. And she had the abortion willingly."

"What?" said Adán.

"No one held a gun to her head."

"Scott—" Dema said weakly, but Scott ignored her.

"Colonel Foster told her it was her duty, and she obeyed like a good little soldier."

The cynicism in Scott's voice churned Adán's stomach. No wonder Dema hated him.

"This isn't about Dema," said Adán. The steadiness of his own voice took him by surprise. "This is about Lainie, and Fess, and Tink—and the seventeen members of our crew lying under four feet of frozen sand."

Scott blinked. Adán continued. "You sabotaged the mission."

"No, I didn't," said Scott.

"Everything points to you. You were our commander. You had control of the damn ship! It did what you told it to do."

"What the hell are you talking about?"

"You switched off communications. And your box was empty, Scott. Jonah checked it. You didn't bring anything with you!"

Adán watched as Scott's once confident demeanor broke down in fear. Adán raised the wrench.

Scott backed up, but tripped over his own feet and stumbled, landing on a knee. "What business is it of yours what I brought?"

"What commander would leave all his belongings at home—unless he never intended to live long enough to use them?"

Scott's expression turned frantic.

Adán pressed on. "Someone intentionally cut the power to the cryo units, but it went wrong. Some of us survived. But then something attacked the shuttle, as if trying to finish the job *you* failed to do."

Jonah, a hungry smirk on his face, took three steps toward Adán. "It's got to be him," he said. "The monster will keep coming back until he's dead. Adán, you've got to stop the monster before it gets all of us."

"No!" shouted Scott. "It isn't me! I-I admit I'd heard rumors about the Beacon, the mole. But I didn't know who or if—" He swiped at his nose. "I didn't bring anything because I didn't think we—any of us—would make it. I was as surprised as all of you to be alive. It wasn't me. I swear, it wasn't me!"

Scott's voice gasped through tears now. Adán didn't know why, but something in Scott's voice, the desperate pleading, sounded sincere.

"If you're not the monster," Adán said, "then what is? What has been attacking the crew?"

"I don't know!" said Scott. "I don't know!"

Jonah, angry now, came forward to stand right in front of Scott. "Just tell the truth, Dryker!" he shouted. "The brotherhood planted you on board in order to destroy the mission. Tell the goddamn truth!"

"No! No, I wouldn't—I didn't!"

Scott melted into a sobbing mess at Adán's feet. Jonah looked away, disgusted. Adán took a step back from the man he had once called commander and tossed the wrench to the ground.

In that moment, Scott lunged at him, growling like a wild beast. His fingers tightened around Adán's throat, clenching like a bear trap. Adán's lungs gasped desperately for even the smallest scrap of air, but his airway was closed off. Then, just as suddenly, there was a dull *thunk*. Scott's eyes rolled back in his head, and his hands slid off Adán's neck as he crumpled in a lifeless heap on the ground, blood oozing from a split in his scalp. Dema stood over him, gripping the wrench with white knuckles.

Adán rubbed his throat, sucking in deep gulps of precious air.

"Thanks," he croaked.

"You're welcome," said Dema.

"Is he dead?" asked Adán.

"He should be," said Jonah.

Dema knelt beside Scott and pressed her fingers to his neck. "No. He's alive. I really didn't hit him that hard, but we need to get him inside and stop the bleeding."

Neither Adán nor Jonah moved.

"C'mon, you guys. You can't leave him here. If you do, then you're no better than that thing out there."

Jonah and Adán reluctantly hauled a limp and bloody Scott inside and laid him on one of the cots in the common room. Dema immediately set to work collecting items from a first aid kit to cleanse and suture his wound. Adán watched for a few minutes, and then removed himself to the cockpit.

He dropped into the pilot's seat and stared numbly out the window through the ever-present sheen of orange dust. Outside, the landscape of Gliese was as still as a photograph. It almost seemed unfair that the planet itself didn't wail and writhe in grief over the death of Tink, over all their deaths. Adán wondered if the rust-colored earth wasn't stained that way from the blood of others who had come before. Had this planet once sustained some community of living beings, and had those beings also been destroyed by the monster that seemed so determined to destroy the crew of the Carpathia?

Adán leaned forward, resting his forehead against the control panel. Thoughts of those he'd lost assaulted his brain. He tried to push them out, but they came in a relentless barrage of vivid images and thoughts and even smells—the bloody slashes across Lainie's abdomen, the way Fess's mouth twisted open when he screamed, Tink being swallowed whole by some grotesque sand creature. But it was the sound of Fess's gut-wrenching squeals that had been the worst, and the way they cut off like that, just suddenly silenced as he got sucked out into the void. Even now Adán's stomach twisted inside of him thinking about it.

Adán lifted his head a couple of inches and let it fall against the cold, lifeless metal panel. He did this again and again, hoping the pain in his skull would drown out the pain inside his head, but it was futile. Their deaths would live inside him forever, like a parasite feasting on his conscience until one day there would be nothing left of him but a hollow shell. All dead. And why? What had done it? They still had no idea. It was some giant invisible beast that existed in a whirlwind of sand. Where did it come from? Could it really have come from the mind of one person? And if it had—how? Why?

He began to think he'd made a mistake, blaming Scott. In the midst of tragedy, of panic, it was too easy to point fingers. Scott had denied everything. He could have been lying, thought Adán, and Scott had tried to hurt him. But maybe that was out of self-preservation. They were all just trying to stay alive, weren't they?

But what if Scott *had* been responsible? What if…?

A thought tickled the corner of Adán's brain. Something he'd seen in the archives. He pressed his eyelids shut, trying to recall the nagging memory. In the archives. What was it again?

Swiping a finger across the panel screen, Adán accessed the shuttle's data banks, returning to the news clippings he'd been scanning through, articles about the sabotaged shuttle.

He slid through document after document, hoping one of them would jog his memory. And after a few minutes, one of them did.

There. He tapped the screen and enlarged the print. He scanned through it quickly. Yes, this was it. He leaned back in the chair, reading it over again just to make sure. He had found the answer, but he didn't know if it made him feel relieved—or more afraid than ever.

Dema

Dema knew the pregnancy test was positive before she'd even seen the pink line across the tiny plastic window, but when her suspicions were confirmed, her reaction surprised her. She didn't feel disappointed or scared. She felt—elated.

A baby.

Her baby.

Well, and Scott's, though she wasn't sure how he'd take the news. He was the Mission Commander, after all. His reputation was on the line. And it wasn't like they were serious. No talk about marriage or any future together at all. It was just a thing between them, and despite precaution, a miracle had happened.

But the mission.

Screw the mission. She'd never really wanted to go into space anyway. She'd been training as an Army medic when NASA's recruitment campaign began. Her friend, Hannah, had coaxed her into applying with her. Hannah didn't make the cut but had convinced Dema to accept NASA's offer to join the team.

She'd met Scott Dryker on day one. He was tall, confident, handsome. He selected her from all the others to be his. Dema didn't know how else to describe it, and she was never really sure why she agreed to his come ons. He was arrogant, like an overgrown high school football star, but he was also a good leader. And he was gentle with her when they were alone together, tender and sensual. Dema had felt wanted.

She knew full well there was nothing more than sex between them, and she was fine with that. Even now, holding the plastic wand in her hand, she had no aspirations that Scott would want a family with her.

But she needed to tell him. She at least owed him that.

But Scott did not react—at all. The news didn't even make him blink. There was no surprised pause, no frown, no smile. His expression remained as disinterested as when she'd interrupted his E-Tab game.

"We're three weeks from launch," he said indifferently. "You should have been more careful."

Dema was taken aback. "*I* should have been more careful?"

Scott leaned back in his desk chair and turned his attention back to his game. "You can't go into cryo pregnant. What are you gonna do?"

So, she'd been right to believe she was in this alone. All the better. She wouldn't even add his name to the birth certificate. In fact, she didn't owe him anything after all.

Dema left his room without answering his question.

She spent two days thinking about what she was going to do. She had finally gathered the courage to resign from the project when she got a summons to Colonel Foster's office. After donning her uniform and going over in her head what she would say, Dema made her way nervously out of the barracks to the administration building.

"Colonel Foster asked to see me," she told the secretary, who told her she was expected and to go on in.

Dema pushed open the office door and stepped inside. The room was furnished with a heavy-looking mahogany desk and two matching bookcases. Photos of the Colonel with various presidents and senators decorated the walls, along with several certificates and diplomas.

Colonel Foster stood beside the desk, dressed in a neatly pressed, navy-blue uniform skirt and jacket. In her early fifties, Foster's dark hair, fashioned into a sensible bun, had hints of gray at the temples. Her face was stark and thin, with fathomless dark eyes.

"Take a seat, Corporal Sarkissian."

Dema turned to look for a chair and was shocked to find Scott already sitting in one in the corner of the room.

"Commander Dryker?" Dema said, trying to mask her surprise. A brief, sharp nod was his only greeting.

Dema took the other chair, closer to the Colonel's desk.

"Is there something you need to tell me?" asked Colonel Foster.

Dema's body went rigid. *She already knows,* she realized. *Scott's already told her.*

When she didn't reply, Colonel Foster answered for her.

"Commander Dryker here has informed me of your— situation. Now before you get angry, let me assure you that as your commanding officer, it was his duty to inform us of any issues that might interfere with the mission. Honestly, Corporal, such behavior during training is not only inappropriate but would normally be cause for dismissal."

Dismissal? Hadn't Scott told her he was the father?

Dema didn't dare look at him. Clearly, he had left that important piece of information out of his report.

"That's actually why I've come, Colonel Foster," said Dema, fear already weakening her resolve. "I wish to turn in my resignation."

The Colonel sat down in her chair behind her desk and clasped her hands together. "That's not an option at this point, Sarkissian."

Dema gripped the armrests. She could feel her heart rate increasing.

"In just seventeen days, the Carpathia and her crew will launch for Europa. This mission is imperative. We cannot delay departure, and there isn't time to prepare your alternate."

"What do you mean there isn't time?" asked Dema. "We just got an alternate last week, replacing a sick crew member."

The Colonel's expression turned icy. "There is a world of difference between a team member coming down with a life-threatening, contagious disease and a girl getting herself knocked up."

Dema squirmed in her seat. Surely Scott would say something in her defense? The baby was as much his fault as hers, but no. The only noise she heard from the corner was the rustle of fabric as he shifted position.

She could speak up, of course, tell the Colonel that Scott Dryker was to blame, but Dema imagined he would deny it, laugh off the accusation. And who would the Colonel believe?

"We find ourselves in a quandary," said Colonel Foster. "But unlike a contagion, this is easily resolved."

Dema looked up. A resolution. Yes, that's what she wanted. To leave the program and raise this baby on her own. She didn't need Scott Dryker. She didn't need anyone.

The Colonel slid a form across the desk and then held a pen out to Dema. "Just sign this consent, and we'll move forward."

Dema hesitated only for a moment before taking the pen. She leaned closer to the desk to read the form, eager to sign it and get on with her life.

But what she read sent ice through her veins.

"What is this?" she asked, though she knew full well what it was. It was clearly printed across the top:

CONSENT FOR ABORTIVE PROCEDURE

"I'm not signing this," Dema said, pushing the form back across the desk. "I want to resign. I want this baby."

The Colonel leaned back in her cushy leather armchair and sighed. "You misunderstand. This isn't optional. You signed a contract when you first joined us committing yourself to this mission. I have a copy of it right here, if you'd like to see it."

Dema wilted. "No, that isn't necessary. I know what I signed."

"Good. So, we're on the same page."

Suddenly, the air in the room felt stifling. Dema instinctively reached up to unbutton her collar but stopped herself. "You can't force me to do this," she said, getting to her feet.

"Actually, I can, though I'd rather not."

Dema stumbled away from the chair and took a few steps toward the door, keeping her eye on Colonel Foster. "It's unconstitutional. I have rights."

Dema turned for the door, but before she could reach it, Scott was there blocking her way like a mountain. "Sit down, Dema," he said in such a calm earnest voice that it startled her. "You need to trust us. Just listen, all right?"

It was the Scott she had grown to care about, the tenderness he'd exhibited in their private moments. And it caught her off guard. He took hold of her arm and gently guided her back to her seat. Dema was too much in shock to resist. And what if she did resist? What would happen then? She suspected the answer was something she'd rather not find out.

The Colonel stood up and came round the front of her desk. She squatted down in front of Dema, a very unauthoritative position for a military leader. Her face softened, and Dema thought she looked almost motherly.

"Corporal. Dema," said the Colonel, her voice uncharacteristically soft, "I know this is a very difficult decision to make. And unfortunately, I am not at liberty to explain to you why we need you to make it. All I can tell you is that this mission is far more important than any of you know. We are counting on you to do the right thing. In truth, you already made your decision when you signed that contract with us, and the reality is I can and will end this pregnancy for you if I must. For the good of the mission." Colonel Foster closed her eyes for just a moment, and when she opened them, her look was intense, almost pleading.

257

"For the good of the human race," she continued. "But it would be easier for all of us if you give your consent willingly."

Dema stared into the Colonel's eyes trying to read what was behind them, but she couldn't. Where she expected to see compassion to match the tone of her voice, she saw only a passionate determination.

She'd been given a choice, but what sort of choice was it really?

She felt the presence of Scott standing behind her, his hands on the back of her chair. She knew the strength of those hands. If she didn't sign, Colonel Foster would force her somehow. She could only guess how that would play out.

Dema gripped the pen in her fingers and with a trembling hand reached for the consent form.

"For the mission," she whispered, tears burning the backs of her eyes.

"For the mission," repeated Colonel Foster.

31

"How's he doing?" Adán sat on the end of a bench and rested his elbows on his knees. "Is he going to be all right?"

Dema nodded sharply. "He has a slight concussion, and he'll have a whopper of a goose egg and a lovely scar, but otherwise he's just fine."

Her sarcasm was not directed at him but at Jonah who stood with arms crossed in the corner, a look of contempt on his face. "You should have killed him," he said.

"Why?" shot Dema. "Because there hasn't been enough death all ready?"

"Because there will be more deaths—ours," Jonah snapped back. "And I, for one, don't particularly want to end up as Zarminan fertilizer, do you?"

Jonah slunk into his corner and went silent. They all went silent. Dema sat cross-legged on the floor beside Adán and leaned her head against the wall. She was covered in dust and looked completely worn out, but Adán thought she looked as beautiful as ever.

"I wanted to keep it, you know." Dema's voice was quiet and low.

"Hmmm?" Adán closed his eyes. He was beginning to feel sleepy.

"The baby," Dema continued. "I was planning to resign my position on the crew, let the alternate take my place. But Colonel Foster said it was too close to launch, that I was bound by contract. I should have fought harder."

"It wasn't your fault, Dema," said Adán. "You did what you had to do."

"No. I did what was easy. Ironic, isn't it? My duty is to save humanity, but first I had to destroy my own."

Adán said nothing. Instead, he brushed his hand down Dema's hair then rested it on her shoulder. She laid her cheek against it, and Adán felt the warmth of her tear-stained skin. He couldn't judge her. She had judged herself hard enough.

Dema went on. "Scott knew, but he didn't care. He was all about the mission."

"I told you, you should have killed him," Jonah interrupted. "You said it yourself, Adán. He's the mole."

"He denied it," said Dema.

"He's lying," Jonah answered.

Adán's patience with his crewmate grew thin. "Listen, Jonah. You have a right to protect yourself, to survive. We all feel the same way. We want to make it to New Earth—alive and in one piece. But isn't it possible we—I—was wrong?"

"We're not wrong." Jonah stiffened defensively.

"Okay, we're not wrong, but what if we're only partly right?"

"What are you saying, Adán?" Dema leaned forward and pulled the blanket over Scott's chest, tucking the edges under his arms. Adán was amazed at her capacity for kindness even toward someone she hated.

"I've been scanning the shuttle's archives again," said Adán, "and I've found things—things that just aren't right. I

260

showed you some of it, but there's more." He told Dema and Jonah about the holos and how each crew member had its own library of them. "But there was another thing I spotted a few days ago that only now struck me as odd. So, I went back and found it again."

He reached for an E-Tab and pulled up the document.

"After the Beacon was sabotaged, there was this massive investigation involving NASA and a whole bunch of higher ups. We had already launched, so this information must have been transmitted after the fact but before Earth—ended."

Jonah shifted impatiently on his bench. "What are you getting at, Adán?"

"They assumed every shuttle was in danger."

"And they were right," said Jonah. "Only the Ensign and Carpathia made it."

Adán agreed. "I uncovered an entire file of documents, all hyperlinked. At first, they seemed to have nothing to do with each other, just a bunch of random articles, but someone created that file and intentionally linked those documents together, maybe hoping someone someday would find them."

Adán swiped a finger across the screen and pulled up another page. "Look here. It's an article about an experiment in Norway, something called the Cognitive Outreach Project. And here's an article about the same experiment from a scientific journal from Prague."

"It's in a foreign language," said Dema.

"It's in Czech, but part of it's been translated into English—here."

Another swipe. Jonah came near to read over Adán's shoulder. Just two paragraphs had been translated, but it was enough.

"The article is dated a dozen years before we launched," Dema noted.

Adán nodded. "But look at the names of the research team. They aren't mentioned in the American article, but they are in the Czech one. Look at that name there."

"Dr. Megan A. Whitlock," Jonah read out loud.

"Vice President of NASA's Planetary Colonization Division," added Adán. "Though not at the time this was written."

Dema shook her head. "I don't understand. This article is about projecting thoughts outside our bodies. So, you think the saboteurs somehow controlled the shuttles with their minds?"

"Maybe," said Adán. "I do think Whitlock somehow used that COP technology on us."

Dema took the tablet from Adán and reread the paragraphs in English and scrolled through some of the other articles Adán had pointed out. "Okay. So, sabotage would explain the shuttle cryo system going haywire, but I can't, for one second, believe Scott or anyone else from our crew was or is capable of conjuring a monster out of sand. It's too crazy!"

"No, you're right, Dema," said Adán. "One person couldn't do that, but what about all of us?"

"*All* of us?" Dema cast a skeptical glance between Adán and Jonah.

"Not us, the four of us. I mean all of us, the entire crew. All twenty-four of us."

"Well," snickered Jonah, "that would be interesting if the other twenty weren't already dead."

"Are they really dead? Weren't we all in a sense dead while we were in cryo? Our bodies were preserved, our brains put on ice—literally. Our minds were recorded, stored in the computer's hard drive system, waiting to be re-uploaded once our bodies were rehydrated. I've seen it. We're all in there, literally one with the system."

The truth was Adán had not thought this all through. He was figuring it out as he went along, but it made sense—didn't it?

"The sandstorms are a natural part of this planet's climate, but in some way I don't understand yet, the shuttle can project some part of us out there—sort of like how it projects the holos."

Dema's eyes widened as she took in Adán's explanation. "Neural function is nothing but electrical impulses firing like engine pistons between synaptic nerve endings. Our unique electrical signatures were stored digitally. It is possible that those signatures, our minds so to speak, are in some sense present in the ship."

"Not just the electrical impulses of our brains," said Adán, getting excited now, "but our memories, our thoughts, our emotions."

Dema went on. "Most of the basic functions of the ship are designed to think for themselves. The shuttle is capable of maintaining life support systems, collecting and interpreting data, creating water from oxygen and hydrogen. Hell, it can even fly on its own once it's in the air. What if its capability goes beyond those basic functions?"

"What if," Jonah continued Dema's thought, "the shuttle itself is the weapon? If it can project one conscience, like Adán said, what's to stop it from projecting all of them in real time?"

"Not as individuals. . ." said Dema.

"But as one single entity." Adán flattened his palm against his tablet's screen, compressing every point of his skin to the cool smooth surface. "All that energy, all those thoughts and feelings fused together into—into what?"

"A monster," said Jonah.

R. Herrera: We've lost contact with three shuttles already. It seems our worst suspicions about sabotage were true. We must assume they're gone.

M. Whitlock: What more could we have done?

R. Herrera: Postponed the launches. Investigated the crews.

M. Whitlock: There was no time for that. We had to take our chances.

R. Herrera: Take our chances? With the fate of humanity at stake? By moving forward, you've jeopardized the entire mission.

M. Whitlock: If we'd waited, the mission would have been dead in the water anyway. As it is, we'll all be dead soon enough.

R. Herrera: What if moles are on every ship?

M. Whitlock: That's the assumption. All we can do, and it's already been done, is reprogram the remaining shuttles and hope it's not too late to save some of them.

R. Herrera: What do you mean reprogram?

M. Whitlock: We've initiated COP.

R. Herrera: Are you crazy? There's a reason the FEDs scuttled it. That catastrophe a few years ago…

M. Whitlock: Has been scrubbed from the archives. We've made huge strides since then. I've already entered commands for the shuttle drives to scour the data for any connection, however remote, to the Terrestrial Brotherhood.

R. Herrera: How, exactly, will that help?

M. Whitlock: The shuttles record and file the crews' brain activity, biochemical fluctuations, psychological data. In essence, the entire person sans the body itself. The shuttles will comb through each record to locate memories or emotions that might reveal the saboteurs' identities: such as guilt, resentment, anger, fear.

R. Herrera: And…?

M. Whitlock: And take them out.

32

Scott remained unconscious for another two hours while Dema fussed over him like a mother hen, which set Adán's nerves on edge.

"He'll be fine," he said finally, pulling Dema away from Scott by the elbow. "We have more important things to worry about than Dryker's headache."

Dema did not attempt to pull her arm from Adán's grasp, and her voice was not unkind. "Adán, we need to rendezvous with the Ensign. Scott is our Commander for a reason. He's the only one of us who knows how to get this shuttle off the ground."

Adán turned to Jonah. "Do you think you can figure it out? Once it's in the air, we can program the destination and let the shuttle fly itself."

Jonah stared at him for what felt like an eternity, and Adán wondered if he had processed anything he'd just said.

Finally, Jonah gave a slow nod. "Yeah," he stammered. "Yeah, I can drive this tank. I just need to read through the, uh, instructions."

"How long do you need?"

Jonah snatched a tablet from the table and started scanning through pages. The tense anxiety on his face did nothing to reassure Adán, but what choice did they have? Unless Scott woke up soon, they would have to fly the shuttle without him.

"Two, three hours maybe?"

Dema guffawed. "This isn't like assembling a Lego model, Jonah."

"Give him a break, Dema," said Adán. "He did have preliminary training in the navigation systems."

"He was a backup, Adán! Just because he can read a map doesn't mean he can take a 50-ton spacecraft into the air!"

"I can do it," said Jonah, with more confidence than he had a moment earlier.

"Good," said Adán. "Get into the cockpit and get started. Let me know when you're ready to go."

"All right," said Jonah, nodding again. "All right." Once he was in the cockpit, he shut the hatch behind him.

On the cot, Scott moaned.

Dema was at his side in a heartbeat. "Maybe he's coming around," she said. "Scott? Scott, can you hear me?"

Scott's eyelids flitted, struggling to open. He moaned again and raised a hand to his bandaged head. "No," he said. "No...no."

"How is he?" asked Adán. "Is he conscious?"

"Yes," Dema said, "but he's really agitated."

Scott's moaning grew louder. He grabbed at his bandages, his fingers scraping at his hair and skin as well as the gauze. Dema grabbed his wrist and tried to force his arm back to the cot.

"Shhh, Scott. It's okay. You're okay."

But it was as if he couldn't hear her, and he was too strong for her. Then suddenly, Scott's body went rigid. His back arched, and his fingers splayed out like ten stiff prongs.

"What is it?" asked Adán.

"He's seizing," said Dema. "Help me keep him from falling off."

Adán hurried to her side, bracing his arms against the side of the cot. Scott's body stiffened even more. His head tipped back, and his eyelids opened and closed rapidly.

"Scott!" shouted Dema. "Scott!"

And then it was over. Scott's body went suddenly limp. Dema hurriedly rolled the commander onto his side and swept a finger through his mouth. She let out a relieved breath, casting Adán a reassuring glance. "His airway is clear," she said.

In the next moment, the shuttle jerked so violently, Dema and Adán were thrown against the far wall. Adán slid to the floor, hitting his knees with a painful thud. Dema managed to stay upright by holding tight to the edge of a table. Scott's cot had been upturned, spilling the unconscious commander to the floor.

"No!" Dema hurled the word like a weapon. "No, not again! Not now!"

The shuttle shook again, rattling like some cheap aluminum soda can being kicked through the street. The shaking was so rough, Adán feared the very seams of the ship might burst apart.

The cockpit door slid open. "What the hell's going on?" demanded Jonah.

Just then something slammed against the side of the shuttle. The impact raised its port side several feet before it

269

dropped back down again with a tremendous shudder. Then there was another impact, just as hard, and another. Each collision sent Adán, Dema, and Jonah bouncing around the common room like rag dolls, hitting walls, floor, tables, and each other. Scott's limp body became wedged between a table and the wall, his arms and legs bent at unnatural angles.

"We have to do something!" shouted Dema to Adán. "You said this—thing—is coming from the shuttle."

"I think it's using our own recorded selves against us!"

"Then turn it off! Shut down the archives, the holo system, anything that might be behind this!"

Adán made his way, not without difficulty, to the large screen in the common room and its keyboard. He'd mainly used the shuttle's computer from the cockpit, but it was all interconnected. He typed in the key that Tink had given him to access the system, but unlike all the times before, he couldn't get past the NASA logo.

He tried again, but the logo was replaced with a red 'RESTRICTED' screen, the first time he'd been confronted with it.

"I can't get in!" said Adán in frustration. "It's like it knows what we're trying to do."

The shuttle continued to rock and quake. Dema and Adán grabbed each other's hands in a firm grip. With her free hand, Dema managed to take hold of the outer hatch's handle. "Then we have to get out of here!"

"What?" Adán couldn't believe Dema said what she had. He'd seen what that thing out there could do. "No! We need to reach New Earth!" He called out to Jonah. "Get this ship off the ground—now!"

Jonah said nothing but groped his way back into the cockpit, leaving the door open this time, and strapped himself into the pilot's chair. From where he was in the common room, Adán saw the control panel light up and felt the hum of the shuttle's engine come to life.

"I'm starting the ignition system," Jonah called from the cockpit, "but I've got to warm up the thrusters. It'll take a few minutes."

"We don't have a few minutes!" shouted Adán.

The shuttle began to move forward, the momentum slowly building. Adán scrambled to a bench and sat down on it. Dema, however, dropped to her knees beside Scott.

"Adán, help me get him back onto the cot and get him secured!"

Adán slid off the bench and grabbed hold of Scott under his arms. Unconscious, Scott was two hundred pounds of dead weight. Adán strained as he slid him out from beneath the table all the while trying to keep his footing as the shuttle moved forward.

Together Dema and Adán managed to wrangle Scott back onto his cot before the shuttle was hit by yet another concussive force, and the impacts kept coming. The shuttle walls creaked from the stress. Then there was a terrible cracking noise below them, and the nose end of the shuttle dropped, smashing into the ground with a crushing blow and shifting the entire shuttle forward at a steep angle. Dema was thrown against the forward wall. Adán landed on top of her, crushing her beneath his body. As he struggled to lift himself off her, he knew at once damage had been done. Dema wrapped her arm protectively against her ribcage, and her eyes were squeezed shut in pain.

"Dema! I'm sorry. I couldn't help it. What's wrong?"

"My ribs," she managed to say through several weak, shallow breaths. "I think a couple are bruised. Nothing broken, thank God."

Adán peered into the cockpit. All he could see through the window was the ground, now only a few feet away.

"The front landing wheel is gone!" Jonah shouted back at them. "The nose is in the dirt! We can't fly like this!"

But whatever had done this wasn't finished with them yet. The next series of collisions pushed the shuttle off balance, tipping it sideways. The massive structure rolled onto its side, its occupants rolling helplessly with it. There was a deafening *pop* as the starboard wing broke away. Dema cried out in pain as she landed on top of the row of cabinets. Jonah was now suspended from the pilot's chair, several feet in the air. Adán landed in a heap with Scott, the cot now dashed to pieces beneath them.

Scott sputtered, blinking his eyes open. He coughed. "Wh—what's going on?" he said feebly. Adán reached for him, futilely trying to hold him in place.

"Just find something to hang on to!"

Scott's eyes widened, but he obeyed, wrapping his trembling hands around the table leg jutting out horizontally above him.

The shuttle lurched violently. Powerful tremors shook through the hull, the shuttle jerking and rattling all around them.

"We're moving! But in the wrong direction!" said Dema.

"You guys need to come here—now!" called Jonah.

Grasping onto table legs and cabinet holds, Dema and Adán scrambled as best they could to the cockpit. Staying upright was difficult with the movement of the shuttle, but they managed to peer through the door. Outside the windshield was a blur of orange sand. From their vantage point, the ground looked as though it were rushing by them like a raging river. Yet it wasn't coming at them, Adán realized. The shuttle was moving across it—sideways. The monster was pushing them across the desert.

"The canyon," Adán said, hardly believing what he was seeing. "The monster is pushing us toward the canyon."

They all watched in horror, feeling helpless to stop it.

"It doesn't want us to rendezvous with New Earth," said Adán, the reality of their situation sinking in. Jonah unhitched his restraint, and the three of them tumbled back into the common room.

"But why?" said Dema. "What does this thing want with us?"

Jonah gestured toward the lab, its door torn from its track and now on the floor along with them. "It wants *us all* dead. Like God and Gomorrah."

"You're right, Dema. We have to get out," said Adán. "If we can get away from the shuttle, draw its attention toward us, maybe we can fight it."

"Fight something we can't see?" asked Dema.

"There's no fighting this thing!" said Jonah. "It wants to destroy us. It's going to push us into the canyon. We can't stop it."

Adán considered their options. There were so few. "I could access the hardware somehow," he suggested. "Damage it. Destroy it."

Dema grabbed his arm, a desperate urgency in her eyes. "We don't have time."

Scott coughed again. He sounded hoarse and raspy, and his breaths came with a struggle. Adán wondered how badly Scott had been injured being thrown about while unconscious.

"What are you guys talking about? What's happening?" Scott asked.

"Without the shuttle," said Dema, "how will we get to the colony?"

"We'll have to take the rovers," said Adán.

"Did Tink find a pass through the mountains?" Dema asked.

"I don't know."

"Even if he did, it's too far. We'll never make it."

"Yes, we will," said Jonah, a big grin spreading across his face. "They're solar-powered, so we've got unlimited juice. And there aren't seven of us anymore, only four. Two per rover. We'll get as far as we can and then comm the Ensign and tell them to send someone to meet us."

He glanced from Adán to Dema and back again as if waiting for their enthusiastic response. He didn't get it. "We've at least got to try!"

"What about the cargo?" Dema glanced toward the lab where the embryos, the future of the human race, still waited. "What about *them*? Without them, we're nothing."

Dema looked up at Adán, pleading. Her eyes tore a hole through his soul. There was barely enough room for all of them on the rovers, how could they transport the cases too?

"We'll find a way," he said, not entirely sure of himself. "Somehow, we'll find a way. Okay. Jonah," Adán added, "we have to get to the rovers."

"How can we do that when this thing is moving?!"

"Both rovers were left outside after we lost Tink. You and Dema have to get out and distract—whatever it is—long enough for you to retrieve them. I'll get to the lab and grab whatever I can of the cargo." He looked at Dema. "I can't save them all. You know that, right?"

She nodded, though her eyes were full of doubt and fear. Suddenly, the shuttle lurched forward. The rear of it raised into the air and then dropped violently, hitting the ground with a horrible shudder. Dema cried out from pain, clutching a table leg. Adán was thrown across the length of the common room when he came down and landed hard against the cabinets. He lay flat on the floor, his heart thumping so hard he felt as though it might explode.

"Adán!" Dema cried.

The shuttle righted itself, so that the floor of the common room was below them again.

A sharp jolt threw Adán to the floor. Dema collided with the edge of a table. Suddenly, the nose of the shuttle rose into the air. The floor tilted, and Adán slid on his back, crashing into Jonah and pinning him against the wall. Then the shuttle fell back again, the entire vehicle shuddering as it slammed into the ground. Adán felt the vibration in his bones, and he bit the edge of his tongue. His mouth filled with the coppery taste of blood.

"It knows we're in here!" hissed Scott who had braced himself in the cockpit doorway. "It's trying to get in!"

"It's okay, Scott," said Adán.

"Don't you get it? We can't hide from it. It'll tear this shuttle to pieces! We're trapped in here!"

A loud thump sounded against the side of the ship, and a low creaking, the shuttle's frame under stress. The thump sounded again and again.

"This is my fault!" said Scott. "You said I was the mole. I thought it must be someone else, but what if it is me? What if that thing is using my brain to hurt us?"

Regret climbed up Adán's throat. "No, Dryker! Not you. Not *only* you!"

"I'm the commander. I'm supposed to protect the ship. Protect the mission!" Scott's eyes were wild with fear. "After I woke up, and I realized what had happened, I used the Quarters terminal to access the archives. What I found—it was wrong. What they did to us was wrong!"

"Why didn't you tell us?" said Dema.

"It was classified," said Scott. "But it shouldn't have been. I disabled the restrictions, used the patches to try and reconnect to the shuttle—to stop it. I was going to tell you, but then Fess died, and Tink. Things have gotten out of control!"

Scott's expression twisted in mental agony. "We've gotta get outa here!" he shouted. "We're sitting ducks! Out there, at least we got a chance!"

"That's exactly what we're trying to do," said Adán with growing concern about Scott's deteriorating mental state. "Jonah and Dema are going for the rovers. I'm going to grab as many of the zygotes as possible, and we're going to make a run for it, get as far away as we can."

"But. . .but how?"

Adán cast glances between Jonah and Dema. "We haven't quite figured that out yet. We have to distract it somehow."

A strange calm came over Scott. He winced in pain as he pulled himself with effort to his feet. "Someone's got to distract it," he muttered. "Get to the rovers."

Scott turned to look at Dema. "There isn't space for all of us," he said, urgently. "You've got to save them."

Dema nodded. "Of course. Adán and Jonah—"

"No." Scott took her by the shoulders. "I couldn't tell you before. I was under orders not to. But the baby, *our* baby, is there—somewhere."

Dema blinked, her face registering shock. "What?"

Scott's voice broke as he fought back tears. "Like you said, we're nothing. *They* are all that matters."

Then suddenly, Scott let go of Dema and lunged for the hatch.

"Scott, no!" Dema reached for Scott as he skidded past her but failed to find purchase.

Scott grasped the hatch's handle with both hands and gave the door a violent shove. He turned to Dema one last time.

"I'm sorry," he said, then flung himself outside.

Adán had managed to roll away from Jonah, and he and Dema scrambled to the open hatch. Sand attacked them with the force of a tornado, but they could see the figure of Scott Dryker running.

All of a sudden, what could only be described as a hand, though it was nothing but sand and wind, snatched Scott right off the ground. They heard him scream as the hand held him by every limb, pulling him taut like a little toy. All at once, his shoulders and hips ruptured, his arms and legs ripping free from his torso. Still alive, Scott's screams took on a gurgling, gut squealing quality. Blood gushed from his mutilated body. Streaks of crimson and bits of limbs swirled around him with the sand, creating a red cyclone. Scott's mass shredded before their eyes, the sand stripping the flesh from his bones and pulverizing what was left of him until Scott was one with the storm. No piece of him remained that was larger than a grain of sand.

"Nooo," Dema whimpered, her hand covering her mouth. Tears sprung from her eyes, and she turned away.

Adán enveloped her in his arms. "Dema, there's no time. The storm—"

And just as it had so many times before, as it had taken each life, the storm abruptly ceased. The winds stopped churning and the sand rained to the ground. Everything fell deathly still.

33

For a moment, Adán held his breath, not quite believing that this sudden respite had actually come, but how long would it last?

"It's gone," said Jonah, with an almost jubilant laugh. "It's gone! It *was* Scott! He's gone and so is the monster."

"We don't know that," said Adán.

"Yes, we do. We're safe now."

"No. Scott's mind, all our minds are still here in the ship. It's just—it's just resting. Jonah, Dema—go now. Get the rovers. I'll meet you outside once I get the cargo."

"But we're safe now," repeated Jonah.

Dema cut in. "No, Jonah! We're not safe. We will never be safe until we get those embryos to New Earth. *They* are the entire future of our species. Now, do what Adán says and get the rover!"

"But—" said Jonah.

"Hurry!"

Jonah grasped his cross and closed his eyes in a brief prayer. "Our Father who art in heaven," he whispered, then snatched a set of gear from the disarray on the floor and quickly pulled it on. Then with only a moment's hesitation, he leapt out of the hatch into the sand, taking off at a run the moment his feet touched ground.

Dema and Adán slipped into their gear as well. "I'm going for the embryos," said Adán.

"And the remote transmitter," said Dema. "We need it to communicate with the Ensign. Without it, we're as good as dead."

"Okay. We'll get the embryos first, and then I'll get the transmitter."

Together they entered the lab. Dema paused, a muffled cry sounding in her throat.

"Are you okay?" asked Adán.

Dema nodded. "If only I'd known—He or she is in here." She looked at him, a fierceness in her eyes.

"We'll save as many as we can," Adán said. "I promise."

Dema and Adán each carefully removed two cases of human embryos and tucked one under each arm.

They turned to leave, but Dema hesitated, looking back at the wall of drawers with regret. "We're not leaving any behind," she said with a hitch in her voice.

Adán said nothing. What could he say? Instead, he quickly coaxed her forward. They returned to the outer hatch. Dema went out first, and Adán handed the cases down to her. She took two with her, leaving the other two behind while she ran for the second rover.

Adán could already hear the purr of the first rover's engine, Jonah coming close. Once he heard the second motor turn over, he returned to the lab for more embryos, but time was running short.

After carefully dropping four more cases into the sand, he headed for the cockpit. He started to remove the transmitter from its casing, but then paused. What if they didn't get away? What if. . .?

He powered up the transmitter and sent out a hail.

"This is Carpathia hailing the Ensign. This is a message of distress. Carpathia unable to fly. Most of the crew is dead. Survivors coming to you by rover. I know that it might not be possible, but please find a way to send someone to meet us. Over."

He set the hail on continuous, then jerked the transmitter free and made for the hatch.

Dema was there waiting for him, the remaining embryo cases already secured onto her rover. He had just tossed the transmitter to her when the shuttle jerked violently, throwing Adán against the wall.

"Adán!" The sound of Dema shouting his name was quickly swallowed up in the cacophony of the shuttle's sudden violent shift.

It was moving again.

The shuttle rolled, its remaining port wing cracking off with a percussive *boom!* Adán could not prevent himself from being jostled freely inside like a snow globe's inhabitant. Every collision against a wall or cabinet sent new spikes of pain through his body. He wrapped his arms protectively around his head. Finally, the rolling stopped, and the shuttle righted itself, but he could still feel the momentum of the shuttle being pushed across the sand.

He looked out the open hatch which now faced the opposite way it had before. Through it he could see the black, snake-like canyon coming ever closer. He had to get out somehow, but if he jumped from the hatch now, he would be instantly crushed by the shuttle itself.

With no time to think, he flung open a cabinet and grabbed a wrench, the same one, he realized, that Dema had used to knock out Scott. Then he ran into the cockpit and began hammering the eighteen-inch steel tool against the windshield. He rammed it against the glass over and over until finally the window shattered, though the fragments held together like a puzzle, bound between layers of safety material. Two more hits, and the glass finally gave way. Climbing up on the console, Adán assessed the distance to the ground. With the front wheel broken off, it wasn't as far as it had once been. He grasped the edges of the frame with his hands and pushed off.

The sand was soft when he landed, but his injuries made him grunt in pain. The shuttle continued to speed away from him, propelled by some unseen force. Adán quickly scanned the horizon, spotting the two rovers not far off. He scrambled to his feet and ran.

Within seconds, the familiar signs of a storm sprang up around him: pitching wind and swirling gusts of sand. In his haste to vacate the shuttle, he had forgotten to attach his comm, so he could not communicate with Dema or Jonah. Would they reach him in time, before the monster tore him to pieces? Or worse, would it kill all of them?

He held his arm up in a futile attempt to block the sand blasting against his visor. He peered underneath it and saw the outline of one of the rovers approaching.

"Get on!" shouted Jonah, his voice barely audible above the tumult of the storm.

Adán clambered aboard. The rover lurched forward, speeding to rejoin Dema in the distance, but they were not alone. As the storm cycloned around them, they were lifted airborne on a powerful gust of wind and then slammed back down again. And then Adán saw what he had feared most— a massive swell rising from the ground, moving across the sand with the speed and power of a locomotive. They were not going to make it. They would never make it. The monster wanted them dead, and it would have them.

As the swell of sand approached, Adan knew there was no escape. At least not for all of them.

Adán leapt off the rover.

"What are you doing?" screamed Jonah, but Adán didn't have time to answer. He sprinted back toward the shuttle, shouting at the tops of his lungs.

"Come get me, you bastard! If you're going to kill us all, you might as well start with me!"

He glanced over his shoulder to see the dazed expression on Jonah's face through his visor. Beyond that he saw the massive dune shift its course. He kept screaming until he reached the shuttle, forsaken by the monster when it went after the rovers. Adán climbed aboard through the hatch, then turned to look out again.

It was as if the shuttle sensed his presence, felt his touch. The moment he stepped aboard, the wave of sand ceased its pursuit and sunk back into the ground like a wave swallowed in its own ocean. The wind slowed as well, and Adán could just make out Dema and Jonah in the distance. They would be safe now, he hoped.

Adán tried to brace himself just as the invisible force slammed into the shuttle's side, but it was no use. Adán was flung inside, his shoulder smashing against the counter. Then the shuttle was moving again, faster than before, but nose first this time. Through the shattered windshield, he saw the canyon approaching and guessed that in just two or three minutes the shuttle would topple into it.

Adán struggled to hold onto whatever he could to get to the lab, but the gloves of his suit made it difficult, so he tore off the gloves and moved on. Once inside, he braced his feet against the wall and reached for two more cases, his fingers gripping their rigid plastic handles. Then he stopped. Scott's final words hit him like a bullet.

"We're nothing. They're all that matters."

But he was wrong. Dema was wrong. Adán thought of the nearly eight billion people who had died on Earth. He thought of Carpathia's crew, of Tink and Lainie and the others.

"We *all* matter," he said out loud, the idea filling him like a revelation. "Every life is worth living, worth saving. Not just the human race as a whole, but each distinct individual."

He pulled the cases free from the storage compartment.

"I'll do my best for you guys," he said, "but I want to survive too."

Then Adán headed back toward the hatch, fighting awkwardly to stay upright. The world zoomed by through the open hatch, the shuttle slicing through the sand like a fin through water. Chances were that these embryos he carried would not survive the fall they were about to experience, and if they did, they might not survive the trip to New Earth. The life-sustaining energy packs on them might die long before they even reached the rendezvous. Yet maybe, just maybe some of them might live. If even one made it, it would all be worth it.

Adán scrambled and slipped across the floor to the hatch and flung the cases out into the sand. In a fraction of a second, they were gone from view. Then he hurried back for more. He had managed to fling out the last of the human cases when he felt the weight of the shuttle tilt forward.

They had reached the canyon, and the Carpathia was teetering at its edge. The truth was, Adán wanted to live. He would take one desperate leap from the hatch, but if he leapt too soon, the monster might release its grip on the shuttle and turn its attention on him, or on Dema and Jonah. As long as the shuttle remained intact, there would be no end to the monster, or to the consciences that controlled it. If he waited too long, he would go down with it, but he'd already decided that was a risk he was willing to take.

The shuttle tilted more steeply, and Adán felt a strange sort of weightlessness as the floor fell away from beneath him. He glimpsed the canyon ridge as it slid past the hatch.

Adán propelled himself forward—and leapt.

34

Adán collided with the canyon rim, his chin smashing into a surprisingly jagged rock. Despite the searing pain, his fingers clawed at the stone, desperate for purchase. He dug the toes of his boots into the cliff face but found no foothold wide enough to stop his descent. He slid several inches down the rock wall until finally, his hand caught hold of a triangular shard of stone jutting out from the wall.

Below him, the Carpathia dropped into the dark, seemingly endless recesses of the planet's gut. It was strange that something that had seemed so alive could die without a sound.

Adán pressed his boots into the rock. Bits of soil broke free, toppling into the grotto. He cautiously tested the wall until he found a grip for his free hand and took hold. Then he released his other hand and did the same, slowly inching his way up toward the crest.

He had climbed to within a foot of the top when he felt something clamp around his ankle. It felt as solid and heavy as an iron manacle, but when he looked down, he saw nothing. It pulled at him, and he clung to the stone by his bare fingertips which were quickly growing numb from the cold air.

When his left hand slipped, he lost his footing on the narrow ridge below him. He screamed out, swinging freely from one hand. Adán tried to shake the monster loose, but it would not release him. He wondered how far the shuttle would have to fall to hit bottom, and would the monster really die once it did?

His fingers slipped, and he strained from the effort of holding on while his other hand desperately searched for a new handhold.

And then she was there. Above him. Reaching down.

"Hold on!" Dema shouted, stretching out her hand to him. He tried to reach her, tried to take her hand, but the force that pulled him would not allow him that extra inch.

"I can't!" he called up to her. "It's got me! It's pulling me down!"

"No, Adán! Don't let go!"

Dema's face disappeared, and Adán feared he would never see it again, but she returned a moment later, stabbing the long crescent wrench at him. The wrench. He had carried it with him when he'd leapt through the shuttle's windshield and had dropped it somewhere in the sand. Dema must have found it.

Adán stretched his hand and grabbed hold of it.

"Can you hold me?" he called up.

"Jonah's got me!" she said. "We'll pull you up!"

Adán released the stone and took the wrench with both hands, but the monster still had him. He groaned in pain, feeling his body being stretched beyond reasonable limits. Would he be ripped apart like Scott had been? The pain was intense. Searing. Something popped in his lower back. He screamed, the pain shooting black daggers across his vision.

He would have to let go. His hands were slipping anyway. "I can't hold on!" he cried. "I can't!"

Above him Dema's face twisted with the effort of holding him, pulling against the force of the monster.

He would have to let go. The monster would never release him.

Dark spots danced in front of his eyes. His head swam. He couldn't fight it anymore. Then somewhere far below him, farther down than human eyes could ever see, there was a sound. A distant echo, a faint rumble like thunder. It drifted up to him and then was gone. And suddenly he felt light, light as air, like he was floating, drifting. And his mind went black.

Adán awoke to a bright lilac sky and the steady thrum of a motor. He lay on a flat, hard surface that vibrated beneath him. He sat up and found himself lying on the flat bed of a rover he'd never seen before. They were traveling across the familiar Gliesen terrain, only the mountains that had always seemed so far away were now very close.

He turned to see the backs of two people in front of him, one driving and the other in the passenger seat. The passenger turned and smiled at him.

"So, the hero awakes," said Jonah, grinning. The driver, an older man with a dark beard, glanced back as well. "How are you feeling?"

"A little dizzy and sore, like someone took a jackhammer to my entire body. How long have I been out?" asked Adán.

"A couple of days, give or take," replied Jonah. "You were in and out of consciousness at first, then you just slept. I seriously thought you were in a coma. I have to admit I did more than my fair share of praying, but Dema was adamant you'd be okay. Guess she was right."

"Where is Dema?" For a moment, Adán felt queasy thinking of everything that might have happened.

"Dema?" said Jonah. "She's right behind you."

Adán turned to see Dema driving Carpathia's main rover, with the smaller one in tow. She waved at him, and he waved back.

Jonah pointed past the front of the rover. "Hey," he said. "You're gonna want to see this."

Adán peered ahead and saw an amazing sight. Green. Everywhere was the color green. The crew of the Ensign had planted crops, and for miles in every direction there were endless rows of green.

And tents. Adán counted dozens of tents of varying sizes. And people. Men and women, and even a handful of children.

New Earth.

They had found a way to reach the colony, or Commander Parks had somehow found a way to reach them.

The rover pulled up beside a large metal dome.

"This is our headquarters," said the driver to Adán. "We built it from the remains of the Ensign. Commander Parks is waiting for you inside where we have a section in the lab set up for your cargo. Jonah here says that you rescued over five hundred human embryos. That's really something."

Dema pulled up beside them. She hurried over to Adán, testing his arms and legs with her hands.

"Are you all right?" she asked. She brushed her fingers over his face, her expression full of concern. "I've been so worried. I've been so worried that maybe—"

Adán placed a finger on her lips. "Shhh," he told her. "I'm fine. Really."

She watched as a group of men unloaded Carpathia's cargo from the rovers. Adán noticed her eyes swell with tears. She smiled. "Thank you," she told him.

They would learn later, from Commander Parks and the archives they had recovered from the Ensign, how NASA had resorted to using a program with unpredictable outcomes to weed out the moles on the shuttles. Yet while the Ensign and some others did in fact have saboteurs on board, most had been destroyed by good intentions. The COP had, as it turned out, a collective will of its own. In its view, every crew member was guilty and deserved to be eliminated.

But the Ensign's crew had fought back—and survived. New Earth and its scrap of humanity flourished. It would become the home of Carpathia's remnant crew and of all future generations. But for now, Adán had only one thought: He was alive. *They* were alive.

"What do you think?" Dema asked him, glancing around the village. "It's pretty amazing, isn't it? They have a whole team here. They'll take care of the embryos. And I'm going to help them."

"I'm glad," said Adán.

"The human race will thrive. We'll make sure of it." Dema's enthusiasm was contagious. "Every one of those lives will have a chance to grow, to exist and fill its potential."

Adán tried to imagine the world Dema envisioned. Like General Berkeley had said in his vid explaining what had happened, it would take generations.

"What about in the meantime?" Adán asked cautiously. "What about us?"

"Us?" Dema replied, though the fervor in her eyes suggested she was thinking about that as well.

"I mean now that we're here," he said, "what are we—you and I—going to do?"

Dema narrowed her eyes thoughtfully and studied Adán's face. Finally, her lips curved into a smile. "I guess we'll just have to take the future one day at a time," she said. Then she leaned close and kissed him.

OFFICIAL DECLARATION
Cristiano E. Barrios, President of the United States of America

My Fellow Americans,

By now most of you have heard the rumors that Earth will soon be facing unprecedented temperatures due to solar radiation. It is my unfortunate duty to confirm that these rumors are true.

Mankind has always been driven toward exploration and survival. The earliest civilizations battled floods, droughts, war, and pestilence. From the Egyptian pyramids to the Phoenician seafarers, from those who travelled the Silk Road of China to the American pioneers and innovators who shaped our modern world, humans have continually sought to expand their knowledge and influence their environment.

This innate instinct landed Neil Armstrong on the moon in 1969, and revolutionized communication with the iPhone in 2007. And since then, our species has only continued to reach toward greater heights and distances, culminating in this year's Planetary Colonization Program, which launched eleven shuttles into space with the anticipation of planting our seed on a distant land.

In light of the news of Earth's impending fate, I ask that instead of fear, we embrace faith. Instead of anger, we embrace appreciation. Instead of despair, we embrace hope—hope for the future of the human race which will endure and increase despite all odds, just as it has always done.

To borrow the words of President Ronald Reagan: "Man will continue his conquest of space. To reach out for new goals and ever greater achievements—that is the way we shall commemorate those who have gone before. And to those who carry our legacy into a new realm, we bid you goodbye. Do not forget us, for we know in our hearts that you who fly so high and so proud now make your home beyond the stars, safe in God's promise of eternal life."

May God bless you all. Farewell, and goodnight.

Acknowledgments

I first thought of writing this book more than ten years ago. When I was a kid, one of my favorite movies was a 50's 'B' sci-fi flick called *Forbidden Planet*. I must have watched it a hundred times. Last year I watched it after a long hiatus, and it was so hokey! But despite the cheesy dialog and bad special effects, the plot still held up.

Writing contemporary versions of classic stories is not unusual, but *Forbidden Planet* isn't like Dickens or Shakespeare or Christie. It's a futuristic tale set on a distant planet, and it probes the very depths of the human psyche. What I wanted was a new plot with new characters, but with a story that remains true to the spirit of the original. I hope I've achieved that here.

I tend to write about sad things. I didn't set out intending to do that, but most of my stories involve emotional pain. I think that's because not only have I experienced pain in my own life, but those closest to me have faced great challenges and struggles. Not to make light of those struggles, but tragedy and conflict make great fodder for novel writing. We can all relate to disappointment, heartbreak, and grief. And when the characters we read about overcome their challenges and come out on top, we feel like we can too. Reading about sad things builds empathy. Reading about facing those things head on and overcoming them gives us hope and courage. I hope that my books, including this one, do that for my readers.

I have several people to thank for *Sand and Shadow*. My dad, first of all, for recording *Forbidden Planet* from TV onto a video cassette decades ago and letting me watch it often. Judi Lauren for her insightful developmental edit which helped me bring my characters more to life. Barbara Groves for creating an awesome cover. Dorine White and Roy Gladden for their insights. And I also want to thank Google search, because without it I would never have known how fast future spacecraft could fly, how cryogenics work, how far Gliese 581g is from Earth, how long it would take to travel there, or any other of the little details I had to research to make this book plausible. And believe me, I researched everything, from telekinesis to what materials are used to repair the exterior of a shuttle.

Finally, I want to thank each of my kids for believing in me. (I included a quiet nod in the book to my youngest, Jarett, by way of Vivaldi.) They've always been my greatest inspiration. I started writing for them. I continue writing for them. They make my life worth living. Thanks, kids.

Laurisa White Reyes

Thank you for reading

SAND
AND
SHADOW

We invite you to post a review on
Goodreads & Amazon.

For a free e-book, join our mailing list at:
www.SkyrocketPress.com

About the Author

LAURISA WHITE REYES is the author of the SCBWI Spark Award winning novel *THE STORYTELLERS* and the Spark Honor recipient *PETALS*. She is also the Senior Editor at Skyrocket Press and an English instructor at College of the Canyons in Southern California.

www.LaurisaWhiteReyes.com
www.SkyrocketPress.com

Read an excerpt from...

CONTACT

Written By

LAURISA WHITE REYES

I

I'M ALIVE?

Yes. Still alive...

Again.

A tube runs from an IV bag into my arm, the plastic needle burrowing under my skin like a tick. Thank God I was unconscious when they put that in. I cringe at the thought of being deluged with so many psyches at once—paramedics, nurses, doctors, all of them touching me.

Where are my clothes? They must have taken them off when I was out. This flimsy gown can't protect me. I want to tear off the tape securing the IV tube to my skin, rip it off like a Band-Aid. I want out of here, but then I see Mama sleeping beside me, her body sloped in a plastic chair. I shouldn't have done this to her again. But I had to try.

A plastic clamp pinches my finger, connecting me to a heart monitor. Three inches further up, my wrist is wrapped in gauze. Two months ago, I would never have had the courage to do this—or any reason to. But now, feeling the staples beneath the bandage, I wonder how deep someone has to cut in order to die?

The curtain jerks back, the metal rings dragging across the ceiling rail. Mama snaps to attention. I half expect her to stand and salute.

"Miranda Ortiz?" says a woman in a beige linen suit and crisp white blouse. She is thin, stiff, and colorless. She reeks of gardenias.

"I'm Dr. Walsh from Mental Health," she continues. The plastic laminated nametag hanging from her neck confirms this.

Dr. Walsh extends her hand, but instead of taking it, I grasp the edge of my sheet and pull it up to my chin. Other than this stupid hospital gown, it's the only barrier I've got right now.

Mama stands up and reaches over the bed to shake the doctor's hand. "I'm Mira's mother, Ana," she says wearily. She starts to sit back down, but Dr. Walsh interrupts.

"It's a pleasure to meet you in person, Mrs. Ortiz. However, I'd like to speak to your daughter alone, if that's all right."

Dr. Walsh is insistent, in a polite sort of way. Mama leans toward me, and for a split second I think she's going to kiss me goodbye. Though deep down I almost wish she would, instead she offers me her gentle smile and tucks the sheet under my shoulder.

"Please don't go," I whisper.

"It'll only be a few minutes," she says. "I'll be just outside, all right?"

Mama brushes a strand of hair from my eyes with her manicured fingernails, careful to avoid contact with my skin. She smiles at me, but her eyes are wistful. As she walks out, my insides tighten up, and I suddenly realize how much I've missed her touch. My instinct is to cling to her like when I was small, but instead I press my arms stiffly to my sides like a corpse.

A security guard opens the door and accompanies Mama out into the hall. Dr. Walsh takes Mama's empty chair, crosses one leg over the other, and lays a clipboard on her knee. "So," she begins, "you cut yourself last night. Is that right?"

Her voice is casual and smooth, as if she's just asked me what I ate for dinner. She waits for me to respond. When I don't, she glances down at her clipboard. "I understand it's not your first attempt. You were here a couple of weeks ago, I see. Overdose, but no permanent damage done."

She glances up at me, pausing in case I have something to say.

I don't.

"Miranda—"

"It's Mira."

"Mira, what happened that made you want to die?"

Her perfume hangs heavy around her. I rub the sheet against my nose, trying to block out the overpowering smell and the awkward silence between us. It's obvious she's going to sit there for as long as it takes. I want her gone, so I might as well talk.

"My boyfriend wants to dump me," I tell her, and it's true. Sort of.

"I see," she says. Her eyebrows lift a little. "Things aren't going well between the two of you?"

"Something like that."

Her eyes narrow as she looks at her clipboard again. She thinks she's got me all figured out. She's met a hundred kids like me, maybe more. To her, I'm just like all the rest.

Only I'm not.

"Mira, do you mind if I ask you some questions?" She looks up at me, a trace of a smile on her lips. "Your answers will help me understand what's happening with you, all right?"

She begins with the same questions Dr. Jansen asked me the last time I was here: Do you have trouble sleeping? How's your appetite? Do you feel anxious or sad more often than usual?

She's so pale with her white skin and bleached hair. Craig's skin is light like hers. I used to relish his touch and let his lips linger on mine as long as he wanted. My skin tingles just thinking about him, but I shove the memories back, burying them down deep inside me where they belong.

Dr. Walsh shifts in her chair, drawing my mind back to the present. "Mira," she continues, "do you believe you have special powers?"

Beneath the sheet my arm jerks, and the clip on my finger pops off. The monitor lets out a loud, piercing beep. I pat around the mattress, but I can't find the clip. Then I see it dangling over the side of the bed. I reach for it, but Dr. Walsh gets to it before I do.

"Here," she says, smiling. "Let me help you."

"No, don't!" I say, grabbing for the clip.

Too late.

Oh God. Please God, not again.

I squeeze my eyelids shut, bracing for impact as she grasps my wrist in one hand and replaces the clip with the other. It takes only half a second, like those commercials where a crash test dummy rockets forward at high speed and slams into a wall. In that instant every thought in Emma Lynn Walsh's head collides with mine—every thought, memory, hope, disappointment, and dream. They come at me like a hailstorm, assaulting me at random. I see her as a child falling off her bike and scraping her knee, and her father scolding her for forgetting to brake. I see the wedding ring slide onto her finger—her yanking it off and flushing it down the toilet. I feel despair at her mother's funeral and relief at her father's. She masks so much pain with poise and self-assurance, but beneath it all she's a mess.

"Mira? Mira."

I open my eyes to see Dr. Walsh peering at me, a puzzled expression on her face.

"Let—go—of—me," I order though clenched teeth.

Dr. Walsh releases my wrist. I turn on my side, rolling up in the sheet, attempting to disappear into my cocoon. I hear the chair legs scrape against the floor as Dr. Walsh slides it closer to my bed.

I stare at the bottom of my IV bag, watching clear drops form, preparing to fall into the tube. One by one they hang there for a moment suspended in time, and then *plop!*

I glance over my shoulder and look at Dr. Walsh. Her smile is gone. Both feet are on the floor, and she's holding the clipboard up now, like a shield. There's a yellow Sponge Bob sticker on the back, staring at me with a goofy, wide-mouthed grin.

"Okay, Mira. Why don't we get back to your boyfriend? You said he wants to break up with you. Why?" Dr. Walsh's tone has changed. It's softer now, more sympathetic, but what can I tell her that won't sound crazy?

"I won't let him touch me anymore."

"So, he told you he wants to break up with you?"

"No. He hasn't said anything—yet."

"Hasn't said anything." Her voice holds a note of confusion. "Then, how do you know?"

She dangles the question in front of me like the proverbial carrot, hoping to draw me out. I don't want to talk anymore, but something inside me needs to. Maybe part of me believes there is a chance, no matter how slight, that this woman might be able to help. That's how desperate I've become.

I open my mouth to say something, but I can't. Instead, I just lay there wrapped up like a mummy, someone who's dead inside. Only I'm not dead. I'm alive. Too much alive.

Just then a nurse comes into the room to check my IV. "Are you comfortable, Ms. Ortiz?" she asks. "Your father called a bit ago. I assured him that if you needed anything, anything at all, I'd see to it myself."

The nurse, a plump middle-aged woman wearing purple scrubs, glances at Dr. Walsh and reacts as if the good doctor had just magically appeared there.

"Oh my, I'm sorry, Dr. Walsh. I didn't mean to intrude."

"Not a problem. We're finished here," says Dr. Walsh, offering a nod.

I hear the snap of the clipboard's metal clasp as she tucks her pen into it. Walking around the side of my bed, she gives me a conciliatory smile. "All right, Mira," she says. "I'm going to have a word with your mother about getting you admitted.

I need you to be somewhere safe, where we can keep an eye on you for a few days."

As Dr. Walsh turns to leave, I find my voice again. "If you hate them so much, why smell like them?"

"Pardon?" She turns, pausing at the door.

"Gardenias. You hate gardenias."

Her lips turn pale as she presses them together. I don't want to do this, but I need her to believe me. My voice chokes when I say it. "It's your mother's perfume."

Dr. Walsh's eyes glisten, and hurt and confusion fill her face. Without a word, she turns and walks through the door, taking the invisible gardenia cloud with her.